MW01677463

Necessary Larceny

Ian Stout

Manor House Publishing Inc.

Library and Archives Canada Cataloguing in Publication

Stout, Ian, 1941-
Necessary larceny / Ian Stout.

ISBN 978-0-9781070-9-3

I. Title.

PS8637.T685N42 2007 C813'.6 C2007-905313-0

Published by Manor House Publishing Inc., Oct. 15, 2007
4522 Cottingham Crescent, Ancaster, Ontario, Canada, L9G 3V6
905-648-2193…. Fax: 905-648-8369
www.manor-house.biz

Printed and bound in Canada.

Special thanks to the National Gallery of Canada and artist Alex Colville for the use of the artist's work To Prince Edward Island on this book's front cover.

We acknowledge the financial support of the Government of Canada through the Book Publishing Industry Development Program (BPIDP) for our publishing activities.

About the author

From an early age Ian heard the beat of a different drummer and was always a step or two out of sync with his peers. The third of five children, the novelty of new babies had worn off and he was left to his own devices, developing an independent streak very much obvious to this day.

A true Gemini, he's always looking for new challenges or exciting pastimes but once the newness wears of, he moves on to something fresh.

At seventeen he started training to become a pilot. Receiving his private license shortly after his nineteenth birthday, he discovered the world was full of Second World War pilots and no work was available for rookies. Losing interest, he left for a walk about in Europe, flying only once in the next two years, at Biggin Hill in an antique Tiger Moth. He said it made him feel like the Red Baron.

Returning to Canada after eighteen months of wandering through the British Isles, France, and Italy, he was preparing to visit Australia when he met Sharon. Smitten, he decided she would be his wife, proposing within weeks. She quite sensibly turned him down.

After several months of courting and a dozen more proposals she gave in. Their honeymoon was an eight thousand mile drive to Acapulco Mexico and back in a Studebaker Lark.

Their next forty years have been filled with travel, adventure, successes, and a few failures. Whether it's walking on the Great Wall of China or driving over a mountain pass in the Swiss Alps during a raging blizzard, Ian believes you keep doing 'till you drop. Just recently he journeyed to the Mayan ruins at Chichen Itza to view the thousand year old Fall Equinox sunlight shadow show on the great pyramid.

Between jaunts to the Grand Casino of Monaco, Corcavado in Brazil and the opera house in Sydney Australia, Ian has found time to father two children, get elected to Hamilton Ontario's city council five times and write columns for local newspapers. His political interests have involved him in elections in the Caribbean and Florida, the latter earning him an invite to the inauguration of a U.S. President.

Necessary Larceny, Ian's first novel, was written while running an automotive import and export business based in Mississauga. His travel takes him to all the places he writes about, and the sequel, well underway, does the same.

Now living with wife Sharon in Mississauga, he complains his grandchildren are growing too fast and the printed word is growing too small. Other than these minor irritants, he feels life is good.

Who To Blame

The impetus for this story came from my close friends, Edward and Katherine Stanley of Bradenton, Florida. As the most active seniors I know, with the youngest and brightest outlooks on life possible, they unwittingly started the thought process involving oldsters doing things not expected of them. They are proof positive that many people no longer retire, they just change careers and get on with life.

Another culprit is my brother William G. Stout, a retired school teacher now running a splendid little art gallery in London, Ontario. He read the draft manuscript, spent hours correcting my grammar and spelling, and never once sent me to the office or gave me detentions. He was the first to read the complete story and will never know how important his encouragement has been.

Manor House Publishing, and its President, Michael B. Davie, deserve blame as well. He saw potential, put up with the author's idiosyncrasies, and stick handled the story through to the final product. There is surely a special place in heaven for publishers who take on a rookie writer and help him with his first book.

Finally I point a finger at the one person most responsible for this effort, my dear wife Sharon Ann Stout. Her faith in me and my ability; her gentle encouragement when I lost hope; and her steadfast belief the book would get finished and published kept me going. Resolutely refusing to read any of ***Necessary Larceny*** until she could hold a finished published book, her blind faith in me will always be a source of wonder. I think marrying her was the best day's work I ever did.

Foreword

Conned out of millions of dollars by slick fraud artists, the senior citizen victims are left impoverished and are too embarrassed to report the crime for fear younger relatives will deem them incompetent and remove what little control they still have over their lives.

Then, a hero emerges with a plan, a sting operation is launched to recover the stolen funds and the Necessary Larceny adventure begins.

Witty, heartwarming and intriguing, Necessary Larceny establishes Ian Stout as an important literary find, placing him firmly in the ranks of Canada's finest story-tellers.

Stout writes about the seniors populating his novel with great warmth and affection: We feel their losses, rejoice in their victories and share their invigorating sense of achievement and accomplishment in a society that for the most part considers seniors irrelevant.

Without ever resorting to preaching, Stout examines the plight of far too many elderly who exist in a state of limbo between irrelevance and death, who cope with constant loss and try to find meaning in a society blind to their value.

The elderly are often victims of scams, many of which go unreported, though the statistics concerning reported crimes are truly alarming. Stout also explores Native poverty and the mindset of those who barely eke out an existence.

One of the most inspiring novels I've read in some time.

Michael B. Davie, author, ***The Late Man***

1

"How the *hell* could you lose a *hundred thousand dollars*?" Nick Archer demanded, banging out the last three words like a hammer hitting a nail.

The silence from the phone in Florida lasted quite some time before Harry Stanton answered, his voice sounding older than Nick had ever heard before.

"It was a business investment that went south and now the money's gone. It's nothing to get your knickers in a knot about." A long silent pause followed; then Nick spoke.

"How's Kitty taking it?" Nick worried about his old friend's wife.

"Oh hell, you know Kitty. She was in from the start and took the loss like a trooper. I'm sorry though. It'll change things a lot." Harry sounded sad, as well as old and tired.

"I'm sorry too," Nick sighed. And he meant it. He and Harry Stanton went back over thirty years and though he was at least twenty years younger than Harry and his wife, the bonds of friendship grew closer and stronger each year. Now, they were more like relatives than just ordinary friends.

"Listen," Nick said, "I've some business in Miami later in the week. I've found some old ambulances in Hartford that are perfect for the Chaves operation; you know the guy I mean, the Cuban. How 'bout when I finish with him I drive over and we have one of our long lunches. I can arrange to fly home from Tampa."

"OK, let me know when and I'll make reservations," Harry offered. A moment later they exchanged goodbyes and ended the call.

Nick Archer started mentally arranging his trip as he placed the phone in its cradle. His Miami customer made a perfect excuse to find out what was going on…

Four days later Nick sat across from Harry, beer in hand, still savoring his chowder and crab cake luncheon.

The sun had long passed it's zenith but still bathed the two old friends in its warming light as they quietly sat by the water. The patio of the Twin Dolphins pub was a good choice for their lunch. Their table was apart from others and their waitress sensed the two would be in no hurry so she left them alone. Over the years she had seen their like many times. Old buddies, possibly brothers, one with a Floridian's tan; the other pale, obviously a northerner, down for a visit and a catch-up session. She knew they'd be relaxing over a long lunch, swapping stories, catching up on news, telling each other a few lies and absorbing the good vibes of just being together.

Once their plates were cleared away she came near only when the younger one's beer ran low. She'd bring a fresh one and the coffee pot for his friend. Around 3 p.m. she knew their long lunch was finally coming to an end as they both sat silently, staring into space, soaking up the late afternoon sun. She started preparing their bill.

"How could it possibly happen?" Nick asked quietly for the third or fourth time.

"I told you. It just happened. Not just to me but to quite a few others as well," Harry answered just as quietly.

He sat sullenly, looking tired and much older than Nick had ever seen. It was as though he'd aged more than half a lifetime over the last three hours of lunch and conversation. Harry looked lost.

Nick leaned forward in his chair. "So are you and Kitty completely broke?"

"Oh hell no," Harry bristled. "I've got my social security. She's got hers. We still have a few small investments that are locked in for a couple more years and I have an old pension from one of the airlines I worked for.

We also have some bonds and a bit in bank notes. We're not broke or destitute but losing a hundred thousand has put a hell of a crimp in our lifestyle. You're looking at near a thousand bucks a month income gone for the rest of our lives. We're lucky though. The house is free and clear. I didn't borrow against it, although I know some who did." He spoke in an old tired voice without looking at his friend.

Nick just nodded his head. He was still digesting the ghastly story spewed out by Harry since lunch ended, trying to sort out the whole shocking tale and not get too angry at those who had taken his friend so badly…

Their reunion had started as expected when Harry drove through downtown Bradenton to the restaurant in the Memorial Pier Building on the Manatee River. It was one of those days the Florida Tourist Board brags about in all its advertisements. As the two old friends got out of the car and strolled across the parking lot toward the waterfront, Nick knew the loss of so much money was troubling his pal. There was no spring in Harry's step. No pointing at buildings or boats and above all, no jibes about the frozen streets of Nick's home town of Toronto. Nick didn't push, but he had a feeling Harry wanted to get the whole story off his chest.

They picked a table at the end of the rail with a great view of the river and the boat docks, settling in for their lunch. It didn't take long for the story to come out.

Nick knew his friend had dropped a lot of money but was stunned to learn Harry and Kitty had lost nearly all their savings in an investment scam. Not an investment, but an investment scam. A well planned con game, run by a bunch of very smart crooks…

The whole unbelievable story started more than a year earlier when Harry and Kitty attended a charity fund raiser hosted by the local Latino Businessman's Association.

Harry had worked for Eastern Airlines in Havana many years before and always enjoyed working with his Latin brothers, as he called them.

The guest of honor at the function was a high ranking member of the Columbian Embassy staff and the aim was to raise some cash to help improve a couple of orphanages in Bogotá and Cali. It was a nice event. There were South American guitar players, finger food with salsa, and lots of drinks. The only penalty involved were some mandatory and vacuous speeches from local politicians and several of the area's prominent Latino community leaders.

Between two of the seemingly endless speeches someone introduced Harry and Kitty to Anthony DiSilva, the president of a large Columbian mining company. The charming Mr. DiSilva, or Tony, as he asked everyone to call him, was six foot tall, in his mid forties, and very well dressed. He was also burdened by the kind of smooth Latin good looks that made men envious and women breathless. With impeccable, slightly Latin accented English, he chatted of non-business things, making women laugh and men smile. By the end of the function he had exchanged cards with most everyone in the room, leaving them thinking well of him. Harry still had his card. It was very simple and rather elegant. Raised gold letters on quality cream colored card spelled out his name, Anthony J. DiSilva, his position, President, Emerald Industries Inc., and a phone number.

Kitty talked quite a bit about 'Tony' on their way home that evening, but Harry gave him or his business little thought.

Then, two weeks later Harry bumped into Jorge Martinez, an old buddy from Continental Airlines who retired to the Bradenton area a decade ago. Harry worked with him years before in Miami and Havana. Each time they got together they re-lived the good old days. This time was different; Jorge had something else on his mind. He was excited and wanted to talk.

He spoke of an investment opportunity he'd stumbled on that was sure to make him a fortune. It centered on an emerald company not just involved in mining, but jewelry manufacturing and retail sales as well. The program looked so good he planned on flying down to Columbia in a couple days to check out the whole operation. Jorge told Harry he would report back if it was interesting. Harry said okay and let it go at that.

To Harry's surprise Jorge called him eight days later and told him he just got back from Bogotá and had a ton of information on the emerald operation he had spoken of. They agreed to meet at a little seafood place on US 41 near the airport.

Over clam chowder and deep fried shrimp he filled Harry in on his discoveries about the mining and jewelry operation. Flying into Bogotá, Jorge had been met at the airport by two well dressed young men. His escorts gave him a running travel dialogue of the sites and sounds during the forty-five minute drive to the Radisson Royal and when there, they just handed him a room key. Apparently everything had been arranged. There was a note in the room from the mining company's manager regarding how the bill was taken care off and how he was looking forward to seeing Jorge in the morning. As he finished reading the note there was a gentle knock on the door. It was room service with a basket of fruit and a bottle of wine, compliments of the hotel. Jorge was impressed.

At the appointed hour the next morning a car arrived at the hotel and a polite young man drove Jorge to the mining company's head office. It was a small place, rather unassuming and set in an industrial development on the outskirts of town. There he spent an hour with the manager who had set up his hotel arrangements. Another man was there, the company's chief financial officer. The three went over the company's books and all the plans for future expansion. Jorge said they were very professional, answering all questions asked, and producing documents to back up all their claims and projections.

The thrust of the expansion, they explained, was in the retailing end of the operation. They were affiliated with one working emerald mine and owned part of a second slated to be in production within twelve months. They also owned a large part of, and had a contract with, a jewelry manufacturing facility capable of easy expansion at very little cost. They were now planning the final stage of their expansion and were currently in the process of creating a new, stand-alone, wholly owned retailing division requiring a great deal of money.

This expansion would follow the model of jewelry retailing giant H. Sterns, created in the early 1950s in Brazil by young German émigré Hans Stern and now accepted as the world leader in marketing Columbian emeralds and Brazilian gold. Emerald Industries Inc. was planning to open twenty retail stores around the world over the next three years and stock them with product from their own manufacturing facility in Columbia. The stores would first go into Miami, New York and Los Angeles. Six would open in Europe, including London, Paris, Rome and Athens. Five would be opened in several Asian Pacific Rim cities and three would be in Canada.

The new stores would be somewhat less exclusive and carry a much less costly line of product than the high end Sterns, but were still designed to attract travelers and tourists. Expensive jewelry would be included but theirs would generally be a middle class operation. This way they could keep each store's cost down to less than five hundred thousand dollars.

After the office visit Jorge was whisked to the airport, helped into a helicopter and flown to the mine. He spent an hour touring it, much of the time underground. When the tour was over he had lunch in the employee's spotless lunchroom. Then they flew over lush forests to a site where the next mine was approved and set to be in production within twelve months. This was a short visit because there really was nothing more than jungle and rock and a few stakes in the ground to look at. From there it was on to the jewelry making facility.

The manufacturing plant was impressive. At least two hundred people were employed in a modern air conditioned building polishing, soldering, tagging and boxing every type of jewelry one could imagine. They seemed happy, relaxed and diligent. It was clean, quiet and well organized. Jorge took several photos and let Harry look them over. It all seemed very impressive.

After the manufacturing plant tour Jorge was taken back into town to a large jewelry store on the ground floor of Bogotá's Hacienda Santa Barbara shopping center. It was full of middle class tourists from charter buses parked out front. Europeans, some with beer bottles in hand, wandered two and three abreast in the isles of this mini emerald mall buying everything from earrings to navel studs. Ranging in age from the mid fifties and up, most seemed intent on spending as much of their children's inheritance as they could. Their Euros were flying about with abandon and everyone was having a great time.

That evening Jorge had dinner with Tony DiSilva, who just happened to be in town for a few days. They were joined by the company's manager and two other senior members of the Emerald Industries management team. Their five course meal was superb, the entertainment spectacular and the drink glasses seemingly bottomless. It was after two when Jorge crawled into his room and flopped into bed. He was happy, impressed and not a little bit drunk.

Harry listened, saying little but taking in all the details Jorge was spreading out before him. He and Jorge went back a long way and Harry knew him as overly cautious about anything to do with money or investing. He remembered him as a man who tossed nickels around like they were manhole covers. Harry figured there must be something good here if an old tightwad like Jorge Martinez was gung ho about it…

Once Nick got Harry started on the story, the floodgates opened and he couldn't shut him up. It was a confessional with no curtain and Nick sat as priest. Harry got deeper into the telling and didn't notice the waitress come and go, refilling his coffee cup and bringing fresh beer for Nick. He needed to tell his story.

Nick took a drink of beer and leaned back. "Does Kitty know all the details?"

"She sure does. We've talked continuously about it since we knew the money was gone for ever. And I must say she's been really good about it." Harry said. "Kitty knows we were both to blame because we were both in it right from the start."

The rest of the story was predictable. Jorge spread the word amongst his circle of retirees and Harry did the same. Several meetings were held in restaurants and homes in the Sarasota-Bradenton area and the group of potential investors grew over the next few weeks. Two more went to Columbia to look over the operation much the same way Jorge did, and they came back with the same conclusions. There was no hint it was anything other than what it appeared to be and no one introduced to the plan had the slightest misgivings. Soon the money started to flow into the company and a bandwagon effect took over with new people jumping in every day.

The method of investing was very interesting. You couldn't just purchase stock in the operation; the principles claimed that would be too risky. To protect one's investment, you lent your money and received a bond from a Cayman Island company called Emerald

Industries Worldwide Marketing Limited. This company would be the operator of the chain of stores under contract to the parent company in Columbia. The loans to Emerald Industries Worldwide Marketing paid a far better rate of interest than any market offered and the money would be used to finance the creation of the stores.

The one thing that made the deal so interesting to many was a side offer involving equity ownership. Emerald Industries Inc. was a privately owned company, which had created the marketing firm as a private company as well. This was the reason given why they were not selling stock, just borrowing money. The owners wanted to grow the company far beyond its present size and then go public, making a killing on the New York Stock Exchange. What they were prepared to do was grant options, guaranteeing the right to buy stock at an incredibly low rate in the new combined corporation to anyone who loaned money.

This guarantee had no strings attached save one; it was not transferable. Your loan paid you a great rate of interest and could be redeemed any time without penalty after one year. The purchase of equity in the combined operation was separate from the loans and could be completed with whatever funds the purchaser wanted to use. Therefore one could loan Emerald Industries Worldwide twenty-five thousand at a great interest rate then purchase twenty five thousand in shares a year later with different funds. It was a win/win proposal.

Nick thought about the deal and all that led up to it with silent admiration. It was smooth, slick, and well put together. These guys were professionals.

"How much did they get?" Nick asked.

"The best we can figure is almost two million, give or take a hundred thousand." Harry said. "That's from about thirty-five of us."

Nick looked at his friend and raised an eyebrow. "What did the police have to say?"

Harry winced. In all their two-hour lunch Harry had been subdued and dejected but now he looked as though he would break down and cry. “Oh, they spent a lot of time questioning everyone who had invested but in the end said there was little they could do even if they found the gang responsible. They said the guys were not selling stock so they didn’t break any SEC rules, and the loans were simply that, loans to a bona fide corporation registered in the Caymans.” Harry shrugged his old shoulders and looked across the table at Nick. “Our local authorities checked Cayman Islands. Their police said an embezzlement was reported by the company several months ago. It seems their bank accounts had been conveniently emptied by an employee who then disappeared. There was an investigation but the thief was sure to have left the island. Both police departments figure it was just another scam by the original guys but there’s no proof.”

Again Nick prodded: “What about the parent company, or the people at the mine or the jewelry factory? Can’t they do something?”

“We checked them,” Harry sighed. “They’ve no idea who these people are and none have ever heard or had any connection with a company in the Cayman Islands. They did have marketing agreements with a host of organizations around the world but none were from the Cayman Islands.”

“Well my friend” Nick said as he stood up with the bill in hand, “if the cops or the Security Commission or the parent company can’t, or won’t, or are unable to do anything, we’ll just have to do something about it ourselves. Let us be on our way, old buddy, we have a lot of work ahead and time’s a-wasting,” He dropped an extra large tip with his payment on the table and headed for the parking lot with his friend in tow.

2

Tony DiAngelo, in the aisle seat, and Al Silvestro, sitting next to him at the window, hardly spoke to each other during the entire flight from New York. One would think they were strangers but one would be fooled. They arrived separately at the airport, stood in line together and checked in without exchanging a dozen words. They were the type of co-workers with little need for conversation and a great fear of detection when setting out on a new project. They had finished two months of research and planning just a week before their flight and were ready to get the show on the road. Besides, neither believed it was a good idea talking about their kind of business in a public place where anyone could be listening.

In fact, as on every flight they ever took together, Al slept his time away and missed the meal service. Tony always told the Flight Attendant to leave his partners food tray and he'd save it for when the sleeping beauty awoke. The Flight Attendant always laughed, agreed, put the meal tray on the large arm rest between them, and moved on. Tony would then immediately switch the full tray with his empty one and gobble up everything on it. After all, it was always pasta and Tony was Italian. Besides, the meal was included.

As the American Airlines flight taxied toward Sky Harbor's Terminal 3 the two businessmen stretched, relaxed and looked out on the parched Arizona landscape. Tony marveled out loud how anyone could turn a wasteland as burned and bleak as this into a desirable retirement destination. He found it amazing how Del Webb, one of the area's original developers, could envision a city of seniors in a desert area know for it's blistering heat, lack of water, and for a long time, tough, bad tempered locals.

Not only did Webb imagine it, he put together fifteen-million dollars, bought twenty thousand acres of cotton fields and adjacent wasteland and constructed Sun City. It was the biggest and most uniquely designed senior's developments in the country. He sold the units in his dream city to seniors and near retirees in places like Camden New Jersey and Yonkers New York who had never been further southwest than Pittsburgh. Salesmanship this good was one of the few things in life Tony respected.

"How did he ever do it?" Al asked.

"Hell, he could do just about anything he wanted. You know, he owned the Yankees when Mickey Mantel played. He was a very, very close friend of Howard Hughes right to the end of Hughes life. In 1946, he was the man who built the Flamingo Casino in Las Vegas for Ben Siegel and Meyer Lansky back when the town had few paved roads. Yes sir, Del Webb was one hell of a colorful man and moved in pretty fast circles. He even owned racing cars and had one in the 1961 Indianapolis 500. It came third." Tony sighed. "He was some salesman."

Al was impressed. "You mean he actually did work for Bugsy Siegel?"

"Not Bugsy, Al. He hated that nick-name and if you didn't want your face broken, you call him Ben, or Benjamin, or if you were really smart, Mr. Siegel."

"Sounds like building a city in a desert for old geezers would be small change for this Webb guy, if he outlived someone like Siegel. I hope we have the same success here."

Tony smiled. He was a good salesman. Not of the stature of a Del Webb mind you, but a good salesman just the same. This trip to Phoenix with his partner of many years was to set up a new sales operation. Since finishing up in

Florida all of them had been enjoying a sabbatical for over a year. It was time to go back to work.

Over the past eight weeks Tony and Al spent endless hours pouring over mountains of paper and internet files, analyzing demographics, incomes and the layout of areas across the nation. They were looking for the next place to restart their unique operation. They researched hospital facilities, especially ones geared toward seniors; studied weather, taxes, banking institutions, real estate prices and a dozen other items. By a process of elimination, the Greater Phoenix area was the best of the lot. All the palms and the constant sun attracted thousands of seniors, making it a natural for their type of program.

The plane finally came to a halt at the bridge and Tony stood with the rest and opened the overhead bin. He handed Al his jacket and carry-on bag and pulled his own computer bag out. His laptop was the gateway to his office and locked away inside behind multiple passwords and firewalls were all the details of their game plan. He once explained to Al everything was on his home desktop while his laptop was virtually empty. That was because if it was stolen, or worse, fell into police hands, it held nothing incriminating.

Al knew something about computers but it took extensive explaining and introduction to a program called 'Go To My Computer' to see how Tony accomplished this. It was a pretty cool setup.

Tony's files included everything from the names of newspapers for advertising to potential office locations and short term furniture rental companies. He was a detail man and this characteristic above all was behind his success over the years. His attention to detail encompassed everything involving his work and his life. In his clothing he only wore hand made suits created by an elderly Italian tailor from his home town. His shirts were of the best Egyptian cotton and had to be from Trimminghams in Hamilton, Bermuda. He wore only understated silk ties.

His hair never needed a cut even when he went to his regular barber. His personal stationary was the best cream-colored bond paper with his name and address in small discreet gold letters across the bottom. Of course there were matching envelopes. With Tony, it was always the same; details, details and more details.

Once off the plane Tony made his usual stop at the first washroom. There was nothing wrong with his bladder but there could be something wrong with his apparel. After a thorough check of his tie, pocket handkerchief, French cuffs and hair, he was ready for the world. Joining Al outside near the bookstand, they headed out, striding through the huge terminal without a sideway glance along the way. Both had been there on separate occasions over the past several weeks and knew where they were going. They marched straight out to the curb into the blistering hundred-degree heat cooking the pavement of the arrivals level.

As arranged, their maroon Cadillac sat glistening in the sunlight, waiting for them with engine running, air conditioning blasting, and liveried chauffer standing near the rear door. His timing was perfect and the door opened five seconds before the two smartly dressed businessmen climbed in. They looked like they were arriving to buy the biggest bank in town. The car door quietly clicked shut and the chauffer moved around to the driver's side and slid behind the wheel. Silently, smoothly, the car slipped away from the curb, blending into the flowing traffic, becoming just another vehicle heading for the expressway into town.

3

Nick caught the last seat on the last flight out of Tampa for Toronto, feeling lucky to get the middle seat in the back row. His wife, a long time Air Canada employee, constantly nagged him not to delay his departure to the very last plane but like most men, he never listened. She was right of course. One could only fly employee standby if a seat was empty. Anyone, absolutely anyone who paid got on before you. Anne bugged him about going early because one of the planes was bound to have one seat vacant but if it was a busy day, overbooked passengers would be moved to the next flight, filling those seats he thought empty. Leaving it to the last could easily result in being bumped and spending a night in an airport hotel, or worse, in the airport. His ticket price was small but it could be a pain in the ass watching "go shows" taking the last seat.

This flight was full of sad and weary tourists laden with cheap bottles of duty-free booze and leading bleary eyed kids sporting Goofy or Mickey hats. It wasn't long into the flight before the sound of snoring gently crept into every corner of the plane. Nick was one of the very few with his overhead light on carefully poking at his laptop and going over reams of note paper.

He spent most of his time between leaving the restaurant and getting his flight running over details of the theft with Harry and Kitty. Now that he knew the story there was no sense in anything other than an open and very frank discussion with no recriminations or blame setting. He prodded their memories, forcing them to recall details they thought gone like their money. He convinced them to tell him everything, no matter how small or potentially embarrassing, making pages of notes for the days ahead.

Nick knew he couldn't walk away from his friend's catastrophe without at least searching for a solution. He was also aware you couldn't fix anything until you had every last detail of what you wanted to fix. He was sure there were more facets of this than he picked up during the lunch meeting and experience told him the devil was in the details, the bigger the problem, the greater the need to know all those details.

Harry said the police had little information on anyone called Anthony DiSilva. There were no warrants outstanding and a deeper check indicated no police record anywhere in the US and nothing at Interpol. With only the first names of a few others they met, there wasn't much more for the police to work on. Harry suggested the cops just went through the motions and had little interest in searching for people they probably couldn't charge and certainly had no chance of convicting. He suggested the officers' enthusiasm under-whelmed him. It may have helped had the victims known who the villains were but it was almost a year since the sting, and law enforcement had moved on to bigger and more newsworthy problems. If anything was to be done it was up to Nick and his friend. Their first problem was finding out who the hell was responsible.

He got things rolling by asking Kitty to spend the next few days writing down every detail she could remember about the handsome and charming Mr. DiSilva. It took him some time convincing her he needed every single detail no matter how insignificant. Did he wear a watch? What kind? What color were his shoes? Did they lace up or were they loafers? Did he wear any jewelry? How about an earring and in which ear? Was his shirt open and did he wear a chain? Did it have a medallion or cross? Did he wear a ring? Did it have a gemstone or was it a school type insignia ring? He asked her to think about his shirt and whether the collar was fused or button down and did the sleeves button or have French cuffs? He asked her to think of anything and everything about him and any other person she may have met.

He pressed Harry to try and remember where they met and who paid the bill and if by cash or credit card. He also wanted to know where these guys stayed, a hotel or condo and to think about how long they took to meet them or go somewhere.

"Most people" Nick explained, "stay close to their home or home base. If these guys suggested a restaurant to meet at it would probably be close to their residence. Think of where they ate and we'll draw a circle around it on map and look for where they stayed. We also need an accurate time line. If we're checking hotels, restaurants or car rentals, we need a start and end date. Check your bank account. It'll say when you handed over your cash."

He wanted to know what make of car they drove, was it new, big and expensive or a small economy model. Did he think it a rental? Did it have Florida plates? He explained how some car rental companies have only certain types of cars so they could narrow their search by a process of elimination. With some reluctance his friends made notes and agreed to follow these instructions. Both were dubious but said they would do what they could until he returned.

Nick sat with a downcast Harry and his slightly more optimistic wife for the better part of two hours going over ideas and was ready to smack his friend on the side of the head. If he heard the phrase 'there's nothing you can do' one more time he thought he'd scream.

"Harry," Nick finally snapped, "shut the hell up. If you want me to forget about this and just go home, say so. Otherwise knock off the whining crap about all is lost and the sky has fallen. All is not necessarily lost. There are far too many people involved and too much money gone to just sit around weeping and wringing our hands. Let's just get on with fixing the problem."

Harry bounced out of his seat. "Well, what the hell *can* be done?" Harry shouted back, storming around the room and waving his arms. "The money's gone. The thieving rats who stole it are gone. We don't even know who they are or where they came from. We don't even know if DiSilva is the bastard's real name. The police did a cursory investigation and say little can be done. Who the hell are you to think you can change all that?" Harry stormed out of the room.

Kitty had been sitting opposite the two men on the other side of the coffee table watching them argue. Now, she leaned forward in her seat and tried to make peace.

"Leave him to me Nick. He's upset but believe me, most of all he's embarrassed. I know he figures you'll think less of him for being stupid enough to get taken. Several of the others feel the same way. No one bothered to check these guys out or call their broker for a simple update on the emerald company. It's amazing how we all ignored the obvious basics of investing and due diligence, but everyone, including me, slipped up.

"None have told their children, or anyone else for that matter. Other than the police you may be the only outsider aware of this." Holding her hands tightly together on her knees, she stared across at him, pleading for understanding. "It's part of growing old, Nick. Any slip from perfection sets off warning bells in the heads of younger friends and all your relatives. They think you're going senile, needing care, maybe have Alzheimer's, just like they saw on CNN. Then they have to step in and take control of your life and all your financial affairs. They feel society demands they get involved, take over, protecting the old fools from themselves; and if they don't, they're bad children. You'd be amazed at how quick they are to get in. I believe many do it to protect their inheritance." She spoke quietly but with conviction.

"Leave him with me a few minutes," she added. "He's

embarrassed and hurt but once he's over that, he'll help, believe me, he'll help." She stood to follow Harry out of the room.

Nick marveled at the lady and her serenity as she moved to join her husband. She was more sad and resolute than dejected or downcast. Standing straight and tall, moving with quiet dignity, she turned away from him to push open the screen door, joining her distraught husband on the lawn. She knew the last years of her life would be different from what she had thought they would be, but no matter. Without hesitation, anger or recriminations, she set her disappointment aside, forgetting about future trips and holidays, and went to take care of her man. Nick hoped Harry knew how lucky he was.

In the stillness of the living room Nick turned to the front window to see Kitty sitting on the bench near the grapefruit tree while Harry picked several large ripe specimens and put them in a plastic grocery bag. Nick shook his head in wonder at how his old friend remembered to do this small thing for him in the midst of such a financial mess. Now, Nick returned his attention to his notes, adding things he thought he might need. He wasn't sure he could do anything at all but it only took a glance outside at his two old friends to make him want to try very hard.

The two came back in as Nick finished the last of his lists. It included a request for as many names of their fellow victims as they could remember, and how much each lost. He also asked them to find out if anyone knew where the gang stayed and what rental car company they might have used while in town. It would take some work but they must have used credit cards and their names could be verified. On top of that, he wanted some idea of each victim's background or work history. He knew there could be a lot of research work ahead and some of the group may be able to help.

"One last thing Harry, find me an artist, a portrait artist. Get me one who can draw a face from a verbal description. You know, like they do in those crime shows on TV. It may cost a few bucks but let's see if we can put together a couple of pictures of these guys to show around hotels and car rental agencies." This suggestion made Harry smile for the first time that day.

The three of them spent the rest of the time before Nick left for the airport discussing how things might go during the next few days. He was sure he left them with a little hope and enough to keep them busy for a while. Finally, when Nick was ready to leave they stood outside on Harry's lawn enjoying the soft Florida evening air.

"Kitty, look after him please. He needs all the care and attention you've got" Nick advised as he gave her a hug and a goodbye kiss.

"And you" he said to Harry, "go over the list, see what you can do with the items on it and don't give me any crap. If you do, I'll come back down here and kick your ass," and he grabbed him in a bear hug. "Don't worry old friend", he whispered, "we're going to solve this one together."

In an instant, bag of grapefruit safely beside him, Nick was in his car, backing up and tooting the horn goodbye. He was heading home to his wife Ann. She had to hear about this; her input would be valuable.

4

Their meal done, Tony and Al were relaxing with coffee and liqueurs. Tony was big on Frangelico, claiming his family lived for centuries on the banks of the Po River in Italy where the liqueur came from. Al, no less Italian, was a Drambuie man all the way. He often said Italians made the best wine in the world but the Scots sure knew how to make a liqueur. Their drinks were doubles, waiting to be quietly sipped from their snifters as their coffee cooled in large mugs. Both men felt well fed, a little boozy and very satisfied with the past few days of work.

From the moment they climbed into the Cadillac at the airport until this meal, they had worked steadily putting their operation into gear. Tony's first job was to find office space and that was accomplished on the second day. He came across a nice second floor unit of about fifteen hundred square feet with a large reception area, a board room and six offices off a long imposing corridor. Although a little larger than needed, it met all other criteria including the most important: it looked expensive. The carpet was better than most, thick and fairly new. The doors overly tall, of beautifully stained oak and when swung shut, closed with a solid click. The place had the air of a very upscale law office and that's exactly what Tony had been looking for. He wanted the feeling of understated wealth and power, properly managed by a group of solid, stable, and honest businessmen.

While he did real estate, Al handled office furniture

and all the other things needed in a well run place. The list he carried into Office Max was long, an exact duplicate of his Bradenton list of many months ago, and included everything from pencils to paperclips. He and Tony learned it was easier to purchase everything their office would need to look legitimate and just leave it when the job was finished. They knew it would all be repossessed, seized by the landlord or stolen by the time someone discovered what they were up to.

Al pushed his shopping cart up and down the store's aisles, grabbing electric pencil sharpeners, three-hole punches, file folders, several different packages of colored paper and multi-packs of scotch tape. By the time he finished he could have outfitted a small corner of the Pentagon. Paying with crisp fifty dollar bills, he made two trips loading everything into his rented van.

After supplies came equipment. Al could have leased everything over the phone but thought that could appear a little suspicious. He spent an hour at the local office furniture and electronics outlet, letting a young salesman display his knowledgeable of the store's wares. He arranged the lease on all the hardware a well run office would need including two computers, a fax machine, photocopier and a projector for large screen displays. He also arranged desks, chairs, a boardroom table, filing cabinets and even a brass coat rack. Al knew that once it was all delivered and set up, he would have his chance to add his touches. With the salesman's card in hand he promised a call back in the morning with the delivery address, then headed off to do phones.

The two villains had done this a few times but Al never got over his partner's attention to detail. No item, no matter how insignificant, escaped Tony's sharp eye.

Tony always looked around and picked up several local calendars from realtors, garages and banks. Patiently he'd sit at his desk and tear off all the past months. Then he'd mark off the days gone by with a black felt pen. Occasionally he'd use a red pen for effect. On all of them he scrawled 'Stan's Stag' on one Friday and 'Stanley the Manley's Wedding' a week latter on Saturday. This done, his used calendars were hung next to the receptionist's desk and over the coffee machine. The latter had 'Cindy's Baby, 7 lb 5 oz.' scribbled across the flowers of its picture. Each desk then received a small folding card calendar from the local bank where Tony opened the corporate accounts.

He then pulled a handful of business cards from his briefcase and walked through the offices sticking them under corners of desk calendars, on cork boards and next to phones. These cards came from realtors, restaurants, taxis and delivery services he had used or talked to over the past couple days or on previous visits to the area. Tony always asked for more than one, ostensibly to stock his pocket, his briefcase and his head office. No one ever refused. He expected Al to do the same.

Tony's final touches included a few small plants in pop bottles or jars placed on desks plus several photos of tiny kids with messy faces spread about. A casual observer would think the place had been in business for years.

Al headed to the local Nextel office and purchased six cell phones in the company name. These would be the main method of communication over the next couple of months. Paying cash, he moved on to the local phone company to arrange the office phones. He was surprised at how fast things went during the day and when he met Tony at four-thirty in their new office, his list was done for the day and he had cleared off a couple of items from the next day's list. He got the exact address and zip code to call in to the office supply and phone company in the morning and then closed his daybook. He had accomplished a lot and it was time to relax.

"How'd it go?" Tony asked.

"Good, real good. I've got a pile of stuff out in the van. Give me a hand and we'll be out of here in short order."

It took only three trips in the elevator to get the boxes of supplies into the new office. They piled them on the lobby floor out of the way so the furniture movers could get through the next day.

While they lugged the boxes from the van they talked about their plans and what was going to happen over the next few days. Tony had called Stan in Cincinnati, Leo in Hartford, their Miami muscle Frank, and the rest of their group around the country. It had been a year since the last job and they were getting a little bored. Most liked the idea of a couple of months in the sun and jumped at the chance of a gig in Phoenix. Stan would be arriving in two days and the rest would straggle in over the next three or four. Tony had leased a fully furnished five bedroom house with a finished basement complete with second kitchen on the northwest side of the city. The guys could sleep there. Things were coming together as they had planned and both felt this venture could be the best yet.

Tony locked the door and handed Al one of the several keys on a ring he held in his hand. They smiled at each other, both feeling good about the project as they strolled down the hall to the elevator. Tonight was a night to relax, have a good meal, a few drinks and maybe some temporary female companionship.

After that, the real work would begin.

5

Nick called Harry minutes after getting up and wasn't surprised when the phone only rang once before his old friend answered.

"Hi Nick," Harry greeted between noisy mouthfuls of raison bran.

"Damn call display," Nick said. "I'm sorry I told you about it."

"I'm glad you did. You'd be surprised at how many aluminum siding salesmen it's saved me from insulting." He laughed at his friend and kept on munching.

"At least I'm some use then. You'd probably have six coats of siding on that place of yours with a new crew getting out of their trucks as we speak. Hell, your house would be the size of a hotel by now," Nick said as he sorted his paperwork on his desk, arranging a list he wanted to discuss with Harry.

"I've got a list of things for you to do. They'll require some work. Are you up to it?"

Without hesitation Harry told him to fire away. His exact words were: 'Your wish is my command, oh mighty master."

"We need a meeting of those burned in the scam. We need as many as possible together in one room to go over stuff I've dug up. We may need all of them involved so I want them to hear my ideas and we'll need some discussion about the plans to recover their money; your money as well, by the way." Nick said, waiting a minute for the request to sink in.

Nick knew he had a tough row to hoe and it would take some smooth talk to convince everyone to get on board, but he was a salesman and salesmen were supposed to sell. His friend and all the others would be tough but he was sure he could convince them to buy in. Harry was slow coming back and all the joking was gone from his voice. “Do you think it’s possible?”

“Of course I think so,” Nick asserted. “Now listen to me. Besides getting as many together as possible, I need the full list of everyone who lost money and how much they lost. I also need their backgrounds and some of the things they have an interest in, you know, hobbies, outside interests, stuff like that. Besides all this, I need to know what they did before they retired and if any of their families are in the same business now or if they still have connections with that part of their life. I have to know what resources these people can call on if and when we need to do some calling. Let’s find out if they have relatives or friends we can beg, borrow or steal things from... Are you getting all this?”

Without waiting for an answer, Nick continued. “I also want to see at the meeting if they have the nerve to get involved in this and if they’re ready to spend a few bucks as well. The process of getting their money back won’t be easy and it’s going to take some money, a pile of work, and one hell of a lot of nerve. Now, have you got all that?”

“Of course I’ve got it all. I’m the fastest writer in the world but just in case I missed a word or two, do me a favor and Fax your list. Put everything you need on paper and I’ll take care of it. And yes, I think they’ll all be in.” Harry said this with authority but Nick felt his friend wasn’t too sure.

“Okay, the list is going into the machine as we speak and you’ll have it in a minute.” Nick didn’t want to waste any time. “Harry, I need some action on it right away. I have a business meeting in Miami tomorrow and I can spare a couple days in your area after that. It's perfect timing for setting things up. Decide who the key players are besides you and Kitty and get them on side. I'll drive over after my meeting to get things started and I haven't any time to waste."

"Okay boss." Harry said in his best Rochester imitation, and hung up his phone…

Nick went back to work. On his return a few days before from Tampa he had contacted Paul Fellows, an old drinking buddy nearing his thirty-fifth year with the Royal Canadian Mounted Police. Over lunch Nick filled him in on the plight of his friends in Florida and asked for help in tracking down some of the villains involved. He gave Paul the few names he had and passed on the comments of the police in Bradenton and the local FBI office regarding the scam. Paul promised to check it out and get back to Nick when he had anything. He said it was the least he could do for a free lunch.

True to his word, Paul called two days later with some information about the gang who worked the Sarasota-Bradenton area, as well as a couple other similar scams they may have been involved in over the years. He was also claiming another free lunch.

Paul had more facts than Nick could have hoped for. To start with, the Florida police knew a lot more about these guys than they indicated to Harry and the other victims. Paul explained why they couldn't pass these details on to the victims. The Police Department could have been sued had they given out private information on people who were not charged with any crime and in effect, innocent of any wrongdoing.

Several were known to police, as the saying goes, in one jurisdiction or another throughout the US. In fact, a couple had fairly long rap sheets for white collar and non violent crimes. Crimes like phony credit cards, bad checks, that sort of thing. It was a gang, a very well organized group headed by two very smart confidence men who were slick enough to stay out of jail so far. In fact, since they got together several years ago, none had crossed paths with authorities for as much as a speeding ticket. Now, all they appeared to be involved in was this sophisticated Ponzi scheme dressed up as a major off-shore industry. Their targets: unsuspecting and vulnerable seniors with money to invest.

Paul claimed the police had scrutinized their scam but could find nothing to sink their teeth into. At present, law enforcement agencies were looking into mail fraud and income tax evasion but at the moment, all were powerless to stop them. They weren't selling stocks, debentures or bonds. They didn't promise any returns other than interest for monies loaned to them and they backed that up with promissory notes. Their company was a real one, based on a Caribbean island and appearing to meet all international standards of accounting and record keeping. It even owned property in several countries including a thousand acres in the Brazilian jungle, a beachfront house north of the airport serving Rousseau, the capital of the tiny impoverished Caribbean island of Dominica. They also had an interest in a closed and seemingly empty emerald mine in Columbia.

Paul laughed when Nick asked him about the possibility of suing the company to at least get interest payments. Paul explained how the system worked.

"Nick, that's a civil matter, not a criminal one. The company is legit. It has a bank account with a couple thousand in it. It complies with all requirements of the country it's based in.

The company asked some people to loan them money and promised a great rate of interest. Then they didn't pay anything on these loans. Big deal, defaults on interest payments happen all the time, occasionally to some pretty substantial corporations."

"The rules where the company is based are certainly not as tough as ours but if one plays by them, there's no way anything can be done. Public records list the President and Secretary and the company's accounting firm and lawyer, that's all the regulations require." Paul took a long pull on his beer and went on.

"It's a private company with only two registered stockholders. They don't have to tell anything more than they have. We have no way of knowing who's on the payroll or what assets they have other than what they want to tell us. In the end it's a civil matter and that's where the fun begins."

He took another mouthful of beer. "If you want to sue, you'll need a lawyer in Florida and one on the company's home island and it won't be a contingency case, they'll want money up front and lots of it. Then you keep paying these lawyers for the next three years and it goes to trial and what do you know, you win." Paul couldn't help smiling here. He waved to the waitress for a couple more drinks and turned back to Nick.

"When it's all over you have a claim on a few thousand stashed in an island bank, a worthless mine, some useless acreage in the 'boonies' of Brazil and a beachfront shack on a lovely dirt poor island no one can find or get to, or, for that matter, cares about. All it cost you was a hundred grand or so and three or four years of your life. Hell, I bet some of your friends in Florida won't live long enough to see the end. I might suggest they accept their losses, lick their wounds till the pain goes away, and get on with life." He sat back, picked up his beer and waited.

Nick just sat quietly thinking. He knew that Paul was giving good sound advice. He was a wise and compassionate person; one who had seen just about all the bad things some people can do to others. If Paul thought there was any possible way to get back this group of senior's money, he'd jump at the chance to help. As it was, he knew the limitations of the law and sometimes it broke his heart being so helpless.

"These guys study the law like university students prepping for finals," Paul continued. "They know every nook and cranny of it and how to get around every rule. It's their business, their life, their career. They've spent years figuring out how to screw people and walk away without a look back. I sometimes think the only way to get back at bastards like them is to apply the golden rule. Do unto them exactly what they have done unto you." Paul chuckled. "I know it's impossible but it sure would be nice."

"Yea, it sure would be." Nick muttered, half to himself, draining his glass and pulling out some money for the bill. "Thanks Paul, I owe you."

"No you don't. The lunches make us even. I'm just sorry I can't help."

Standing next to his car outside the bar, Paul stuck out his hand and smiled. "I know you Nick. We've been friends a long time. You've got that glint in your eye. You're off on another crusade and I have the feeling I'll hear more of this as time goes by. Just remember, if there's anything I can do to help, call, just don't tell anyone where you're getting your information or where that list of names or other facts came from." He gave Nick a light slap on the shoulder and climbed into his car and was quickly gone, leaving his friend deep in thought, standing in the restaurant parking lot.

Paul didn't know it but he had given Nick the solution to his problem. Now it was time to get to work.

6

The next day Nick arrived in Miami and found it much the same as he left it after his last visit; hot, noisy, brassy, and lots of fun. He loved the vibes of the place, its Cuban atmosphere and revived Art Deco style. He flew into South Florida every chance he got. Many suspected he arranged his business there simply as an excuse to visit.

This trip wasn't arranged though. Nick had found several well used ambulances near Hartford Connecticut and was trying to sell them to Orlando Chevas, a Cuban expatriate who owned a small automotive exporting business near Miami Airport. Orlando, now in his seventies, escaped north with many of his countrymen when Castro took control of his homeland. Arriving on a packed, leaky old fishing boat with less than $300 US in his pocket, Orlando herded his wife and three children into a world he'd only visited once or twice. All of the family's possessions were stuffed into four hastily packed suitcases he dragged into his new homeland. Not in the bags but tucked away in his head was the one thing Orlando owned and Fidel could least afford to lose; the priceless experience and knowledge of an excellent administrator.

These skills were honed during more than twenty years of managing the largest General Motors car and truck dealership in Cuba. Orlando was determined to use this knowledge to make good in his new country, and he did.

A fellow Cuba escapee offered a job near Disneyland but after some thought, he turned it down. His command of English was good enough to realize an Orlando working in Orlando might not be a good career move. He knew a lot of goods were exported from the port of Miami, including cars and trucks. Staying near the harbor made sense.

His friends and business associates considered him the most knowledgeable truck man from Cuba and news of his arrival and plans quickly spread through the Latino auto community. He started a used car and truck operation, specializing in exporting vans, busses, and other specialty vehicles to Spanish speaking countries in the Caribbean basin. Soon he was shipping to Costa Rica, Nicaragua, Panama, Guatemala and Mexico. Rumors had him dealing in other, more sinister places but little proof existed. It was said one would occasionally see his clients on TV in handcuffs or in gory newspaper photos, bound and bloody, thrown into the dirt of a jungle road; reportedly killed as a revolutionary or patriot, depending on who did the shooting. These episodes always upset Orlando, who said customers were hard enough to find as it was.

This trip involved older Ford diesel ambulances that might be interesting and Nick had brought pictures and specs for consideration. He could have emailed everything but both businessmen were a little old fashioned. Orlando hated computers, and although Nick could use them, he liked working face to face. Mind you, if Orlando's business was in Wisconsin, and it was dead of winter, Nick would have mailed everything in a nice fat brown envelope.

Orlando was waiting in a No Parking zone on the arrivals level of Miami International. After tossing his bag and computer in the back seat, Nick jumped in front beside him.

"Buenos dias, me amigo," he said.

"It's 'buenas tardes' and your Spanish still stinks, buddy," Orlando admonished playfully, making Nick smile, because his friend was right. When they first met a few years back, Orlando told Nick he must learn a little Spanish. Nick agreed, and it was settled that during each visit, a new phrase would be learned and memorized. The first such phrase was easy. It would be 'La cuenta, por favor'. Orlando and his staff made Nick repeat it over and over during that first morning while they went over possible sales and the types of vehicle of most interest to the Cubans. As each employee passed on the lot or in the showroom, they would demand with a good natured smile "hey, gringo, what's the phrase?" and Nick would shout back "La cuenta, por favor." Then they went to lunch.

Orlando and his sales manager picked a fabulous little Cuban restaurant filled with dark mustachioed men looking like they were plotting to overthrow some government in a far off land. The car lot gang ate a lot and emptied several bottles of wine during two hours of guy talk. Nick was the only one there whose native tongue was English and Orlando asked him if he remembered the Spanish phrase.

"Sure I do." Nick said.

"Then try it on the waiter and see if he understands you. It'll be a good test."

"Alright, watch this," Nick said. "Senor, senor," calling the waiter and smiling, he asked "La cuenta, por favor."

"The waiter smiled back, pulled the bill from his shirt pocket, gave it to a stunned Nick saying "gracias, senor."

The laughter in the restaurant was deafening. Everyone in the place seemed in on the joke and there was much cheering and whooping by patrons and staff alike. Orlando could barely speak and almost fell off his chair but through his peals of laughter, he told Nick his accent was excellent.

Nick never forgot the phrase or the lesson, but Orlando did buy three vehicles so Nick could well afford the lunch. Since that memorable day he'd learned a few more phrases but Orlando was right, his Spanish did stink.

"I think a student's failure is mostly the fault of the teacher," Nick said and both had a good laugh. "By the way, who's picking up lunch this time?"

"I will, but these ambulances better be good."

Nick assured him they were and the topic changed to politics, sports, women, and Nick's friend in Bradenton and how he wasn't flying out of Miami but renting a car to drive over later that day. He knew the deal had all but been made and they could get on with more important things. It was a pleasant morning topped off with another great lunch at a superb little Cuban restaurant, and Orlando did pay.

Nick left for Bradenton with a handshake deal for up to six of the Hartford ambulances and Orlando's offer of any help needed in Bradenton. He made it a point to stress the 'any' part of the offer of help. He then phoned a friend who owned a rental agency and a car was brought over for Nick.

The drive across Alligator Alley was a favorite and if Nick had the time, he always checked at one of the bridges to see if any of the ugly beasts were relaxing in the water. The first stop had none but he got lucky fifteen miles further along where a whole family had come out just for him. About thirty feet below the highway, half out of the water in the mud, lazed five alligators soaking up the sun.

One was very large, one pretty large and three that looked like they'd be able to eat him in a couple of chomps. Nick waved at them and shouted obscenities but they took no notice. He figured they were full from the last driver who bothered them, so he waved goodbye and moved on.

Harry knew Nick was coming but Harry knew better than to expect him at any specific time. Nick would get there when he got there and he always checked into his hotel before letting anyone know of his arrival. As a very private person well set in his ways, Nick enjoyed being alone. Not only that, he was by far the world's worst house guest and never stayed at anyone's home when he visited.

The Hilton Garden Inn was exactly where he had left it across from the airport the last time he was in Bradenton. The staff were just as pleasant and the rooms just as nice. It was like coming home. Tired, he decided to read a paper beside the pool, get dinner and hit the sack early. He would call Harry first thing in the morning to set up the meeting.

7

Much to Nick's surprise, Harry was able to put together all the asked for arrangements in less than twenty-four hours. He had a list of every person in his area stung by the scam and it contained a little over thirty names. The meeting was also set up. Twenty-six of the victims from Harry's list had agreed to attend and several others suggested they would try to rearrange golf games or doctor's appointments. The get-together was for two o'clock that afternoon at a local restaurant owned by one of the victims. He generously offered Harry his small banquet room plus light refreshments for the gathering.

The second list, the one with everyone's background and previous employment, was not yet complete but Harry faxed what he had to the hotel. As Nick looked over it he was a little surprised at the vast breadth of experience throughout the list of retirees. Several people worked or owned business in a wide variety of very diverse and interesting backgrounds.

One listed himself as a sign painter but in fact had built a large Paterson, New Jersey printing and sign making operation now run by his two sons. Another New Jersey native retired once as a police officer in Trenton and then retired ten years later as chief of security at one of Trump's casinos in Atlantic City. Also near the top of the list was the aforementioned semi-retired restaurateur from Michigan. There was a Moore, Oklahoma car and truck dealer, whom Nick made a note to talk to; an Indiana insurance executive and a woman who managed a welfare office for the City of

Hartford. Near the bottom was a name with one word after it: Marine. He made a note beside that one. This meeting promised to be very interesting. Nick was looking forward to meeting this gang.

His scheme was now a fully developed plan and he was ready to present it at the meeting. It had received Anne's personal seal of approval before he left for Miami but only after she had spent some time getting her laughter under control, which required a very stiff drink. She told him he was nuts but it might be possible for such a nutty plan to work. Then she kissed him on the forehead and told him she was happy she married such a madman and left the room, drink in hand, chuckling away.

After returning from Tampa, Nick had sat Anne down and filled her in on all the details of the problem in Florida. They went over several possible ways of solving the problem but all required lawyers, courts, investigations and tons of money. None seemed any good so he went back to his original idea prompted by the bar chat with Paul, his RCMP friend.

Adjourning to his home office, Nick worked for several hours, plotting the program on paper. He knew it would be a hard sell, especially to a diverse group of retired people relaxing in Florida who wanted nothing more exciting to do than learning to e-mail their grandchildren. For all Nick knew, they might all appear at the afternoon meeting slowly pushing walkers or riding in electric wheelchairs or tricycles. He also expected most would be complaining about the government. No matter, he said, as he presented his plan to his wife, this was the best and possibly only way.

Anne's reaction clinched the deal. If she thought it was a good plan, although somewhat hilarious, it must be a winner.

8

Harry, always a natty dresser, was standing in his usual sartorial splendor in Arrivals, awaiting Nick. He always drew attention when he stood around a busy place such as an airport and often people came up requesting his autograph. Harry loved it. When asked, he would whip out his gold-banded black Waterman's fountain pen, slip the cap off with a practiced flourish and ask to whom the autograph was to be made out to. When they answered he would graciously pen a nice note and sign it with broad sweeping strokes. Harry would then smile like a Prince bestowing honors, pat any accompanying little child on the head and shake hands with the requestor, indicating their interlude with greatness was over. Happily clutching their autograph, the thrilled recipient would move away, never knowing whether the autograph came from a political leader or an aging movie star but quite sure it came from a very special and very important person.

Nick always had a good laugh with Harry when these incidents happened but also enjoyed the looks of awe and respect from those nearby when Harry greeted him, shook hands like an old friend, and headed for the parking lot carrying one of Nick's bags. He was viewed as important because they saw someone they thought important treating Nick with respect. As they walked out through the arrivals area, their conversation usually centered on how many autographs Harry signed. It was a great joke and both got a great kick out of it.

On the long drive out of the Tampa Terminal to the airport exit ramp Nick asked Harry to take the Howard

Franklin Causeway across Old Tampa Bay on I-275. This route south to Bradenton took them over the spectacular new Tampa Bay Bridge which Nick always loved crossing. The drive was longer than taking I-75 on the east of the Bay and the bridge toll was a whole dollar, but he liked the drive through the St. Pete's area and the scenery of the long crossing of the new bridge.

He recalled the old dual bridges towering side by side above the entrance to Tampa Bay and well remembered the day a ship collided with the base of one, bringing its center span crashing down onto the ship and into the water. Several cars fell with the bridge, taking those inside to a violent watery grave.

For many years Nick drove to Harry's place over the remaining high span, reduced to single lanes to accommodate the highway. It seemed forever for the new bridge to be built and the remaining reminder of the tragedy torn down, but the wait was well worth it. The structure was a beauty and most people said it looked splendid to anyone on board a ship passing on the way into or out of the bay. Two great spires reached to the sky with multiple long single lines of yellow painted suspension cables that made it a work of art as much as engineering wonder. At night, bathed in a soft glow from strategically placed lights, the sight was even more spectacular. It was Nick's favorite way to get to the south side of Tampa Bay.

The two old friends chatted about everything during the drive south. Politics, weather, and especially the state of Kitty's real estate career, were the main topics of discussion.

Kitty, or, 'She Who Must Be Obeyed', as Harry called her, surprised Nick a few weeks back when she lightly informed him she was going to real estate school and intended to get her license and start selling houses in the Bradenton area. Nick had trouble getting the picture straight in his head.

Kitty was an aristocrat. Although tall and slender like her husband, they were as different as salt from sugar.

Harry was a veteran of the Second World War and looked every inch an officer and gentleman except for his only unmilitary feature, a great shock of white hair that always seemed to need cutting surrounding his craggy old face.

His wife was a different matter. She was imperialistic, even majestic. Kitty oozed elegance, and a style many would think no longer existed in this world. She didn't walk into a room, she entered it. When she offered her hand during introductions, one would ponder whether to shake it or kiss it. Her taste in clothes was superb and the furnishings in their home made one think of Park Avenue swank. Kitty was a woman of style and grace and if Nick ever cast a film involving Russian Royalty, she would definitely be his pick for the role of Dowager Empress, complete with floor length black dress with a high collar encircled by a priceless pearl choker.

It would take Nick a long time, maybe forever, to accept this grand lady, fast approaching her eighth decade, as a lowly real estate agent, no matter how successful she may become.

Harry was still a very active Republican in the local organization and constantly prodded Nick about his outsider's view of the American political landscape. Since their primary season was just starting up, there was much in this area to talk about.

Weather took only a few seconds chat, mainly because Florida's never changed and he was tired of Harry's jokes about mukluks, igloos and freezing in the Great White North. That left the real estate lady so the rest of their trip centered on Harry's wife.

Kitty's burgeoning real estate career wasn't going as anticipated. She was having problems getting listings and she had yet to make her first sale. Harry claimed she was getting more and more depressed as each day passed.

Nick knew what she was going through. He had been a successful real estate agent many years before in southern Ontario and knew only too well how hard it was getting started, inking the first sale or seeing the first of your listings sold by another agent. He suggested a chat with her during a quiet period over the next couple days to pass on a few tips she could use that might help.

Minutes passed in silence as they drove past the exit to Isla del Sol toward the bridge. On their right, jutting out into the water for at least two thousand yards were the remnants of the approach to the old destroyed bridge. Retained, refurbished and well maintained by the state, these roads were now popular fishing spots thrusting like piers into the deep waters of the bay beside the new busy interstate. As always, scores of fishers and their families stretched along the railings, patiently hoping to get the big one. Nick always marveled how some politician could have the brains to create such a wonderful public sport area out of the tragedy of the bridge destruction and loss of life. He doubted if many casting into the dark waters beneath knew their fishing pier was once a busy highway.

Harry finally broke into Nick's musings, raising the subject of their afternoon meeting. He requested some details. "Not until the meeting, please." Nick said. "I want you to hear my idea along with everyone else, so you can evaluate the plan with the rest. I will tell you this, though. It will require a lot of work and effort by everyone involved; and some money too. Remember, you're one of the victims just like them and you'll have to gauge this plan the same way all the rest do. You'll only have to wait a couple more hours so hang on my friend."

Harry wasn't happy but he knew Nick was right and he would wait. Ever since Nick claimed he may have found a way, Harry had wracked his brain trying to figure out what it could be. He had drawn a blank so agreed he'd have to wait. He changed the subject to the flight Nick just arrived on and the general state of the aviation business.

The rest of their drive to the Hilton on US 41 near Bradenton's small airport passed smoothly with small talk about the years they had known each other. They joked about old times at St. Pete's airport, remembering the gravel parking lot and car rental agencies, like the fledgling Alamo, operated out of construction style trailers. Those were the days when the sleepy local airport was being visited by small charter companies out of Canada flying 737s full of frozen sun-seekers.

Companies like Nordair, Quebecair and Eastern Provincial Airways ferried a hundred and nineteen passengers at a time, helping turn Pinellas County into today's number two tourist area in Florida. Back then both Harry and Nick were trying to make good in the aviation charter business.

It was fun recalling peoplc, some dead, some retired, many still working; laughing at silly events and crazy passengers of that era. Harry recalled taking a drunken passenger into a lavatory, making him throw up, then pouring a pot of coffee into him before sending him home. Today, agents call the police, have the drinker arrested, and ruin the family vacation and possibly the life of the wayward traveler. Both agreed people problems were handled with more tolerance and sensitivity back then. It was a pleasant drive and a fun bout of reminiscence for two old friends.

9

From the outside, the restaurant was small, nondescript and well worn. It was a typical Florida one-storey flat-roofed building, constructed long before the present owner was born. All its fresh paint couldn't hide the dents and wear caused by decades of burning sun, pelting rain and hurricane winds. Once you were inside though, it was a whole different matter. The place was spotlessly clean, sparkling even, and well lit, with furniture less than a few years old. They also served very, very good food in a bright, efficient manner. Their New England clam chowder was legend in this area of great seafood restaurants and the shrimp could almost be heard begging people to eat them. Their catch of the day came straight from Gulf fishing boats and were usually still flopping about when the chef bought them at the pier.

Nick had strolled across the road from his hotel to check out their meeting place and have some lunch. He was impressed by both the food and the people who served it. Watching how they moved and interacted with patrons, it was obvious both the help and their customers had many years in the restaurant under their belt. Business wise, Nick always believed sludge and honey ran downhill, and in this restaurant, it was honey running. The management must treat their staff pretty well, he thought. After a second beer, he paid his bill and wandered back to his room; he was ready.

An hour later he found out it was a damn good thing he was ready. On returning to the restaurant he was directed into the small banquet room in back where he walked smack into row upon row of silent, sullen, old people; looking toward the front while waiting for something to happen. This was not a group of happy campers.

Thankfully, there were no electric wheelchairs or powered scooters and try as he may; he could see no walkers, just lots and lots of grumpy old people. They were all well dressed, sitting in color coordinated outfits purchased in places somewhat beyond K-Mart. They seemed fit, healthy, and well groomed; but not very friendly. All glared at him, obviously in no mood for games.

The only one not seated was standing near the back. Nick had seen him merrily working the cash register during lunch and assumed he was Edward Fisher, the owner of the place. He reminded himself to compliment his food later. At the front sat Harry and Kitty so he headed there, his footsteps the only sound in the silent room as all heads moved as one like spectators in a slow tennis match, eyes glued on him. The air of skeptical expectation hung like an invisible fog. They may be ready to listen but they looked like a tough audience.

He smiled down into his two friends familiar faces and got a small ‘thumbs up’ from Harry. Casually tossing his bundle of papers on the head table, he turned to the waiting group of silent, serious, seniors. They all glared back without moving. He felt as though he was staring at a Norman Rockwell cover of old people on the Saturday Evening Post.

Nick knew they were checking out his well tailored slacks, polished loafers and the crisp, white, short-sleeved shirt with the expensive silk tie. They were trying to determine if he was just another bag of wind here to waste their time or maybe even dip into their pockets to steal more of their money. There was no microphone or sound system and no lectern, just the head table that held his papers behind him and the group of cheated bad tempered investors in front. Nick took a deep breath and dove in.

“My name is Nick Archer, I own a small car and truck import and export business in Toronto, Canada and I’m a longtime friend of Harry and Kitty Stanton, sitting up front here with you." He walked over and stood next to his friends.

"I'm here because I recently learned that my friends were victimized by a gang of villains who seem to think it's a good idea to move around the country setting up scams to bilk money out of people just like my friends here. Harry didn't tell me about it for a long time; I might think due to embarrassment, and it was only with a great deal of effort and a rather expensive lunch that I managed to drag the details from him. I now have a lot of the story of what occurred and I'm going to help him get back as much of his money as I possibly can." He paused to let his words sink in as he walked back to the table.

"During our discussions he told me that all of you are in the same boat as he and Kitty and I thought maybe together we can get a lot more done for all of us than if just the three of us work on our own."

No one moved or even flicked an eye. For a moment he thought they had all been turned to stone by angry fish restaurant gods but one finally coughed and Nick knew they were still alive. He forged ahead.

"Except for Harry and Kitty, none of you know me from Adam and you've no reason to trust me. I understand and accept that. When I'm finished speaking today, you can tell me to get lost, or stuffed, take some time to think about my idea, or start things moving; it's your decision. Whatever you decide, I'll still work to get my friends money back, whether you're in or not." Nick scanned the room and not a movement flickered across the faces pointed at him. Even Harry and Kitty seemed in a trance. Tough house, Nick thought.

"All of you lost money in the scam perpetrated by a gang of rats who now have your cash and are probably relaxing right now at some all-inclusive beach resort, sipping Pina Coladas, on your dime. In fact, some of the money they're using belongs to my friends Harry and Kitty Stanton so I think it's only fair to get a few things straight right from the start. I'm not a do-gooder trying to help you as some type of charitable project. I'm not from social services or some other government agency and no one is paying me to get involved." He paused and let this sink in. "I've got a successful business of my own and it demands a lot of my time. I'm here for only one reason, to help my friends. You may benefit from these efforts and if you do, fine."

A voice from the back called out, indicating at least one live person in the audience. "How old are you?"

"Fifty-eight," Nick called back.

"Hell, I got socks older than that." The voice growled, causing quite a few smiles and a couple outright chuckles from the statues in the chairs. The voice had broken the ice and you could feel the tension start to flow from the room. Everyone seemed to relax a little.

"I doubt if your socks have seen as many miles as this old body of mine but if you're referring to the fact I'm the youngest person in the room, you're right, I am, and if the ladies in the room will forgive me, I'm pissed off at what has happened here in the Bradenton area and I mean to do something about it." This time heads moved up and down and a few looked around indicating some support or encouragement. There was a positive feeling taking hold in the room.

"Who are you and what do you do?" the voice from the back called.

Nick smiled. "First, who are you and how much did you lose?"

"My name is Louis J. Livingston, my friends call me LJ so you can call me Louis, or Mr. Livingston until I let you know different. I'm a retired printer from Paterson, New Jersey, I'm eighty-one years old and I lost fifty-five thousand dollars." Mr. Livingston sat down.

"Well Mr. Livingston, that's a hell of a lot of money and if you're prepared to work with me and some of the other people in this room, you might get back some of that fifty-five thousand." Nick recognized the name from Harry's list. He knew this Mr. Louis J. Livingston was a lot more than just a retired printer from New Jersey. Harry's notes had suggested the printing business was the biggest in the area and had got that way through political connections and mob acquiescence. It was obvious he was a man of substance and one Nick would need on his side for this to work.

"I'll listen to what you have to say." Mr. Livingston said. "If I like it I'll tell you, if I don't, I'll tell you."

"Thank you. A straight and honest answer from someone involved in these losses is all I ask." Nick carried on.

For the next half hour he proceeded to fill in the group on all the information he garnered from his RCMP friend in Canada combined with the details he and Harry had gathered from the local police. He told them of the gang pulling the same scam in Palm Springs and how the police expected it to happen again, soon, somewhere else.

He detailed how the company in the Caribbean was structured and the trickery at the emerald mine and jewelry factory in Columbia. His explanation of how the bad guys kept just inside the law in most matters caused eyes to roll. He was a little surprised to learn everyone in the room already knew a civil lawsuit was out of the question. The fact there was very little to seize or derive revenue from only confirmed what their legal advisers had told them.

They all listened intently and no one interrupted, simply nodding or grimacing as each black detail was rolled out before them. He had them all to himself right to the end of the presentation and sensed the group understood everything he said. When finished he held his hands out, palms up and said "That's my presentation."

As Nick expected, the first to open his mouth when he had finished was Mr. Louis J. Livingston. Tall, slender, with a face molded on ski slopes, golf courses, sailing yachts, and a few barroom brawls, Mr. Livingston looked like the Marlboro Man's grandfather.

"Thanks for the history lesson son, and for the extra information you've gathered about the gang. It's an interesting story and shows we were screwed by a group of professionals, but it doesn't do us much good. They have our money and are gone God only knows where, and we seem to have no legal recourse to get it back. What do you propose can be done to bring this gang of crooks to justice?"

His question was greeted by grunts of agreement and much nodding of heads. In the second row a woman who looked a hundred took her husband's hand and sadly looked up at his proud old face. There was a lot of misery and hurt and some fear in the room but they all had too much pride to admit it. Like Harry and Kitty, they kept the problem to themselves. Not one of them had informed their family or friends of the problem for fear of being thought stupid or even worse, senile. Many feared their children. Feared they would be considered incompetent and unable to handle their money, causing the family to move to take control of what was left of their estates. Some of the older ones had seen this happen with smart assed lawyers hired by worried offspring who were sure they knew best. With a stroke of a pen a judge would remove all semblance of independence, leaving all decisions in the hands of a son or daughter or worse, an in-law. These were good hardworking citizens, long time contributors to their society, now out to pasture, who had been conned by a group of very good confidence men. You didn't have to be old to be tricked but unlike younger victims of swindlers, they could lose a lot more than money. They could lose their freedom and independence. Nick knew he had to do something, but it had to be with them, not for them.

The audience waited for his answer to Mr. Livingston's

question. It was the proverbial moment of truth and Nick knew if he could sell his idea, Harry and Kitty had a good chance to get some of their money back and that of everyone else there.

"We know this gang of villains has done their dirty deeds before in at least one place other than the Bradenton-Sarasota area. We know it's safe to assume they are going to do the same thing somewhere else to another bunch of people just like you. They seem to operate on a twelve to eighteen-month schedule and it's been almost a year since the last scam so I would expect they're getting ready as we speak. We as a group must find them. We must find out where they are setting up for the next fleecing of seniors. We must know where they are working."

Everyone in the room was leaning forward, straining to hear every word Nick was saying, hardly breathing; wanting to believe there was hope.

"I propose," Nick solemnly said, "we find out where this gang is putting together their next job. Once we know that, we will figure out a way to get them to give us back your money. There's a lot of brainpower, experience and determination in this room and if we put our mind to it, I'm sure we can do as good a job on them as they did on you. When we agree on what kind of scam our group will operate, we will set it up in a way they can't ignore, and sell them a part of our venture for cash. Once we've done that and have their money, we'll simply drift into the sunset and disappear just like they did. It's a simple plan but if it's properly organized, it will work. It also follows the golden rule. Do unto others as they have done unto you."

Mr. Livingston broke the stunned silence in the room. Rising from his chair to his full six foot plus height he said firmly and slowly "Young man, are you suggesting we, this group of upright law-abiding citizens, become common criminals and confidence men just to get our money back?" His voice indicated his disbelief as he continued. "Are you saying we must crawl down into the gutter with these scofflaws and wallow in the mud with them, trick them, lie to them; all in order to relieve them of their ill gotten gains?" By now he was fairly shouting, seemingly furious at the very idea being proposed.

Nick swallowed hard. "Yes… You seem to have a pretty good grasp on my line of thinking."

"Well hell, I love it!" Mr. Livingston exclaimed. "It's a great idea. I wish to hell I'd thought of it so let's get on with it. I don't have that many years left and if we're going to get the best of these damn people, we had better get a move on. Besides… it sounds like it could be fun!" He looked around the room as though searching for someone who might dare to disagree and finding no one who would, he fired off some questions at Nick.

"Who's going to organize this? What will it cost? How many of us will be needed?" He seemed ready to throw several more questions at him but Nick held up his hand.

"Hang on," Nick smiled. "I propose I take some time from my work and organize this project myself. As for cost, there is none for me and I don't think everything else will be much, probably a couple hundred each for basic expenses. The most important items we'll need are expertise, knowledge and time, time, and more time from all of you. Lastly, we are going to need every person in this room and maybe a few more, so I hope you'll all get on board." The last part was important but one look at the intensely eager faces staring back convinced him they would all welcome the challenge. He was amazed at how years seemed to disappear as unhappiness and despair was shed, replaced by hope and purpose. As they chatted to each other excitedly about the project, they seemed to grow younger.

The lady who looked a hundred leaned close to her husband and shouted: "Isn't this exciting, I'm going to be a moll." She brought the house down.

When the laughter died out, Nick continued: "I have some papers here I'd like each of you to look over and fill out if you wish. It's the usual stuff, age, address, phone numbers, both home and cells and next of kin. Don't worry, we won't tell them what we're doing, I promise, but we should have the information." As he talked he handed the papers to the hundred year old moll who now looked only ninety. With surprising agility she grabbed the sheets and started passing them out to everyone in the room.

"Now," Nick said as the paper passing continued, "how many here have computers and are hooked up to the internet?" He was stunned when almost every hand in the room went up.

"You guys are making this too easy," he grinned as he reached for another pile of papers just as his distributor headed back to her seat. "Excuse me" he called "You're not done yet" and handed her the next bundle. "What's your name?" he asked.

"Bella, short for Isabella. That's Richard, my husband of sixty-nine years and we lost thirty-thousand. I knew you were going to ask." Nick laughed and asked Richard to stand so everyone could see him. He did, to a round of applause, and Bella got back to work.

"This next sheet has the names of several members of the gang that cheated you. The first order of business is, knowing who your enemy is. When you go home today, get on your computer and Google, Yahoo, Dogpile, anything else you can think of to find information on these people. Nothing is too small. I'll try to find out where any of them started their criminal career and maybe we can discover what school they went to, if they played football, if they were or are married. Remember, nothing's too small."

From the back of the room came the voice of their gracious host announcing the arrival of refreshments in ten minutes. Nick waved for him to come forward.

"Ladies and gentlemen, this is Edward Fisher, a suitable

name for the operator of the area's best seafood restaurant. He has generously offered his banquet room and even more generously, is providing refreshments." Restaurateur Fisher glowed in the applause that followed. "And by the way, Mr. Fisher is not as young as his good looks might suggest. He and his wife were stung to the tune of twenty-thousand, so he's one of you."

"The last item to be tackled immediately is a search for this group of thug's next hit. We have photocopies of the advertisement the gang placed in the Bradenton Herald for the charitable event where DiSilva first appeared on the scene. I need some ideas on where they might hit next. We'll narrow the list of places down and then search the newspapers for a possible advertisement similar to our copy. Harry Stanton will organize the internet search over the next couple days so keep in touch with him." Nick moved about the room, handing out the photocopies as he spoke. This done, the meeting broke for refreshments.

He felt good about the get together. People were moving about the room, most with plates of shrimp and scallops in one hand and an adult beverage in the other. A few knew each other but most were strangers, drawn together by the actions of a common enemy. They introduced themselves to anyone near and soon chatted like old friends. Most found they had a lot more in common than money.

Almost every one had retired from a successful business or high-paying corporate positions they had worked hard to achieve. Those with businesses either sold them or passed the operation on for their children to run. All were long married and the wives generally had a lot to do with the success of their men. In moments the gathering was more than a partnership in a plan to right a wrong; they were a group of friends on an adventure.

Before they broke up the meeting, Nick asked if they could meet in two days at the same time in the restaurant. All agreed.

10

Just over a week had passed since the call went out summoning Tony and Al's gang to Phoenix. All six men notified made their way into town without hesitation.

First to arrive were the Augastino brothers of Detroit. Actually they were residents of Sterling Heights, a northern suburb of Detroit with several nice golf clubs. It was here the brothers had spent the past ten months overseeing their Registered Importers business, and playing a lot of golf.

It had been a good year for Alberto and Mario, who legitimately imported cars and trucks from Canada. These activities were started as a cover for their more lucrative operations, which centered on smuggling guns, drugs, people, and lately, tobacco products, in both directions across the Canada-US border. The past few years had seen some major fluctuations in the value of the Canadian dollar relative to the US buck, making some people who were capable of reacting quickly, very rich. Alberto and Mario could move quickly and made so much money honestly with their legal importing business, they almost decided to go legitimate. *Almost* was the key word.

These brothers were the business face of the operation. They looked and acted like the business brains because they truly were legitimate businessmen who ran a very successful operation in a very competitive commercial environment. There was nothing phony about them. Over the years their rough edges had been polished smooth by meetings in Lansing and Washington with government officials and politicians. Both knew sales and marketing, accounting, customer satisfaction, and presentation. The last item they considered the most important. At receptions, sales presentations, or casual functions, they were the picture of extremely successful and knowledgeable businessmen, never too far from a good thing.

Unlike the Augastino brothers from Michigan, Stan of Cincinnati and Leo of Hartford represented the muscle. They arranged to meet at Pittsburgh and flew together the same day as the brothers from Michigan. Stan had an eastern European background and Leopold DiSousa's family had been run out of Portugal for some unknown nefarious dealings many decades ago. Their big asset was they looked like brothers, Latino brothers. It was this look that prompted the original scam involving South American Emerald mines. They moved to Miami for a year and stayed with Frank DiPietro so they could learn Spanish, which they did with ease because they spent the whole year hanging around Cuban bars and dating Cuban women. Their Spanish was a little low life but Stan said gringos couldn't tell the difference anyway, so why worry. Tony liked them because they were sharp, smooth, totally without scruples and took orders without question. They were the perfect players.

Two days later Frank flew in.

Frank DiPietro of Miami was their "go to" man. Six foot three, two hundred and seventy five pounds with not an ounce of fat, Frank was a formidable member of the team in more ways than just size. He was their scrounger, the man they turned to when a strange or unusual requirement came up to keep the scam going. There was absolutely nothing in the world from jet planes to hookers that he couldn't arrange at the drop of a request.

One story tells how he got a phone call at his Miami home around 3 p.m. one afternoon. He was offered a bundle to set up a fake Drug Enforcement Agency raid on a home near an apartment complex on Crawfordsville Road on the northwest side of Indianapolis. The raid took place at 11 a.m. the next morning complete with DEA agents wearing jackets and caps, flashing photo ID's. A stolen

Indiana State Police cruiser was there and even a camera crew from some imaginary local TV station was on the scene in their own van, complete with antenna on the roof. No one could figure out how he arranged this.

The raid went like clockwork. The phony drug enforcement officers managed to confiscate almost a ton of pot and hash, some coke, two bags of cash and several guns from the dealer's house. After loading everything into their black DEA vans, they read the "arrested" villains their rights and left them handcuffed and sitting in a black van in the driveway of the raided home to await transport to jail. They were found hours later when a tenant of the apartment complex next door heard noise coming from the van when he came home from work. He called police.

This was all set up by phone over a period of about sixteen hours and earned Frank a very large fee for his efforts. It also earned him almost legendary status amongst those who knew of the caper, on both sides of the law.

Sal Papullia followed everyone two days later. He was always the last to arrive for a new job but no one minded. He owned a nationally acclaimed restaurant in Denver and it always took him several days to leave detailed instructions for his manager. He would call back many times during the project to make sure all was well. The only thing more important than his restaurant was the money he would make over the next month or two.

Larry Silver was the seventh member, and their wheel man. He arrived in Phoenix the day before Tony and Al flew in, checked into a motel and rented the Cadillac that met them at the airport. Larry had a collection of chauffeurs uniforms complete with caps and black leather gloves. At sixty, Larry was the oldest of the gang. He looked like a chauffer, played the part well and loved every second of it. He had driven what he called the short distance into Phoenix from his home amid the vineyards north of Valejo on the Saint Helena Highway in California's Napa Valley. It was there his passion for cars, especially old cars, reached it's zenith in his twelve car garage and superbly equipped machine shop. There was little he didn't know about the world of automobiles and he only worked for Tony and Al to help fund his collection.

Each member of the gang had a specific role in the endeavor and each knew exactly what was expected of him. Tony had selected them over several years from the many scoundrels who had done jobs for him. Each had certain valuable skills which when combined with their lack of morals and past criminal activities, made them perfect for his projects.

Al Silvestro was the money man. A defrocked accountant who lost his license for not following generally accepted rules of accounting in a condo development in which he had a sizeable interest. He could rig any balance sheet to look like a Warren Buffet favorite with just a few strokes of a pen over some white-out. His effort with the books of the emerald mine and jewelry factory was pure artistry and did much to make their Florida project successful. Tony loved the way he painted financial pictures with simple words that elderly investors could understand. When he presented the fiscal end of the operation and answered questions from the 'marks', he was worthy of an Academy Award. Al looked good, having a gentle face, as one old lady had said, and people tended to trust him.

When all had arrived and settled in, Tony called a meeting and briefed them on the new project. He went over the details but it was so similar to the Sarasota-Bradenton effort, little explanation was needed. Each one of the group had done well on that caper, making a lot of money for not too much work. This one would be much the same, just with more sand and a lot less water. Most of the first meeting was spent on where the best restaurants were and the locations of any casinos. Tony was confident this Phoenix job would go well.

11

When Nick heard the news from Harry of where the gang was setting up their next sting, he dropped everything and started working on how they would handle things.

Since the meeting in the restaurant, Harry had taken hold of the local organization and teamed up with Louis J. Livingston to get the computer search teams up and running. Through experience they both knew it would be better to separate long married couples when setting up each unit. With this in mind the internet search began with teams of two wives or two husbands hunched over home computers normally used simply to email grandchildren or check stock portfolios. It took a few days for most to get the feel of the various search engines and their power but by the end of the first week most searchers were jokingly calling themselves geeks and beginning to amass an impressive pile of information about the gang members.

The phone lines between the homes of team members began to ring continuously as small problems arose or situations sprang up involving the search engines. Some of the searchers liked Google, others swore by Dogpile, while still others found Yahoo to be the best. The local discount bookstore was raided and all their people-searching editions were purchased and passed from home to home for study. The email flowing between each team was continuous and, as the week progressed, often ribald.

Most of the group had fairly new equipment so there were few major problems and in no time at all words they had never heard before, like Google, Dogpile, XP or Jeeves became common phrases in their everyday conversations. When not sitting in front of the small screen they were talking about it over tea, coffee or more likely, a strong adult beverage on the back patio.

They crawled happily into bed each night after ten or twelve hours tracking tiny details through scores of obscure websites, book-marking relevant facts and dumping them into holding files for future study. All did their job like one would expect of their generation; flawless work carefully done, exactly as Nick asked. Many of the wives had spent long years beside their husbands in family businesses, filing papers and keeping things in order so much of this work came easy. In Nick's view: They were one hell of a group and they did one hell of a job.

Early one evening Harry got the news to drop by and look at a newspaper ad found by one team. The phone call came from LJ and although he could email it, he thought Harry should be there in person because their chief newspaper searcher, Bella Brown, was the finder and she was pretty excited.

She had spent days slowly going through newspapers, carefully looking for anything to help. When she finally stumbled on what they all wanted to see, she phoned LJ and was so excited she had difficulty getting her words out. He thought she might need some calming and a whole lot of congratulations.

Harry agreed and hopped into his car to drive the several miles to the Brown's condo on Longboat Key. He considered it a bit of a pain in the ass but Richard and Bella Brown, both over ninety, were the oldest members of the group and without question, the most adorable. Everyone loved them and never stopped fussing over them. They were also the only couple who refused to split up for the internet search and they were quite emphatic about the things they would search.

Bella would not do research into peoples background or private lives. She felt it to be an invasion of privacy; something a well bred woman didn't get involve with.

Besides, she said, what if she came across something sordid or distasteful, what would she do? Goodness, she couldn't tell anyone those kinds of things, could she? No, Isabella Brown was too much a lady to get involved in anything sordid and even the return of her money couldn't change that. She would look for the advertisement they expected to pop up in a newspaper somewhere, and that was that.

When everyone understood what the Browns were going to do and let them get at it, the job was completed in a little more than one week. They systematically listed every area of the country where seniors retired in large numbers and found the local daily and weekly newspapers and their web addresses. They then set up a daily routine where Richard would review newspaper ads for an hour while his wife did normal household duties. Then Bella would work the ads the next hour while Richard got the mail, handled household bills and took care of the garbage. Then they would both stop, and depending on the time of day, have a cup of tea or a small glass of sherry. After the break, Richard would get back to work for the next hour. They did this for twelve hours a day and kept a log of every moment invested in the project in a large black diary style book. Considering their advanced age, they did a fantastic job, and both were having a great deal of fun.

LJ had noticed the change first when he was delivering papers and instructions to search teams around the area. He mentioned to Harry how animated Richard and Bella Brown seemed. He told Harry how the two had re-arranged their home and set up the computer in the dining room, dragging a filing cabinet in to sit next to it. They had a large chalkboard hung on the wall across from the monitor so a quick glance upwards showed all details needing attention. They were dealing with their part of the overall project like two old intelligence officers slowly digging up details to be used in an upcoming battle.

As they slowly shuffled about their condo one never

had to worry about them bumping into each other. They seemed to know exactly where the other would be at any given moment, no matter what. They were a joy to watch as they moved about, looking like two very experienced ballroom dancers moving in slow motion to a familiar old tune. Theirs was a routine rubbed smooth by many years of comfortable companionship.

Richard and Bella were beaming when Harry arrived. They both looked like a cat that not only ate the canary, but made a nice feather boa out of the leftovers as well. They welcomed Harry at their open door with joy and excitement. Both knew their successful discovery of the advertisement was the one part of the puzzle everyone needed. Now they could get on with recovering their money, and these two old devils had done it.

"Phoenix," they yelled at Harry. "Phoenix is where the rats have set up to do it all over again. The blaggards have an ad in the Republic just last week." They shoved the papers proving them right as Harry came into their condo. The gang had indeed placed an advertisement in the Arizona Republic almost identical to the Bradenton-Sarasota ad of a year ago. It was an invitation to interested citizens to attend a reception for some obscure Latino consular agent who was promoting a fund raising effort for orphaned children in Columbia.

Harry studied the printout and compared it with the copy Nick had passed around at the meeting in Ed Fisher's restaurant. Except for time and place, the ad was identical to the one from the Bradenton Herald. It was indeed by the same bunch and the Browns were right: the gang was in Phoenix.

Harry grinned at the beaming couple and held up one finger for some silence while he pulled out his cell phone. Nick needed to know about this right away. They would party over a bottle of sherry after the call.

12

Nick eased into his seat on Air Canada's flight 683 for Phoenix with his laptop safely on the floor in front of him. He looked forward to the long trip because it was his best time to think out problems and then make lists of necessary tasks. This was how he got things done.

List-making was a trick he learned from his wife and it worked. He always laughed at Ann's lists because there seemed to be no task she tackled without lists of things to do and lists of things to buy and lists of things to think about and just lists of lists. She claimed they helped her do things and he learned, begrudgingly, they did. He still was far from attaining Ann's skill at making a list out of thin air but when he secretly used her methods, they worked. When alone on long flights he would make a list of the lists he would need to sort out. He knew by the end of the flight his head would be straight on what would have to be done.

Over the past week he had wracked his brain searching for a plausible method of tricking a pile of money out of the gang. He knew he would need some unique kind of product to sell and a plausible line to make the bad guys believe the sale had to be on the QT. What the hell the product or the line would be, was, for the moment, beyond him. He was on his way to Phoenix to find what he needed.

Nick was surprised and happy with the way the group of seniors in Florida had gelled so fast into a smooth and cohesive machine. Harry, with the help of LJ, arranged all the search teams, training some who were still a little green about using search engines and organizing data gathering with results he found astounding. They accomplished far more than he ever expected.

Their research had found the names of every member of the gang and in all but one case, their home address. They found information on any who held a federal or state license for anything. These included the brothers in Detroit who held a US Registered Importers License and a Federal DOT number plus the restaurateur in Denver who had a Colorado license to serve alcohol. One, from California, held a master mechanics license.

They dug up marriage dates, the names of family members and birthdates and with some, the names and addresses of their mothers and fathers. These last details were dug up by a few couples who were genealogy fans, taking on the family history part of the project. They carried their searches deep into the Mormon data banks in Utah, shipping records of immigrants, military records and government sites in half a dozen different countries. There are a vast number of sites on the internet where details of family history lay buried and the seniors seemed to have visited them all. It appeared if you ever even talked to someone in a government, Harry's gang would find you.

Included in the gang were the aforementioned brothers from the Detroit area involved in the same general auto importing business as Nick. A phone call to a Registered Importer Nick often used in Brighton, Michigan, and a second call to another in Warren, a suburb of Detroit, filled in all the details of these Augustino brothers. They were clean, with no record, running a legitimate operation much respected by most of the RI's in the Michigan area. There were some suggestions floating about of a mob connection but nothing solid. Both were married, each with several children, substantial homes, and, similar to most Italians, an active family life. They went to church most Sundays, visited their still vigorous parents each week and generously contributed to local charities in both time and money. On the surface, the Augustino boys were model citizens.

They belonged to a couple golf courses, one being a very exclusive club catering mainly to Detroit's high rollers. They also enjoyed good restaurants, saucy night club entertainment and the gambling casinos in their area. They started first as regulars at the Windsor Casino, just across the border in Canada, but now frequented the new local Detroit casino. They believed in keeping their hard-earned money at home. Nick's connections suggested the brothers were big shots; big tippers, big gamblers and all round fun guys. There was only one small problem. One nobody knew about. They were high rollers and fun guys on stolen money cheated out of a lot of old people.

There were other members of the gang but none caught his eye like the brothers from Michigan. It was probably because they were in the same business as Nick but there was something else about them he couldn't quite put his finger on. Given some time though, he knew he would.

The rest of the gang were from all over and most had legitimate businesses or were retired men of leisure. The restaurant owner from Denver, Salvatori (Sal) Papallia, was a very wealthy man. His steak house had a great web site listing such facilities as banquet rooms for any size group up to 250. Smart and expensive, it was "THE" watering hole frequented by Denver's power elite, including the mayor, both senators and most business leaders. Reviews in the Post suggested it ranked as one of the top five restaurants in the city. Obviously Sal needed these ill gotten gains like Nick needed a kidney stone.

Frank DiPietro was the Miami man and although he lived on a fast track, he had no visible means of support other than spending a great deal of time gambling. The search also turned up an interesting fact. Mr. DiPietro was the only member of the gang with a gun permit and being from Florida, it included the right to carry the weapon concealed. Nick stored this small fact away in a corner of his memory.

Frank spent a lot of his spare time in Nassau or Biloxi practicing blackjack. Although not a counter, he was good and his many years at the tables in every casino from Vegas to Atlantic City helped him stay in the black.

This love of gambling was a common thread throughout the gang, including Leo, one of the thugs from Hartford who knew the inside of the Foxwoods casino like the inside of his fancy five bedroom home in Windsor Locks. Leo had a few minor convictions over the years, mostly for bar room brawls were he used his size to intimidate people. They were quite a crew and Nick was looking forward to sticking it too them.

The next list to be made from Nick's list of things to solve was not a bad problem but a situation needing attention just the same. It involved the army of old warriors now assembled in Florida awaiting their next set of marching orders. He would never have guessed what a force his original efforts had started in motion. What had emerged in a very short time was far more than a group of old farts outraged over being cheated. They had once again become what most had been all their lives; independent members of society with a purpose for getting up each morning and goals to strive for. No longer were they like so many in their golden years; ignored, joked about, shoved from pillar to post and generally expected to keep quiet and stay the hell out of the way until they had the courtesy to die and stop being a nuisance. They now had organization, money and leadership. They had power, and by God, they were going to use it.

Harry had asked Nick when he phoned that morning if he wanted some of the Florida group to start packing for Phoenix. Nick told him to hold off a few days until he had a chance to check out the town. He wanted to see if he could find out where the gang was headquartered and pursue some possible plans for recovery. One thing he did ask Harry to do was canvas the group for any Arizona or

Phoenix area connections or friends that might come in handy down the road. He also asked him to check and see if any of the group owned a motor home that could be used as a command centre in Phoenix if need be.

Again, Harry, using his best Rochester voice, said: "Okay Mr. Benny," and hung up laughing at how funny he was.

Nick couldn't help but smile at the thought of his old friend joking on the other end of their phone conversation. Harry was having a ball and let Nick know this project could go on forever as far as he was concerned. He claimed he was even getting along with Kitty.

He closed his lap-top and slid it into its case and then under the seat in front of him. It was now 12:30 p.m. Phoenix time and as they started their descent Nick changed his watch from Toronto time. He had rented a car and booked a hotel on the internet and looked forward to a couple days in a town he hadn't seen in a few years but had always liked.

13

Harry and LJ were waiting for Nick at 'Arrivals' in the Sarasota-Bradenton Airport. He had taken US Airways from Phoenix to Charlotte North Carolina, spent an hour over beer watching the news and then flew south to the Florida west coast. By the time he walked off the plane his spirits were high, his lists all done, and his plan of attack was in place. He knew it would work and he knew Harry and Mr. Livingston would love it. The plan had all the elements of a great joke combined with a very good chance of getting their money back. It would be worth all the hard work they would have to put into it.

"Hello Harry. Anyone ask for your autograph today?" Nick laughed and stuck out his hand at LJ. "How are you, Mr. Livingston?"

"I'm fine and please, call me LJ." He shook Nick's hand with a grip far stronger than his years might suggest. His face was even more creased due to his grin, the smile of a man enjoying himself. They headed for the exit.

Walking out into the blazing sunlight and crossing the hibiscus bordered scorching tar of the airport parking lot, Nick asked if the evening meeting had been arranged. Earlier that morning, before boarding his flight in Phoenix, Nick called Harry, asking him for an after diner get-together at the restaurant. He wanted as many of the group in attendance because this was the big one and he was prepared to put it off for another day if necessary.

"It's all set." Harry said. "I was surprised at the response of everyone. They jumped at the chance, all of them. I think most understand the information search is about over and it's time to move into operation mode, as they now call the next stage of this effort. All I ever hear now is 'when will the operation start?' Hell, some of them even want to give it a grand name, like 'Overlord 2' or 'Operation Getting Even'. You'd think we were back in the Second World War preparing for an invasion." He laughed at this. Nick joined in then asked about any possible connections in Phoenix they could use and LJ jumped in with his findings.

"I think we're going to be lucky there" he smiled. "Elizabeth and John Hardy, they're from Kansas City, well Independence, actually, have a son and daughter-in-law who own a motel in a place called of all things, Apache Junction, just on the east side of Phoenix."

"I know Apache Junction" Nick interrupted. "I drove past it on the expressway yesterday morning looking for a site to use in our project."

"Well, their son has this thirty-room motel that runs pretty empty this time of year so he said we could use it anyway we want. If you let me know what you need I'll get John to email a request tonight."

LJ paused a moment, then continued: "Another couple, Herb and Thelma Sayer lived in Sun City up to two years ago before moving here. Herb said they moved to Florida because there was no fishing in Phoenix. Thelma claims he never fished before, doesn't own a fishing pole and doesn't like fish. I've never seen him eat fish, let alone try to catch any since I met him, but, what the hell, it's his story and he's sticking to it." LJ chuckled and shook his head. "Anyway, both know Phoenix pretty well. Thelma will do whatever we want and Herb will do whatever she tells him, within reason. Herb still has some connections in town and should be a big help in our planning. As well, Vince, the pharmacist, the one with the unit at the tennis club on Longboat Key next to where the Holiday Inn used to be, has a twenty-four year old granddaughter doing post graduate work at the University of Arizona. She might be able to lend a hand. That's about it so far."

Harry smiled and put his hand on Nick's shoulder. "LJ has been just great," he offered. "He has these computer geeks so organized and so keyed up he can get just about anything out of them."

Nick was pleased. "The motel sounds great. We could probably use it as a base of operations as well as home for some us while we're out there. We'll also need Herb's connections and knowledge. This granddaughter of Vince sounds good too. Depending on her availability, and how she looks, we could use her as a receptionist in the office we're going to have to set up."

"You think her looks are important?" LJ asked.

"Yes I do. These guys move on a fast track and we have to attract their attention. It will be a lot easier if she's pretty, has long legs and smiles nicely." Nick stated. "I'd prefer our receptionist to be part of our group, like this girl, with a direct connection so she can be in on everything but, if not, even though some may think it's not politically correct, we'll need a looker for this job."

They climbed into Harry's car for the short trip around the corner onto highway 41 and the Hilton. Nick was a creature of habit and usually stayed in the same hotel, on the same floor and even in the same room if available. He liked the comfort of being surrounded by familiar things and being served by people who recognized him. By now, this was the way he felt about the Bradenton Hilton.

Once at the hotel, they retrieved their bags from the trunk. LJ handed Nick his bag and his hand on Nick's arm, stopping him as he turned to for the entrance doors. "I just want to thank you" LJ said. "I know you're doing this mainly for Harry and Kitty but the rest of us appreciate your effort and want you to know how we feel." His steely eyes didn't waver; the firm grip on Nick's arm was steady.

"Thanks LJ." There didn't seem to be much more to say so Nick just gave him a friendly pat on the arm and turned for the hotel lobby. "I think you'll like what I have for tonight. See you then." He pushed through the doors to disappear into the hotel.

14

The gathering in the banquet room of Ed Fisher's seafood restaurant was a lot different than the first one Nick attended. That had been almost silent, filled with sullen old couples and a few individuals, all wary of everyone, ready to take issue with anyone or anything. This group mixing before him was as different as salt from sugar. They greeted each other with smiles and friendly slaps on the back. The room was filled with laughter and good natured jokes along with robust hugs and warm cheek kissing. As they milled around the small refreshment table near the entranceway, filling coffee mugs and tea cups, several turned to holler at Nick and give him the thumbs up sign.

It took a while to get some semblance of order in the room but soon most were sitting, or heading for their seats. A buzz hung in the air and all heads were turned to the man at the front asking for silence. Within a few moments they settled down, attentive, motionless; excitedly awaiting Nick's presentation. They didn't have to wait long.

"How's everyone doing?" Nick asked his bright-eyed audience. It was a dumb question because it was obvious they were doing just fine. Not many days ago they were a disillusioned bunch of cheated oldsters with little hope of getting their money back. Tonight they were an enthusiastic and well organized band of buddies well on their way to achieving a common goal. The transformation was astounding. They looked younger, moved younger, and all were eager to get on with life, not wait around for it to end. For several seconds Nick just stood and stared in wonder.

They stared back expectantly; waiting for the words that would keep a ball rolling that most thought had stopped a long time ago. They now had a reason for getting up in the morning and staying up at night and they enjoyed the feeling. Nick doubted if any would ever go back to the days of simply waiting to die.

"I have a plan" he said. "It's a good plan but it can't work without your whole-hearted support and complete commitment plus one hell of a lot of effort, and, I might add, one hell of a lot of luck. My big concern is if you're game for something a little out of the ordinary."

A voice from the back dispelled any misgivings Nick had. It was TJ. In his gravelly New Jersey accent, he expelled any doubt he spoke for every person in the room. "Get on with it Nick," he said. "We all want to know what we have to do and we sure as hell aint getting any younger." Heads bobbed up and down throughout the crowd so Nick did as he was told.

"All right folks, here's the deal. We all know who cheated you out of your money, it's ancient history and I won't go over it again. We also know how they did it and we all know there will be a next time. In fact, they are, at this moment, getting ready to do it all over again. Thanks to your squad of web searchers, we even know where they've set up and started doing their dirt again." He looked around the room and saw several heads nodding in understanding.

"I think if we go into their area of operations and break up their program, whether by alerting police or getting some newspaper or a TV station involved, we will accomplish only one thing. We'll stop this one effort of theirs and they will simply close up shop, disappear from the scene for a short while, and then start up someplace else." He stopped for breath, then forged ahead. "This in itself is a good and decent accomplishment. It will save a lot of seniors in Phoenix the same grief you've gone through but it won't get back one dime of the money these bums stole from you. The idea is to get your money back, screw up their operation, and make it harder for them to do it again in the future."

Nick paused again, letting everything sink in. A couple of them were repeating his words to the hard-of-hearing, but most everyone had a bright understanding look on their face. Harry sat in the front row, calm and trusting. TJ sat quietly at the back with a look on his face that made Nick think he knew exactly what was coming. He must have been speaking with Harry. Undaunted, Nick carried on: "We're going to Phoenix to get your money back."

"All of us?" a voice from the group asked.

"All who want to go." Nick said. "We'll need a lot of people to make this a success. We'll need drivers, office workers, researchers, lookout people and computer geeks. The motel we'll be using as a base will need help in keeping our section of the place clean and tidy. We're getting the place for free and we can't expect the owners to carry upkeep expenses as well. We'll need help with meals for the whole crew and bag lunches for those on the road. The list goes on and on."

"What exactly are we going to be doing to get our money back when we get there?" called out one of the men in the middle. The question caused more than a few heads to look up from their notepads to hear the answer.

Nick knew this query would come up and he had prepared an answer. "I can't tell you right now. I know I'm asking for a lot of blind trust from you but all the details are not in place yet. I only found out about the motel a few hours ago from John, and Vince is still waiting for word from his granddaughter. This project is going to be very complex and I may have to make a lot of changes and adjustments over the next couple weeks. There's no sense telling you one thing now and then changing the plan every few days. It'll just be too confusing and could cause problems down the road." He stopped for a breath and hoped they would go along with him. The answer came quickly.

Hilda, one of the oldest and probably the deafest member

of the group asked with a grin "When are we going?" and everyone laughed. Several people had said Hurricane Hilda was a sparkplug who, despite her eighty odd years, was always on the go. She was ready, willing, able and impatient.

Nick laughed and acknowledged Hilda's enthusiasm. "We'll be out of here within days, Hilda, within days. Will that be soon enough for you?"

"Well let's get on with it." She said. "I haven't got that much time left to sit around waiting, you know."

"Oh come on Hilda. You'll outlive us all and dance on our graves." This remark came from a woman near the back who was almost as old as Hilda.

"Of course I will. It's from clean living and an ample application of gin and tonic. If you'd stop being such a bunch of goodie two shoes, you could live as long as me too."

Laughing, Nick had to raise his hands to settle down the crowd and get back to the matters at hand. "Come on you guys. Leave poor Hilda alone and you" he said, pointing at Hilda's tiny white haired and grinning agitator "you can hand out these," and he passed a stack of papers to her.

As she moved about the seats giving each person a stapled bunch of papers Nick spoke about what they were getting. "These sheets will give you some idea what we will need for this project. I figure we'll be in the Phoenix area close to a month so all of us need to be prepared." He thumbed through his papers. "I know a couple of you have large motor homes and we'll need them. First off, we need them to transport some of our stuff out there and then we'll use them as secondary headquarters while we're there."

"For your personal use there's a list of things you might want to take. If you're driving you'll have no problem but if you're flying, your stuff will have to be tagged and loaded into one of the motor homes. Remember, irons, ironing boards, microwave ovens, that kind of stuff." He paused, watching everyone going over the papers he had prepared. A couple had pens out, making marks and nodding. It appeared most were planning on the trip.

"Another thing," Nick called out to them. "Make sure you have a chat with your doctor and get enough of any needed medication; enough for at least a month, maybe a bit more."

Larry DeLong, their chief computer geek got Nick's attention with a question. "Hey Nick, what about communicating with friends and families while we're on this junket?"

"No problem. This isn't a secret mission behind enemy lines. We're just heading for Phoenix for a get together of old friends in an area that's interested all of us for a long time. Sort of like an unofficial reunion out in Indian country. The vast majority of your family and friends won't be interested in what kind of reunion. In fact, the Motel's address and a map to it are in your package. Redirect your mail out there if you want."

"Don't have to." Larry said. "Everything I do is online so I seldom get any snail mail."

A few other questions were thrown his way but they seemed to accept the list of instructions and suggestions and most were discussing travel details.

"Okay folks." Nick hollered to be heard. "Lets all meet back here tomorrow night at the same time and we'll make our list of who's going and how. I'll also have another list of stuff we'll need once we're out there. And remember, target departure date, one week tomorrow." Everyone looked a little shocked, but no one raised an objection.

"One last thing" Nick hollered over the activity. "How many here have ever read anything by Tony Hillerman?" The query prompted several hands to shoot up.

"Good. If you still have the books, pass them around and I want as many of you as possible to read them. Go to the library and grab everything you can find by him. Read them. I'll tell you why later. Besides, they're pretty darn good books."

That ended the meeting.

15

One night later Nick walked into the banquet room of Ed's restaurant and was stunned by the gathering. What had been one happy and enthusiastic gang the day before was now raging fanatical mob. Almost everyone who walked, hobbled, crept or strolled into the room had a clipboard, pencils and even roadmaps. Someone had even brought a photocopy machine and set it up near the refreshment table. It was constantly in use.

This group was not just planning to be away from home for a month or so. They were planning the route they would take to get there and back, the best places to buy fuel and food and someone even had a map showing the location of all the Wal-Marts between Bradenton and Apache Junction.

Nick wandered through the room while everyone exchanged information.

"Hey Harry," he called to his friend. "What the hell's going on?"

"Not much," Harry answered. "Just some old farts taking care of business. After last nights meeting, they started on the phone and 'net setting up for the trip. One made a personal information sheet and sent it out. Now we have details on everyone; next-of- kin, lawyers, doctors, required medications, etcetera, etcetera. Hell, they even list their executors." He grinned as he waved his information sheet under Nick's nose.

"We've made Hilda the project archivist. She loves the title and went out this morning and bought a filing cabinet and a box of legal sized file folders. She's not very computer oriented but don't mention it to her. She'll keep track of all the info on everyone so if you need to know anything about anyone in the group, see Hilda."

LJ joined them and handed a typed sheet of paper to Nick with the names of three couples owning large bus-like motor homes set to head out to Phoenix. Over the next couple of days they would have them serviced and checked out for the long trip. Each had already arranged for three other couples to travel with them. He was pretty pleased with all the evolving arrangements.

"We're putting half a dozen microwaves, six ironing boards and six irons and three small bar fridges in the motor homes." He handed Nick another list. "I got John Hardy to call his son at the motel in Phoenix so we could pin down what they have and what we'll need to bring for a long stay. This list covers that issue. We'll be taking quite a lot of things with us so it'll be one hell of a convoy heading west."

Nick took the offered sheets of figures and wondered if they had enough space for all they wanted to move west. LJ waved away the question with a comment about U Haul trailers or one-way truck rentals.

"Not to worry." He said. "If we need more space, we'll get it." And with a laugh he walked off to join the others near the refreshment table.

Over the next two hours Nick moved through the room offering encouragement and assistance where needed although not much of either was required. He was amazed at how much had been put together and how well organized they were. In only a few hours, strategies were thought out, discussed over the phone, the internet, and in person, and preparations made for something akin to the invasion of the beaches of Normandy. Eisenhower sure could have used these guys. Hell, Nick thought, from the age of some of them, he probably did.

The convoy to Phoenix was set. LJ owned one of the motor homes, the slowest one, so he would lead. Harry would bring up the rear. In between was a convoy of another motor home, a fifth wheel trailer behind a dually pickup truck and eleven cars and vans. Thirty- eight people in all were heading west.

They had all subscribed to the new Nextel phone service, the one that allowed interphone contact so everyone could keep in touch. On top of that LJ and Harry had separate two way radios operating on a different frequency. They all had new Rand McNally roadmaps with the route marked, fuel stops and restaurants noted, and motel reservations made. Everyone had a three ringed binder with page after page of information, details and hints.

It was 2240 miles from Bradenton to Phoenix and their departure target date was Friday morning, less than five days away. They felt they could make about five hundred miles a day so their first stop would be just east of Pensacola. LJ expected the convoy would be in Phoenix by Tuesday afternoon barring any unforeseen problems. Nick felt that town would never be the same.

As the gathering broke up Nick, LJ, and Harry stood at the door saying goodbye, wishing everyone well and promising to see them off when they left. All who stopped and shook their hands were as excited and upbeat as kids going on their first overnight camping trip. If Nick didn't know better, he'd have thought they had made supper with the Alice B. Toklas cookbook but he knew theirs was a natural high. This gang was heading out on a great adventure.

The next few days were spent getting ready. Bags had to be packed, material loaded, homes closed for an extended shutdown, and papers temporarily cancelled. Neighbors were notified of the holiday being taken and arrangements for mail and parcels to be picked up and safely kept. It was a major undertaking but one helped by the ever present lists Harry and LJ kept passing out.

At six a.m. Friday morning Nick arrived at the appointed marshalling place in front of a giant bookstore for the start of the great trek west. He was expecting chaos and confusion. What he found was an exercise in good old American know-how in event organization. Any casual observer would have thought the gang had done this every year for the past two decades.

LJ strode about the parking lot of Books A Million at Cortez and US 41 in a way you would have expected Marshal Zuckov did while arranging his tank divisions for the final assault on Berlin. This present day marshal lacked the baton but his baseball cap and two way radio made up for the shortfall. Followed by his harried wife, who scurried about, scribbling his instructions on a clipboard, LJ marched from car to van to motor home chatting, joking and giving final instructions. Logistical skills, learned and perfected in the marines and forgotten for nearly twenty years prior to becoming a printer, suddenly sprang forward as though never set aside. Abilities to assess the situation in an instant and make a decision seemed not to have been asleep, just dozing for a few seconds.

Nick marveled at how well this gang of people, none under seventy, planned, organized and executed the project. They were truly a force to be reckoned with.

As the last of the drivers climbed into their vehicles, LJ came over to where Nick and Harry were standing and stuck out his hand. "I haven't had so much fun since Grenada," he said with a grin. "I guess we'll be going. Keep in touch."

Nick grasped his hand and held it firmly. "We're flying out this afternoon and we'll meet you at the motel in Apache Junction. Please drive carefully."

"Don't worry about us. You just take care of yourself. If you're not there when we arrive, what the hell are we to do?" This came as another shot because Nick had refused to give them details on why they were heading west in the first place.

"LJ, we'll be there but if it's any comfort, the reason you're heading to Phoenix is to do unto others as they did unto you."

"Damn." LJ grinned and gave Harry a smack on the shoulder. "Well, whatever the details are, you know we're with you. Damn. This is going to be a great trip." And he marched to his unit and his poor disheveled wife, climbed in and without a wave to Nick or Harry, hollered into his radio: "Alright gang, let's move 'em out."

Nick couldn't help but think of John Wayne's Rooster Cogbourn as the vehicles, led by a weather beaten old Marine, started snaking out of the parking lot. One after another they passed Nick and Harry at the exit onto Cortez Boulevard. Once out of Bradenton they would head a few hundred miles up Interstate 75 and then swing west on I-10 for their first stop. As each vehicle passed, those inside waved, smiled, and gave Nick and Harry a big thumbs up. The line was long and the sun hot but neither Nick nor Harry noticed. They knew they were watching something important.

16

Tony's new offices were open and ready to go. All the rented furniture was in place, telephones connected, and a pretty girl sitting ready to answer them. Potted plants dotted the floor in the reception area with several others installed in the offices. Local calendars with dates marked in red or black hung on walls or sat on desks. Assorted older magazines lay neatly piled on coffee tables near the very attractive receptionist's impressive curved desk.

The receptionist, who called herself Malita, was Latin, leggy and luscious. She sat primly behind her desk checking out everyone who came near with old eyes in her young and attractive face. On close inspection, someone worldly would know immediately she was far more than just a pretty face above a great body. She was a cleaned up, high priced hooker who knew more about the world than most who ventured into her bailiwick.

Neither Tony nor Al knew if she could type, or even spell, but she "talked nice" and they knew she impressed when she uncurled from behind her desk, smiling with hand outstretched, greeting the clients of her two bosses.

A radio played soft elevator style music in the background while Malita answered the gently ringing phones every few minutes. There was activity behind closed doors down the hallway as well. Occasionally someone would open one of those doors and head through the reception area with papers in hand, on some important mission. This was a setup that would have fooled anyone.

The phone ringing system was a new gadget of Tony's, picked up from an online electronic supply company. It was a $69 program loaded into one of the office computers that was set up to call specific phone numbers whenever, and as often, as you wanted. He had put in the three numbers of their office, his cell phone number and Al's cell as well. The result was terrific. The three phones in the office each randomly rang about four times every hour and his cell phone rang at random about five or six times an hour. When it did, he would answer, talk to himself in a manner appropriate to the person he was with and then hang up after giving some instructions or noting some important details. He loved it and had great fun with his partner recalling all their imaginary calls each night over drinks.

Al came through the glass doors into the reception area and waved at Malita, who smiled brightly and waved back. She knew who the bosses were. "Is Tony in?" he asked as he stopped at her desk and picked up a couple messages.

"He's in his office." She said and shifted a bit so Al could get a better look down into her new crisp white blouse. She knew he was looking and figured for a thousand a week he could look and see all he wanted.

Malita had been hired right off a barstool in the lobby bar of one of the best hotels in town. She had caught their attention that first evening with a skin tight red jersey wool cocktail dress that clearly showed the only thing under it was her. The four inch open spikes held tight by thin ankle straps made her great legs look fabulous and her waist length glistening blonde hair swung across her back like a shot from a Miss Clairol commercial.

After some preliminary chit chat they asked if she wanted a job working for them. She told them it would be $500 an hour for a threesome and $1,500 for the night. Tony and Al burst out laughing. She took umbrage at this and got quite indignant, making to leave before they could tell her it was a real job, in an office, for a couple weeks.

Their negotiations went on over drinks for the next hour and they agreed she could keep her evening job as long as she was in the office at nine sharp each morning looking like the best, friendliest and most efficient secretary receptionist in the world. She was to wear blouses, preferably white, or some muted color, and a skirt only a few inches above the knees. Theirs was a business dealing with wealthy seniors and she had to be classy.

When they said they'd give her a thousand a week she almost fainted and Al mentally kicked himself for not offering $750. Of course she agreed and suggested they close the deal up in their room with a freebee. It was without question the most money she had ever made vertically and she wasn't going to let it slip away.

The deal was good for both sides. Tony told her she didn't have to know any intimate details about their business and she was happy with that. She sensed these guys were heavy hitters, possibly mob connected, and she was smart enough to know the less she knew, the better for all concerned, especially her. Their clothes and style had a certain tone but when the rest of their associates arrived on the scene she was sure they were connected. She loved her new job and knew she'd be sorry when it ended. In the meantime, evening work went on as usual but happily she was able to turn down some of the rougher clients. For a few weeks it would be quiet businessmen away from home and looking for some glamour after a hard day at work. It was going to be the easiest two weeks of her career.

Al told Malita he liked her blouse and headed down the hall to his partners office.

"Howdy pardner, how's things?" Al drawled, pushing the door open. Tony, at his desk reading the sports section of the paper, waved to Al without raising his head.

As Al pulled a chair closer to the desk Tony folded the paper and placed it carefully to his right. "I don't think you've quite got the western accent down yet, but everything's fine." He smiled. "Malita's taken over and is doing a great job. She's very good handling the phantom phone calls. Hell, we should keep in touch and use her in the next one." They both shrugged and grinned, thinking of the first night they met her as Tony reached for a file folder on his left. “We got a couple who would like to look at the operation in Columbia already. I’m setting that up for maybe next week so prepare for a trip. Who would you like to go with you this time?”

“How about Stan and Leo?” Al said. “They look like hot South Americans, both can fake some Spanish and they deserve the trip, they missed the last one.”

“Okay, let them know. Let’s aim for late next week. See if our new secretary can make some of the arrangements.” Tony grinned. “You don’t seem to have much trouble working with her.”

Al laughed and waved the comment away. “You hurt me Tony. You know I’m all business and no play. Even when she wears a blouse that lets you see down to her kneecaps.” They were both laughing now.

“Sure, sure, just get everything done and give me a heads up on the timetable. I’ll need to call the boys down in Bogoto so they can get ready.” Tony knew his friend and colleague would take care of all the details and be ready for the trip. He could do this, fix a car, balance his checkbook and fool around with Malita at the same time. Tony was beyond being surprised at Al’s ability to do many things well at the same time.

“What about you? What’s up for you in these next few weeks?” Al wondered why his friend wouldn’t be heading for Columbia. Tony seldom missed one of these trips.

“I’ve got a couple functions. You know, Rotary, Kinsman, that sort of thing to take care of; besides, one of the gang who want to see Columbia is a seventy two year old pushy bitch who thinks her husband and all other men are dunces. You can have the pleasure of this one.” He smiled across his desk, leaned forward and said “Have lots of fun and keep an eye on the mouthy one.”

Al said “sure,” and got up to leave. At least he’d have the chance to work a little with Malita. Life wasn’t all that bad.

17

Nick managed to sweet talk upgrades into business class for Harry and himself on the Charlotte to Phoenix leg of their trip. It was unusual for an airline to be that nice, but the pretty young agent checking them in said Harry reminded her of her grandfather and two more were needed up front for balance. This was all done with a big smile and a cute little wink.

Kitty was in one of the motor homes driving across the country, claiming it was a great opportunity to get away from him for a few days and telling Harry she expected their room all set up on her arrival. Nick thought she'd be lucky if Harry had an extra set of keys by the time she got there. Anyway, the two men had a chance to relax on the way out in big comfortable seats with good service. It made it easier to talk over their plans.

They chatted about all kinds of things but most of their conversation centered on the amazing world passing so clearly below them as they flew across the continent. It was one of those brilliantly clear days when one could look up and see a plane at thirty-five thousand feet leaving a long white vapor trail behind. The same clarity applied to passengers on the plane. The world was spread out in all its glory.

Nick pointed out what he thought were the straightest man-made things in the world. Hydro rights of way that charged across the land as though shot from a gun, looking like they had been marked on the ground with some giant ruler. He also showed Harry how railway lines were almost as straight but would change directions to service a town or city and would sometimes change course for a river or mountain range. After these two came the interstate highway system laid out across the land like a giant grid. They were built after the towns and cities were established so the system connected each place, like lines connecting the dots on a child's giant picture puzzle. Cars and trucks could be seen moving along the dual black stripes far below and the perfect symmetry of interchanges stood out like small flowers positioned irregularly along the road. Harry had never looked at his country quite like this.

"How come you see it this way?" Harry asked. "I've flown all over this country and never noticed any of the things you've pointed out."

"I don't know," Nick shrugged. "I love looking down when I fly and I study everything I see. One time I flew from Beijing to London largely during daylight. I had my nose pressed against the window most of the way and I couldn't get over how different the landscape was from here. I saw vast empty deserts in northern China and across Mongolia. Once we were over Russia, I was amazed at the almost endless miles of forests rolling across the horizon. Occasionally you'd spot a small community clinging to the edge of a lake or carved out of the wilderness on a riverbank, but the vast majority was just never-ending forest. There were no roads, no hydro lines, and no railroads. It struck me how the land in that section of the world was totally in control, as apposed to here. In your country, it's exactly the opposite: you control the land and make it serve you. Maybe it's because you let people own it as opposed to so many other places." Nick paused, a little self conscious at his musings.

"I never thought of it that way." Harry said. "You may be right. Three-hundred-million people, most owning their own little piece of land sure would seem to make some difference. Of course, having a few million lawyers looking for someone to sue could make some difference too." Laughing, they discussed these and many other things before they got around to the real reason for their trip.

Nick knew where the bad guys had set up shop and he had a line on an office in the same building, possibly the same floor. It would be pricey but he thought it would be worth the extra expense. He brought his laptop with all his lists and suggested he drop Harry off at the motel so they could meet the owners and then get started setting up.

"I'll call the real estate agent and set up a viewing of the office for later today. You stay at the motel and start figuring out what we'll need there and where we can get it. The room arrangements have to be worked out as well." Nick handed him a sheet of paper with several items listed. "This is LJ's list of items loaded into the motor homes and cars on the way here. We'll need some long tables and chairs but the motel may have them on hand. I don't know. You'll have to see."

"I'll take care of the office for now and you handle the base at the motel. LJ can oversee the satellite units and any field work when he gets here. We'll keep in touch, making sure everything runs smooth and each group knows what the other is doing."

Nick passed a photocopy of a greater Phoenix map to Harry highlighting the airport, motel, location of their new office and the two satellite locations. One was directly north of the motel in the northeast quadrant of the area, the other sat in the northwest sector. He pointed to the northwest spot. "This is where the action may be. You might want to head out there before LJ gets in. Find the best exit to get on and off the Interstate and check out the local stores, bars, hotels or any other thing you might think we'll need. I've some instructions for LJ about this area and you can help bring him up to speed. In fact, get as much information as you can and take some pictures. You brought your digital camera, didn't you? Good, take a bunch and burn them onto a disk, I'll need them. I'll be taking some people out there for a look around and I'm going to need everything you can get me."

Harry took the map, scribbled some notes on the back and stuck it in his shirt pocket. He was going to use his Rochester voice again but thought better of it. No one on the plane but Nick would get the joke because none were old enough to remember the Jack Benny Show, so he just told him not to worry. Nick reached over and patted him on the arm. If there was one thing in this world he knew he didn't have to do when he asked Harry to take care of something, it was worry. The idea wouldn't even enter his mind.

18

The Apache Junction Motel sat like a thousand other roadside places dedicated to tired drivers that sprung up across the US as the Interstate highway system developed. It was a one story building with thirty six rooms spread in two wings of eighteen each from a small office, meeting room, and operators living area in the centre section. It looked like a clone of many others except for much better landscaping, fresher paint, and the general air of being a lot cleaner than most of its kind across the land. The tiny office was stuffed with local tourist brochures, a newspaper rack, soft drink machine and a genuine, imitation potted plant in the corner. One wouldn't call it the Hilton, but it was clean and appeared serviceable.

Sitting on six acres of dust, sand and rock south of the Superstition Freeway near the Tomahawk Interchange, Robert Hardy's well kept little motel was the perfect place for a base of operations. There was lots of space for parking and the pool out front would probably be well used by some of the gang. The meeting room slash banquet hall between the office and the left wing of rooms was big enough for a seventy-five person wedding reception, so it would do just fine. All in all, the Apache Junction Motel fit their plans perfectly.

Nick and Harry parked near the pool and sweated through the blistering sun to the office, checking out everything as they walked. The grounds were in pretty good shape. The landscaping was decent with a variety of cactus and palms growing through river rock used as ground cover. These areas were all bordered by neat curbing beside walkways and a parking area recently paved. The building had been painted within the last year and there was no garbage or litter anywhere. Nick was impressed by the level of maintenance and knew there would be few complaints from the convoy now on Interstate 10 somewhere in Texas.

"Not a bad looking place." Harry commented. "It should work well."

"It does look good. Let's go in and see if Bob or Linda are here. John Hardy said he explained everything by phone and email and we can just walk in." He pushed open the glass door and moved into the tiny office.

Stepping to the counter, Nick tapped the bell perched to one side. Instantly a pretty girl of about ten or twelve years of age bounded through a door from some back area behind the counter and grinned at the two men. "Can I help you?" she asked with perky experience way beyond her years.

"You sure can Miss," Nick said with fake solemnity. "Is either Mr. or Mrs. Robert Hardy here? We're friends of Mr. Hardy's father and we're from Florida."

"Oh cool," she almost shouted, bouncing up and down. "Is granny and pompa with you?"

Nick smiled at both the bright-eyed youngster and the notion that all kids seemed to have a special name for their grandparents. "No, I'm sorry. They're on the road somewhere in Texas and should be here in a couple days."

She was disappointed for a moment then brightened. "That's okay. I'm Amanda, their oldest granddaughter and I've already got their room ready. It's the first one past the banquet hall. That's so they'll be near. We live here you know, and I wanted them to be close." She pointed back to the doorway she'd bounced through minutes ago and before either Nick or Harry could utter a word, she turned on her heel and in a flurry of blond pony tail shot back through the doorway, hollering; 'Dad, Dad', at the top of her lungs.

Within seconds a six-foot plus younger replica of John Hardy strode into the tiny office making it seem full to overflowing. He grinned at the two of them and stuck out a big tanned hand that was no stranger to hard work. "Howdy guys. I've been expecting you. Come on in and have a cold one," and he literally pulled both of them into the living quarters. "Grab a seat. Beer okay? In this heat it's almost a necessity of life." He pointed at some chairs and disappeared into what they guessed was the kitchen. Nick and Harry pulled two chairs out from the dining room table and sat down, awaiting their host.

They sat in a large room, called a great room in trendy places like California, and it seemed to stretch across the back of the banquet hall. On the long window side was the dining room table they now sat at, with one end guarded by a credenza and the other, a china hutch. The other side had a giant TV in one corner with sofas and armchairs around it. In the furthest corner was a large metal stove for chilly nights. Scattered all around the room were assorted books, a sound system, electronic gadgets and toys plus a computer on a small desk near the corner with the TV. This was the room of a busy family, much lived in, and Nick liked it instantly. He looked over at Harry and knew he felt the same way. Their host returned with the beers and pulled out another chair from the table.

"Here's looking at you," he said with a grin and took a long swig from the can, savoring it like a man who deserved it. "Hang on a second." He held up a finger and turned toward the kitchen.

"Manda! Do me a favor? Get some more beer from the store room and stick it in the fridge, please." The three men heard a "yuck" sound from somewhere and a door bang.

"Some young lady you have there," Harry said between sips. He wasn't a beer drinker but he was very polite.

"Oh she's a handful, I'll tell you. Flies around here like a whirling dervish and gets her own way on just about everything, but she's a big help and she's cheap, so we put up with her." This as she flitted across the room and out into the office muttering something about his yucky beer being in the fridge.

"Just be glad she still thinks beer is yucky," said Nick and they all laughed.

Bob Hardy sat back and looked at the two older men sitting across from him. He was a big man, probably a college football player, defensive back, Harry figured, and a guy who marched to his own drummer. Both men liked him. "What are you guys up too and what has my dad got to do with it?" he asked.

"Didn't your father tell you?" said Nick.

"Nope. Dad called and said he and a gang of his friends needed this place for a week or so or maybe more and wondered if we could help. I said sure. Hell, who argues when their dad needs something. You'll have to take care of your own cleaning and laundry but otherwise the place is yours." Nick and Harry smiled and nodded agreement.

"As you can tell from the heat," Bob hardy continued, "this is the slow season. Tourists don't come to play golf when the temperature hits a hundred and ten. We have thirty six rooms and we're lucky if we rent half a dozen a night. It'll be like that for the next two or three months. In fact it may generate a little extra business having you and the cars around. It'll make me look like a popular place. Hell, lots of owners around here close down their places at this time of year and head for a better climate. It's cheaper than staying open." Bob drained his beer, thought a moment, and then asked, "What the hell are you all up too?"

Nick looked at Harry then back to Bob. He was wondering how much he could tell about their plans. He didn't like exposing Bob or his family to any problems but he knew they couldn't stay at the motel and finish the project without Bob's full co-operation. He was sure they wouldn't get it done without him being on the inside. Nick suggested the three of them go for a drive. He didn't want little ears hearing his story.

19

The convoy from Florida rolled onto the motel parking lot about 4 p.m., two days later. LJ, in the lead vehicle, parked at the far end of the property, climbed out of his motor home and strode across to where Nick was standing in front of the office. His first words were a demand to know where he could get a cold beer. The air conditioner in his rig had stopped working about twenty miles west of El Paso, making the final four hundred miles of scorching highway through New Mexico and Arizona somewhat unpleasant. It made his already bad mood worse, if that was possible.

Nick took him into the office to meet Bob and asked Amanda to get a cold beer for the grumpy old man with him before she went out to greet her grandparents. She had put on a pretty dress for her granny and pompa's visit and when she brought the cold can to LJ she looked up, giving the hot tired old man a shy smile. Without a word being spoken LJ's bad mood melted away and he instantly became a nice guy again. From that point on he and Amanda were co-conspirators and buddies and he got a cold beer many times over the next few weeks just by winking at her as she followed him about the property.

"Nice kid." LJ said as she flew out of the room to find her grandparents.

"Ya", said Bob, looking him over, "I think I'll keep her. You must be LJ. I heard quite a bit about you, nice to meet you." He stuck out his hand and another friendship was established.

"You'll have to tell me some day just how you managed to herd that wacky looking mob out there across the country without getting thrown in jail or losing half along the way. You wouldn't get me trying that for all the cold beer in Milwaukee."

"Well it sure as hell wasn't easy, I'll tell you. What with meal breaks, pee breaks, dead hearing aid battery breaks, more pee breaks and flat tires, I was beginning to think we'd never make it. Some day, if you have a week to spare, I might just tell you all the horrid details." LJ finished his beer, crunched the can in his big fist and tossed it in the waste basket behind the desk. "I have to get out there and arrange the parking or that gang of loonies will be all over the place. If you could get the room keys for me, I'll start herding them into their pens." LJ turned and headed for the chaos developing outside the office.

Bob started pulling room keys from the board on the wall behind the desk, passing them to Nick. He figured they'd need all the units on the banquet room side of the office and handed over keys numbered one to eighteen. "Do me a favor, will you? Give number eighteen to my mom and dad," he asked. "Amanda would kill me if they're put anywhere else. She spent all day in that room, scrubbing down every square inch and smoothing down every towel. Then she headed out into the brush behind us an hour ago to pick a big bouquet of wildflowers for the room. It's her first chance to do something for them and she took it very serious." *Lucky grandparents,* thought Nick as he headed out the door with the keys.

Some semblance of order was taking hold on the parking lot as LJ moved about the vehicles directing traffic like Patton directing tanks at Bastogne. He had the motor homes parked on the gravel area behind the motel and the cars were all lined up some distance back from the units. Nick handed LJ the keys, explaining the Hardy arrangement and what Amanda had done. Within minutes Elizabeth and John Hardy were parked in front of number eighteen and climbing out of their car with their granddaughter, who had jumped in with them several minutes before for the short ride across the parking lot. Bob and Linda were waiting for their daughter and her grandparents in front of the room with big smiles. They were very happy and excited.

The rest of the weary wayfarers spent the next hour unloading bags and suitcases from cars and vans into their designated rooms. Clothes were shaken out and hung in closets. Medicines and pill bottles found preferred places by bedsides or in washrooms. Pictures of children, grandchildren and even great grandchildren were positioned on TV sets, desks and any space by the bedside not occupied by medicines. Tired as they were from the day's 450 mile drive, the travelers were quickly turning their rooms into a home away from home.

LJ had called Nick a couple hours out of Phoenix to give him an estimated time of arrival and Nick knew they would all be weary. He then arranged for Chinese food to be delivered, and he, Harry, Linda and Amanda set up a simple buffet dinner in the banquet room while the move-in was taking place. Nick then strolled down the line of rooms, knocking on doors, renewing old friendships and inviting everyone over for dinner. All of them were tired and didn't feel much like going out looking for a restaurant so his gesture was well received.

Bob, Linda and Amanda acted as hosts and met each couple arriving for dinner. Amanda was an instant hit and her parents didn't do too badly either. It didn't take long before it was a party of friends chatting about the long drive and telling stories that brought laughter and good natured ribbing throughout the room.

LJ told how he couldn't take a shortcut in Texas because there were just too many Republicans in the convoy and the shorter route would go right through Johnson City, home of the LBJ museum. This story brought calls back and forth across the room of "damn Democrats" and "damn Republicans." The biggest laugh came several seconds later when a voice muttered "damn independents."

After the meal Nick helped clean up, dragging a green garbage bag around the room and asking each tired traveler to meet again the next morning in the same place. As the job neared completion several gathered around him inquiring of plans for the future. They still had little idea of what Nick was putting together. He waited for the noise to settle down before announcing the next day's plans.

"I'm glad everyone made it with little or no problems, and I'm happy to see all of you, whether Democrat or Republican, alive and well and in one piece." This last remark brought a laugh and a bigger one came when the same voice as before asked what about the independents. "Them too," said Nick.

"While you were all relaxing on your cross-country sight-seeing tour, Harry and I have been working our butts off trying to set some things up here. We have a lot to report and we'll need at least an hour of your time to go over everything. So, how about all of you being here at ten-thirty tomorrow morning and we'll fill you in on all the details? I've arranged for lunch to be brought in at twelve." He looked around to field any questions but there were none. The group was tired, fed, burped, and ready to turn in.

"Ok gang." Nick called out "let's call it a day and have a nice rest. We have a lot of work ahead of us. Tomorrow we have to empty the stuff we brought in the motor homes and set them up in the appropriate rooms. We also have to set up this room", and he waved his arm around the banquet hall, "with our computers and other stuff. So sleep well, I'm going to work you to the bone in the morning."

Within minutes the banquet room was empty, trash bags hauled to outside containers, and the Apache Junction Motel quickly grew quiet. Everyone seemed to understand that the heavy lifting was about to begin.

20

The gang straggling into the banquet room between 10 and 10:30 a.m. all seemed in a good mood. They were well rested and, due to the close proximity of both a Denny's and a Waffle House, well fed. There had been a general grouping of couples into foursomes or sixes but once in the room they were as one. They all had the same goal, getting back their money. An air of anticipation hung over the group and they all felt it while waiting the appointed hour.

At precisely 10:30 a.m., a serious looking Nick strode through the door and went straight to the head table. He placed his briefcase on it, snapped it open and set out several different piles of paper in various locations on the table. The room was silent for the 30 seconds he spent with his back to them. When he turned around, he looked into the faces of a group of people who, unlike the first time they met, were excited, intent, happy, and ready to get on with the job.

"I'm happy to see everyone here and I have a couple comments to make before we get to the meat of this project." He stood before them with his hands in his pockets, moving his weight from one foot to the other, almost shyly. "The first thing I want to say is thank you. Thank you for trusting me. Thank you also for putting some of your remaining savings into this endeavor. Most of all I want to thank you for piling into your vehicles and traveling, at your own expense, across this country, simply on my say-so. I know Harry vouched for me, but I was a stranger and you trusted me. I sincerely thank you for that." He paused for a moment and then continued.

"Secondly, I'm pleased and impressed with how well

you've all worked together to get as far as we've come. I thought at first there would be problems, arguments, and out and out fights. Nothing could be farther from the truth. It has been a smooth transition from a loose collection of retirees with varied interests to a cohesive organization that can probably accomplish anything it wants. I know something important has happened over the last few weeks and I think it will live with us all forever." Nick took a deep breath here because the last item could cause some consternation in the room.

He took a sip of water from a glass on the table and forged ahead. "Lastly, I think you should know why I've been reluctant to tell you my plan to get your money back. There is a very simple reason. Had you known what I wanted to do before you drove over twenty two hundred miles to get out here, I think most in this room would have thought me nuts, and decided to stay home. Now you're here and I know it would be difficult to back out. You can see I'm serious, and now that you're aware of what you are capable of doing, I know you will support me." Nick stopped as several of them turned to a mate or friend to pass a comment or two back and forth.

Sylvia Brenner, a quiet, no-nonsense member of the group who seldom said anything at these formal meetings, rose to speak. Facing Nick, she stood in front of her chair at the far end of the front row with her hands clasped in front of her like an old fashioned school teacher; something she'd been for almost 45 years. Sylvia was the group cheerleader and constant voice of encouragement, moving slowly about the room at meetings and work sessions, softly offering praise and commenting on efforts as she must have done to students in hundreds of classes during her long career. Her husband Allan claims more than six hundred people showed up for her retirement party overwhelming the school gymnasium where it was held. He was very proud of her. When she spoke people listened so she had every attendee's attention in this room where Nick stood.

"Mr. Archer," she said in her tiny old voice as the room became as silent as a grave and all leaned forward to catch her every word. "We are here for two reasons. One you can see and understand, and one you can't see and may never encounter and therefore might never have to understand. The first reason is easy. We are here to try and get some or all of our money back from that nasty group of villains. They tricked it out of us and we were lost, very despondent, and resigned to a life much different from the one we had planned. Then Mr. Stanton introduced us to you. He said you could be trusted. Those of us who know Mr. Stanton listen if he says someone is good. Since then you have proven several times over you can be trusted and I think I speak for all of us when I say we believe you do sincerely mean to help us. We like you and we probably would have come out here even if you had told us your plan back home." She stopped here and looked about for encouragement and got it from all her colleagues. Heads nodded up and down and she turned back to Nick.

Mrs. Brenner continued, "The other reason is far less obvious. It's one most retired people in this country know well and resent above all other things. We resent how so many think a person must turn in their brain as a condition of receiving a pension. Not only do we have to stop working at sixty-five, everyone wants us to stop thinking, stop participating, in fact, stop being a part of the world around us. We become a nuisance when we retire and the un-retired world wants us out of site and out of mind."

"You, Mr. Archer, have never treated us that way and all of us in this room appreciate it." She was punctuated here by several quiet comments from the seated group. "You didn't ask us if we could use a computer. You asked us to get online and find out everything we could about the bad guys. When it came to this trip, there were no questions about who 'could' do it, the question was, who 'would' do it. Sir, I am eighty- eight years old and no one ever once asked me if I was capable of an assigned job. It's a good feeling to know some people feel I can keep up to the seventy-year-old kids in this gang." This last bit brought a broad grin from her husband and laughter from the rest. Someone called out: "You tell him Sylvia," from the floor. She smiled and carried on.

"We live in a world where old people are supposed to go somewhere to sit quietly, try hard not to be a bother, and patiently wait for death. We're not allowed any input into the raising of our grandchildren, no matter how bad a job our kids are doing. The courts even allow grandchildren to be kept from us if their parents break up." She was on a roll now, eloquently laying out something close to her heart.

"No one thinks we can take care of our own retirement investments and if we make a mistake, like this last one, it's not because the crooks were very good at their job, it's because we're just stupid and senile. A problem like ours is just additional ammunition to others in their fight to show how stupid we really are. On top of this, if we make a fuss about anything, all the 'beneficiaries in waiting' try to have us declared incompetent so they can make all the decisions, like Jim Simpson's family tried last year." To emphasize her point she looked over at Jim and his wife who both nodded vigorously in agreement.

"It's refreshing to meet someone who treats us as we were accustomed to being treated before we retired. Never once have you suggested we can't do something because of our age. If we can't do a particular job, it may be because we haven't been trained, or we don't have the tools, but you have never suggested it's because we're too damn old. Pardon my French. So, Mr. Archer, on behalf of all of us in this room and those still back in Florida, thank you for pointing us in the right direction and giving us a shove. We appreciate your confidence in us and we're ready to do whatever you want. And believe me we're going to accomplish what we've set out to do, mark my words." With this, Sylvia Brenner sat down to a round of enthusiastic and prolonged applause from her fellow group members. Several leaned forward to pat her on the back or called a hearty, 'well done'. It seemed there had been much discussion amongst them prior to this meeting. She was obviously speaking for everyone there.

It took Nick several seconds to process what he had heard and the reaction of those in the room. This was a special moment and he was overwhelmed by this display. He was truly at a loss to find the right words of response. Over the past few weeks the key word to describe these people would be reserved. This statement of confidence, support and even friendship was more than he ever expected. The applause had faded for some time before he spoke.

"I'm overwhelmed Mrs. Brenner, all of you, just overwhelmed." He was much more animated now, hands in front of him, feeling more comfortable. It was the first time he felt as one of them. Sylvia Brenner had articulated a group message to Nick and all knew he received it and understood its meaning. All doubts were now gone, this was a do-able project.

"I appreciate all your kind words but they're not going to get you out of any work you know. Sucking up to the leader won't work." This was the right comment at the right time and amid laughter he handed Sylvia a bundle of papers to be handed out. As she took them she stood on her toes and to a chorus of cheers, planted a kiss on Nick's cheek. Then she started passing out the papers with a jaunty step and a big smile.

21

"Now let's get going," Nick called out as Sylvia Brenner finished her job and sat down. He picked up a clip board and flipped through the top two or three pages. He was ready to start giving them the details.

"You men are now going to find out why at the beginning I asked you not to cut your hair if you didn't have to. It wasn't a plan to save you money, and I know it's been a source of amusement for some and I'm sure there were times you thought me a little nuts but I must say some of you've done a great job. LJ, your hair was quite long to begin with but now it's beautiful. In the next couple days you're all going to learn to wear it like the Native Americans of this area, in a bun tied tightly on the head or in a braid hanging down the back."

Nick smiled as several of the men ran their fingers through their long hair. One asked if he could cut his now and his wife said "Nothing doing, I like long."

"You are all probably wondering as well why I asked you all to try and read as many Hillerman books as possible. Were any able to do that?"

Once again they surprised him by their response. Every hand in the room reached for the ceiling. Nick grinned, shook his head and muttered: "I love you guys!"

"There are two things we must do before we start our program," Nick continued. "The first is a short excursion up into the Fort Apache Indian Reservation. I've arranged it for tomorrow and I'd like all of you to go. It's a regular tour with a guide who'll answer questions and I think you'll enjoy it and I know it will be a help down the road. The bus will arrive early for an 8 a.m. departure so no sleeping in tomorrow, get up early, have a good breakfast and wear good sensible walking shoes."

"We'll go first to Fort Apache," he added, "have a walk about, and then move on to the Kinishba Ruins to steep ourselves in some of the ancient culture. After that, we stop at Whiteriver, a small community north of Fort Apache. Last on the list of stops is Show Low. We'll visit there for an hour or so, and then head home.

"During this trip I'd like you to pay special attention to the residents of these towns we're visiting. Please check out what they wear, how they move, stand about or relax; anything you may find interesting or special. You may take pictures but please, ask permission first. These are a proud and noble people with a history much older than some in this room. Common courtesy and respect is the order of the day. It's important to our plan for you to familiarize yourself with the original people living in this area, so don't be afraid to smile, strike up a conversation, or chat about the weather; and listen carefully to what is said." He shuffled his papers to give time for his comments to sink in.

"The second item may be some fun. I need you all to go on a little shopping trip." This brought cheers from the ladies and some groans from the men. "I've done a little research and there are a few items I'd like you to look for. Ladies, mature Navajo women like to wear silver, squash-blossom necklaces. They can be found in good jewelry stores or pawn shops, just ask to see their selection and I think you'll love them. Women of this area, and I think most other women as well, love turquoise and silver jewelry and you can find that almost anywhere. The Navajo are famous for their designs and workmanship in silver and turquoise and most are quite beautiful. Just remember the quality can vary dramatically so check it out carefully. There are notes about all this in the handout, and you can do a little research on the net if you like." He tapped his clip board and turned to the next page.

"Gentlemen, you need a few things as well. First off, every man needs jeans. I know most of you have jeans but they look like you bought them last week at a ritzy store in a fancy mall in Sarasota. That won't do. Everyone out here wears jeans and they must look like you've worn them constantly for thirty five years. No jeans or new jeans will mark you as a tourist as much as shorts and a Hawaiian shirt. Secondly, you need boots. Cowboy boots. Boots that look like they've seen many miles of bad road and the repair shop on several occasions. Remember, this is an area of sand, gravel and dry river beds. Anything you walk around in is going to get beat up pretty fast. Try on as many as you like and make sure they fit. Don't worry about getting used to them. If you've never worn cowboy boots before you'll be surprised how comfortable they are.

"You'll also need a hat. The usual hats worn in this area by Indians are wide brimmed felt hats usually with a decorative band. Some hat bands have silver and turquoise, very elaborate and expensive looking. They're a mark of stature so don't get something too elaborate or showy that might attract too much attention. Just a middle of the road hat band will do."

"Some of these things would best be picked up in a second hand store, such as Goodwill, Salvation Army, that sort of thing," he continued. "That's for the jeans, hat possibly, without a band, and a shirt or two. The boots can be picked up in a pawn shop. You can get the hat band there too or you can purchase one at any jewelry store or quality souvenir shop." Nick stopped here and let what he had just said sink in.

"One thing to keep in mind. You are not looking for a uniform. You're searching for the kind of outfit that will help you blend in. Please don't come back all looking like clones."

Most of the people sitting in the room had never been inside a pawn shop in their life, let alone a second-hand store.

Some had never been in the type of neighborhood where a pawn shop or second-hand store might exist. Here he was asking them to go out and buy clothes in them and he expected them to wear the stuff. These people donated clothes to Goodwill, not shopped there. This trip was going to be a very interesting adventure for many of them.

Nick continued: "When you find the clothes you want, bring them back and we'll run them through the washers here at the motel with soap and a little bleach. I'll also pick up some cans of spray disinfectant so we can do a thorough job on the inside of the boots and hats: can't be too careful, you know."

He was sure several of them would be more than a little squeamish about wearing some other person's old clothes.

"I think most of this can be done over the two days after our tour. I'll get someone to put together a list of pawn shops, second-hand stores and souvenir shops throughout the area. You can go out in pairs and foursomes and spread across the area. Each will have a map and a list of addresses. I don't think you'll have any problem." He hurried on to the next item on his list before they had any chance to ask questions about the shopping.

"This afternoon I'd like to get this room set up. We have several long tables, some chairs, a couple cork boards and a large blackboard. I don't think we should stick anything into the walls or use tape. Otherwise we'll all be painting before we leave." Nick checked his list.

"The computers you brought from Florida need to be unloaded and set up. This very well-run motel already has high speed so we can connect right in if you have a wireless card. If you need one, we'll get it.

"The coffee maker, filing cabinets, copier, you know, all the good stuff, will have to come in and be arranged. You have a list; Harry and I worked out a floor plan, and he has a copy of it so he'll work with you. If you have any suggestions, we want to hear them. This roomful of people has more experience and know-how than just about any other room in this country right now, so let's not hide our candles under a bushel.

"Now, while you were all snoozing," Nick smirked, "Ed Fisher, our chef de maison, and his dear wife Liz were slaving over a hot sandwich board preparing lunch. Let's take a break, do a critique on their handy-work and then start getting this place in shape."

Nick set his clip board on the table, gave the group a grin and a wave to follow as he headed for the table stacked with sandwiches, pickles, cookies and donuts. It looked like enough to feed an army. Behind him, he could hear that army coming.

22

The hall of the second floor of the Encanto-Central Business Plaza was abuzz with movers, phone technicians, executives and assorted staff all moving every which way trying to get their job done as best they could in the chaos caused by a new business moving in. A burly delivery man with a large desk on a two-wheeled dolly rolled up to the doors of the new offices of Lasenda Casinos Ltd. and motioned through them for the person on the other side to come and hold it open. He knew what he was doing because the only one behind the doors was the receptionist, and she was special.

Jennifer Strong, 24-years-old, five-foot-ten, one hundred and twenty perfectly positioned pounds with long brown hair, was more than special, she was downright spectacular. The delivery man had come up to check the address before bringing the desk and several other pieces in, arriving just as Jennifer was bent over unlocking the doors. She looked up, smiled at him, said "Good morning," and he hadn't been quite the same since. She had that effect on males between the ages of twelve and ninety-nine.

Vince and Isabel Strong were two of the group now at the motel in Apache Junction and they suggested their granddaughter Jennifer may help. She was a business major at the University of Arizona with a minor in theatrics. Although Jennifer's mom and dad had sporadic contact with Vince and Isabel, Jennifer was constantly in touch with her grandparents, mostly electronically. Despite almost weekly email contact with her grandparents, she hadn't seen them in person for almost a year and their phone call from Florida excited her. They told her they were coming to Phoenix shortly and wanted to know if she could do them a favor and play receptionist for a week or two at an office in town. Jennifer jumped at the chance. They gave few details but told her of a Nick Archer, suggesting he would contact her, and asked if she could help him out.

Nick called, arranged a meeting at the University and took Jennifer to lunch in a very upscale restaurant where every man in the place, waiters, cooks, dish washers and customers openly envied him. He reveled in the attention, noticing rapt faces peeking through the kitchen door window and knowing full well every man in the place was wondering who he was to have such a beauty on his arm. It was by far the best service he had ever had in a restaurant. After their lunch he took Jennifer to see the office and joked about how every male employee of the eatery had provided some service during their meal. Nick suspected a couple customers may have joined in as well.

The next day he spent about four hours at the new office with her, going over every detail of his plan. Jennifer was the first to know it all and he made her promise to keep it to herself for the time being. Nick liked her and was impressed with how fast she grasped the situation. She asked endless questions, made several sensible suggestions and worked with him through a few scenarios she might run into. When he was finished, he knew this was a girl with more brains than looks, if that was possible, and he had no qualms about leaving her alone in charge of the office. She was gung-ho about helping retrieving her grandparent's money and Nick figured there would be no holding her back.

Now here she was; receptionist for an organization called The Lasenda Nation Casino Corp. Inc. and at this moment, the door holder for an infatuated furniture mover.

Down the hall from the new offices of the Casino Company, the small office of Santa Maria Emeralds Inc. was slowly waking up. Tony DiAngelo was, as usual, in first and had the coffee brewing before Malita arrived. She came through the door just ahead of Al and the Augustino brothers wearing a denim mini, three inch spikes, and her usual crisp clean white blouse. It was understandable why the three thugs climbed the stairs behind her. All of them swung through the doors wearing broad grins a few seconds after her and within minutes the home office of Santa Maria Emeralds was up and running.

"Hi Tony," Al said as he stuck his head through the half open office door, "what's going on up the hall?"

"New organization," Tony looked up. "Just as I left last night someone was painting the name on the door, some Indian Casino operation. I don't know what it's all about but the young beauty unlocking the door this morning makes Malita look like a chump," he grinned and made a face. "Hard to believe, isn't it?"

"You mean they're going to set up tables and slots down the hall. Hell, Alberto and Mario will be dancing all over the place. We'll never get any work out of them. They told me last night they were tired of driving out to that rinky-dink casino north of Scottsdale. They're going to love this," he grinned and did a little dance.

"No tables or games," Tony laughed. "I'd think this is only their executive office, I'm not sure but if you want to check, wander in and ask. You've got nothing to lose and you'll have a chance to check out the best piece I've seen in a long time."

"I just might do that," Al grinned and headed for his office. He had some work to do and a few calls to make before an afternoon golf game with a potential investor. He always liked to get the work out of the way before the fun.

They were all in a good mood around Santa Maria due to how well things were going on their project. To this point thirty-one people had indicated a willingness to get involved in the financing of the chain of jewelry stores. Four had already been to the site in South America and returned enthusiastic about the potential to make a fortune. Three more were setting up to go sometime in the next week with Tony.

They had discussed their schedule at a meeting several days before and decided to extend the program an extra three weeks. It was going so well and the reception had been so overwhelmingly good it now appeared the Phoenix operation would far outstrip the Florida one of last year. Al had never seen such action with people calling every day to ask if they could get information. The sums being tossed about were much larger as well. He felt good about this one and quietly considered his share to be close to somewhere around half a million. That figure alone was incentive enough to get his work done and calls made. In the back of his mind he figured if he got it all done soon, he could head down the hall and check out the receptionist at the Indian casino office. She must be good if Tony said so, and he wanted a look.

An hour and a half later, Al pushed open the glass door of the Lasenda Nation Casino Corporation, found the reception area empty and called out politely if anyone was around. He listened and was about to call again when around a corner stepped a woman who simply took his breath away. She was tall, maybe five ten, slim, beautifully shaped with long dark brown hair hanging almost to her perfect little backside. Her eyes were dark pools of sparkling water and her high cheekbones made Al think she must be a princess from some ancient line of Indian chiefs. Without doubt she was the most stunningly beautiful woman he had laid eyes on.

"Hi, can I help you?" she purred, with a smile that lit up the room as she moved across the foyer to her desk and set down the heavy bundle of paper she was carrying. Al said nothing, unable to take his eyes off her legs. Her skirt was only a couple inches above the knee, not an obscenely short thing like Malita was wearing that morning, but as she stooped down to place her load on the floor beside her desk, he knew he was looking at the best and sexiest legs and bum he had ever seen. It took him several seconds to find his voice and answer.

"Yes, well I mean not exactly. I'm from the office down the hall and I thought I'd drop in and say hello and welcome you." He pointed back to his place and wished he had put on his best suit instead of the casual golf clothes he was wearing.

"How nice of you to come by," she smiled. "Are you from that emerald place? How exciting." She turned from her desk and moved toward him, looking him straight and steadily in the eye. "Our people love green stones, you know, that's why we have turquoise in everything of value. Emeralds would be nicer but they are so expensive. By the way, I'm Jennifer Greatstone. I'm the receptionist, office manager, coffee maker and paper hauler. You just name the task and it's in my job description." She laughed and stuck out her hand to shake Al's.

Al took her hand, not believing how warm and friendly she was and almost ashamed of himself for thinking she did indeed have great stones. "I'm Al Silvestro and I'm vice president in charge of marketing at Santa Maria Emeralds." He gave her one of his cards. "What do you guys do here?" he asked, thinking how much he didn't want to leave and knowing a few questions would prolong his visit.

"Oh, this office has been set up by the Lasendas, we're a branch of the Apache nation, to make all the arrangements for our new casino. We're going to build the largest Indian casino-hotel complex in the country. It will be even bigger than Foxwoods, up north, and this little office is where it will all be put together." She spoke with great pride, eyes sparkling and cheeks a little flushed. Al was enthralled, totally lost to this perfect lady, thinking she looked better than she did five minutes before, if that could be possible.

"Yes," she continued, "we have our site picked out, northwest of the city, our architects have started preliminary concept drawings and we're just putting together our fund raising program which should start in a few weeks. It's really rolling along very well. Actually we should have opened our office weeks ago but we just received our approvals from the authorities on Thursday. Getting everything up and running properly will be difficult but I think I'll manage." She said this last part with a big grin and her right wrist placed theatrically on her forehead. Al just stood and watched her as she rattled on about the casino. She could have been reading names from a phone book and he would have just stood there listening and watching all day.

"I'm sure you're up to it," he stammered, smiling and turning on what he thought was his natural Latin charm. "You say you already have your site picked?"

"Oh yes. It's on the east side of Interstate 17 on the way to Flagstaff just north of a little town called Adobe. There's a race track out there, Turf Paradise, I think it's called, we're just beyond it. Of coarse it's all pretty barren right now, scrub grass more brown than green, occasional stunted trees, and spotted here and there, a run down shanty with a bunch of junk cars littering the place. You wait until we're done with it though. Huge buildings, palms, fountains, it'll be fantastic." She was on a roll now. This project excited her and she loved to talk about it. "It also means a lot of good paying jobs for our people. That's going to be the best part."

"It sounds great" Al said, "I'll have to drive out and see. You said something about fund raising. What are they doing, selling stock?"

"I'm not really sure. I know there's some rule about only Indians owning the casino but anyone can own the hotel and resort part of the complex and I heard someone say something about condos. That part I leave up to the men who are putting everything together." She shrugged and gave him her best, 'I'm just a girl' look, "Nick has all the details."

"Who's Nick?" Al asked, keeping the conversation going.

"He's the tribe's casino business manager and legal advisor. He could answer all your questions much better than me; he's bilangi," Al's puzzled look prompted her to correct herself. "I'm sorry, I mean he's white, you know, not one of us, but he's a good man and knows his stuff when it comes to casinos. Our tribe is very small and we must get a lot of our help from the white world. It's okay though, we never do anything without presenting it to our elders first, so we seldom have any mistakes."

Interesting, Al thought, and figured Tony would find it so as well. Smiling at Jennifer he thanked her for all the information. "I've learned a great deal and I'd sure like to talk to this 'Nick the white man' or whatever you call him, if he has some spare time. Could you ask him to call me? I have to go now, appointment, you know, and I'm sure you have lots to do."

"I'll do better, when he comes in I'll find out when he's free and come down to your office and let you know. Maybe you can show me some of your emeralds." She came out from behind her desk with a smile that would warm a Minnesota football stadium in January and stuck her hand out once again. "It's been nice talking to you Mr. Silvestro, and please, don't hesitate to drop in and say hello again."

Al floated out the door, hardly touching the floor as he headed back to his own office. Tony was gone but Al knew he, and the rest of the gang would be interested in this project being set up by a bunch of backwoods Indians from out here in the boonies. It could be worth looking into.

23

The shopping expeditions were a blast for everyone involved, including the shopkeepers who had to handle each gang of seniors pushing through their doors every half hour. The women loved wandering through the second-hand stores because clothing, kitchen items and children's stuff was the main stock. The men enjoyed the pawn shops, joyously searching through the display cases of handguns, racks of rifles and shotguns, and shelves of tools and electronic equipment. Before they finished many not only bought their clothes, hats and boots, but a lot of the men purchased power saws, drills, and hand tools, while a lot of the women had gone for jewelry; lots and lots of jewelry.

These junkets deep into a segment of the retail world most would never considered visiting, came as an eye-opening revelation. With almost a hundred pawn shops in the greater Phoenix area and countless thrift stores and second hand shops dotting the city, there was little problem finding a place to look. What surprised the seniors was the length of the list Nick had given them and the fact no store was short of customers when visited.

On arriving at their first target store, they were struck by the old age and poor condition of the cars and pick-ups parked in front. Most looked like they had gone through more than a dozen owners with the present one a lot more interested in keeping it running, rather than clean. Once inside, the age and gender of the patrons struck them. Almost all were either very old or very young and all were female, and the younger ones all seemed to have a couple small kids with them. Thrift stores sure didn't seem to be the kind of place men frequented.

The regular clientele spent a lot of their time checking quality, condition and size. Small children had to stand still while outfits were held against them to make sure the possible purchase would fit. Buyers were very careful about each item considered and carefully checked every inch before parting with their limited resources. When the shopping was done and it came time to pay, they counted out the small bills and coins with the same great care. The Florida group of well off seniors left the shops humbled, carrying a new understanding of the importance such places meant to people on fixed or low incomes. On the almost silent drive back to the motel in their shiny new cars, a few commented on how they meant do some donating or even volunteering when they got back home.

Evenings at the motel had all the trappings of a senior's social club. Within days the routine developed that everyone congregated in the banquet room after their evening meals for coffee, liqueurs, sherry and much gossip. From 7 p.m. on, couples made their way, many carrying bottles and glasses, to the meeting place for gossip and note- comparing of the day's adventures. It worked well for Nick because every time he had information to spread or needed help for the next day, he'd head for the banquet room about 7:30 p.m.

This night was no exception as he found almost everyone relaxing, laughing, milling about swapping stories, mostly about their shopping exploits. He needed a few men to set up a sign on the casino site the next day so he just waved his handful of notes over his head to get everyone's attention and stepped to the middle of the room.

"Listen up everyone," he called as he looked over the crowd. "I have to say you all look pretty spiffy in your new old togs." This brought a pretty good laugh and a few catcalls. "No, I mean it. Most of you look like you've worn this stuff for years. In fact, some of you look like you should be thinking about buying some new gear." This was enough to bring the house down. Nick felt like a stand-up comic in a Vegas hotel.

"Okay, okay, enough of the serious part, let's get down to business. I need several men to help put up a sign tomorrow. The job's a little difficult and as usual it will be hot as hell so you'll need a lot of time to get it done. LJ will lead the team and he'll need at least one pick-up so anyone wanting to help, see him over at the corner table." Nick pointed to where they should gather.

"Another thing, the office downtown is now open and we're going to need some people to come and go and also to spend some time there helping out Jennifer. By the way Vince, your granddaughter is terrific, doing a great job and is probably one of the best suggestions we've had. She's not bad looking, either." He donned his best wicked grin and gave Vince a big 'thumbs up'.

"Remember, if any of you spent a lot of time with these villains last year while they were in Bradenton, don't go near our office. Their operation's on the same floor just two doors down the hall from us." This last comment drew boos and hisses from the floor.

"As a final item I want you to know that my son Alexander is flying in tomorrow from Toronto to give us some cosmetic help. He works for Corkboard Entertainment, a large production company in Toronto that specializes in music videos and commercials. He's an expert in making things appear to be what he wants them to be, which is quite often not exactly what they are. He will bring his make-up kit and there will be a session the day after tomorrow on looking a little browner than we are. Questions anyone?"

"Yes Nick," Herb Sayer called out. "I know some of the people in the room had a lot of contact with these guys, but some of us only met them once and I think a few never did meet them. Do you think they will recognize any of us?"

Nicked stared at the floor for several seconds before answering. “Well Herb, let me put it this way. Back then, you were in Florida with money, position and nice clothes. They needed you to make their thing work. Now you’re in Arizona, God knows where you live, you have no money and your clothes leave something to be desired in the haute couture department. You’re of no interest to these crooks so I don’t think they’ll even notice you, let alone recognize anyone. Not only that Herb, your hair’s much longer and in a couple of days you’ll probably be a little darker. No, I don’t think they’ll catch on but remember, you are all simple poor people looking for work in the new casino.” This last bit brought a few more comments.

Nick checked his notes and carried on “The place has to look a little busy at times, so we’ll need a flow of people in and out. Those who never had contact in Florida will be needed to work in the office and be around more often. Could you please gather at the table over there so we can get details and set up a schedule.” This time he pointed to the other side of the room.

“Now for the last part of this program” Several had asked for details and it was time to tell them.

“You will notice on the door of the office when you see it, the name ‘Lasenda Nation Casino Corporation’. That is the name we are going by. We are the Lasenda branch of Apaches Indians and we are going to build the largest native owned casino-hotel complex in North America. The casino will have almost two hundred thousand square feet of gambling floor space and include every game of chance known to man. The hotel will have six hundred rooms in two towers, plus three swimming pools, nine restaurants, a day care centre, spa, barber shop, and beauty centre. This will be a first class operation. My son is bringing the preliminary drawings and artist’s rendition with him.” Everyone sat in stunned silence and stared at Nick. It was several seconds before anyone found their voice.

"What the hell is this all about?" a voice demanded.

"It's about getting your money back; remember, do unto others as they would do unto you. That is exactly what we are up to. We are going to sell a share of our fabulous new undertaking, this great shiny glass and marble casino, to our friends just down the hall from our office. They are going to want a piece of the action so bad they'll be able to taste it and we are going to get cash from them for that piece and then quietly close up shop and go home."

The following noise took several minutes to subside. Finally, LJ was the one who started the questioning and for the next two hours Nick patiently answered in detail every one thrown at him from members of the group.

He explained how he got the idea from a policeman friend of his and how he had worked it out over the past few weeks. When asked why he choose to build the sting around a casino he said most of the gang loved gambling – it seemed a natural attraction.

He explained how an architect friend of his in Hamilton, Canada, spent several days modifying drawings he had access to for a hotel complex in Abu Dhabi in the middle east. This architect even had concept drawings of several elevations sitting in a barren desert plus some with palms and landscaping. They would look like the real thing. In fact the paperwork and drawings for the hotel weighed over fifty pounds and had to be checked on the plane.

To a question about the Lasenda Apaches, Nick laughed and told them he had just invented them out of thin air. In fact the name comes from a golf club not far from them right there in Phoenix. The whole story was based on a tribe in New England where they opened a casino even though the tribe really didn't exist as an entity.

Taking a sheet of paper from his briefcase, Nick read to them a list of efforts to make the 'Lasendas' a real tribe. He recounted how Harry Stanley had asked a columnist friend at the Bradenton Herald to do a story on the Lasenda tribe. It was published and archived and appeared on their website. He sent letters to the editors of dozens of daily and weekly newspapers across the United States using the 'Lasenda' name extensively. Several were published, many also appearing on websites. He even had a computer savvy friend in England plant the name on several other websites. This would leave a broad trail for anyone researching the Lasenda band and its casino efforts.

Nick explained he'd sent letters on Lasenda letterhead to scores of state and federal agencies requesting information about Indian bands, Indian casinos, and the rights to operate a gambling establishment. He figured anyone checking out their operation would run into a flurry of hits and lots of information about a tribe of Indians called Lasenda and assume the whole story was legitimate. His carefully woven web of deception was quite extensive and far reaching.

The questions soon came not with skepticism, but respect and wonder at the thought and planning and brazen audacity of the scheme. By the end of the two hours everyone in the room sat looking at Nick, believing it would indeed work. LJ summed it up. "You seem to have done a lot of work on this Nick, and I guess we all owe you some thanks."

"Let's not be too quick with the thanks, LJ. I appreciate your words but we have to make this work and we have to be careful." He could see they were with him and Nick knew they would do just about anything he asked. "I want everyone to know one very important thing. You must not tell anyone about this program. No phone calls to friends, no letters, no discussing it in restaurants. You just never know who may hear you so remember, the less we talk about it the better. At the moment, the only safe place would be this motel but even here, keep idle chit chat about our program to a minimum." All had their eyes glued to Nick, listening intently, and for the first time, they really believed they had a chance.

24

Alexander Archer, Nick's somewhat wayward, but always interesting offspring, flew in from Toronto on Air Canada the next afternoon. His dad met him just outside security and led the way to the baggage carousel where they stood with others waiting for their things to come down the belt. They chatted about everyday things like his work, his new girlfriend's parents and the house he just bought near the Beaches area of Toronto. This lasted until a large red bag of golf clubs came around. Alex pulled them off the belt and shoved them at his dad as he grabbed a large cardboard box and a small suitcase right behind the clubs.

"What the hell did you bring these for?" Nick asked of the clubs as they made their way to the car park.

"They're for digging ditches, why else does one lug golf clubs two thousand miles?" he laughed and slapped his dad on the back, who happened to be the one carrying the clubs. "Hey dad, I know you've got a job for me but there's bound to be a little time for important things like golf, drinking, maybe even some bar hopping. Otherwise, I doubt I would have come." They both laughed and Nick just shook his head.

On the drive along the expressway to the motel Nick filled in his son on all the details of the project he hadn't explained on the phone. Alex had a few questions but basically he just listened. When Nick finished, he whistled and looked at his dad with more respect then usual.

"You're telling me you thought this all up by yourself?" he asked.

"Well, yes. I guess so. I got the original idea from Paul. You know, the Mountie from Burlington I drink with occasionally who almost got me thrown in jail for 'chug-lugging' with him in the basement of Terminal 1, but that's another story. He suggested we do unto others as they do unto us and that got me thinking. It all just seemed to fall into place and with Harry's help we set it up. This is the group who were screwed. Every one drove out here and they're as good a bunch you'll ever meet. You'll have fun while your here, I guarantee it, besides, when I introduce you to Jennifer, the granddaughter of one of the couples, I think you might even forget your golf clubs."

That evening after an expensive diner, paid for by Nick of course, he introduced his son to the group. As his dad expected, it took him just a few minutes to charm everyone in the place. He flirted with the ladies, talked sports, especially hockey with the men and quickly had them eating out of his hand.

When the social part of the get together was over and everyone was finding a chair, Alex strode to the front with his putter in hand. Positioning himself in front of them at a spot where he wouldn't take anyone's head off, he took a swing. He then talked to them, occasionally swinging at an imaginary ball and sometimes shaking the putter at them, explaining he expected full co-operation because he had a two o'clock tee time the next day and he never ever missed a tee time. Besides, he claimed, if by some odd chance he missed his tee time he would lose his green fees and that would just double the bill he was sending his dad. Nick just stood back and let the good-looking thirty-two-year-old rampage on with the gang of oldsters. Alex was having a ball and Nick had never heard the group laugh as much, nor as loud.

He told them of his work in Toronto with a movie and TV production company and how he has done just about every job you could think of in the creation of film illusion. He regaled them with stories of improvised solutions to problems that popped up during shooting and how they were solved. One was about the time they had built a false building for a hamburger commercial shoot on a lot in north Toronto. To save money it was put together in a rather flimsy manner and the whole thing began to fall down when an unexpected wind sprang up. The producers didn't want to delay the shoot for better weather because of cost and begged for a solution. After studying the story board and doing some thinking, he nailed rope handles all over parts of the building the camera couldn't see and enlisted everyone available to hold onto them to keep the walls from fluttering. Before the shoot was over he had senior staff from the production company, executives from the Hamburg chain and strangers passing by on the street holding on for dear life while the cameras rolled. It worked and the exec's had a story to tell at their next cocktail party. Alex also had some very funny and unflattering shots of the restaurants big shots fighting to hold their place together. Of course the executives never saw that footage, they were for private parties only.

Amidst all the joking, arrangements were made to start their make-up classes at eight the next morning so Alex would have lots of time to get to the golf course. He told them they all needed note books and pens and clothes that could take a stain or two. He said he would take care of everything else.

It took almost an hour for the room to empty and Nick was quite proud of his son and the way he handled himself. The gang loved him, especially the women, and most stopped to chat on the way out. Alex patiently answered each question asked and offered encouragement and support to everyone. LJ seemed impressed and Harry beamed like a proud grandfather. He had told everyone about Alex before his arrival and many of the crowd mentioned on how Harry's positive assessment had been right on. Harry claimed all his knowledge came from many Thanksgiving and Christmas diners sitting around a table in

Toronto laughing at the 'off the wall' comments and antics of Alex.

The next morning started right where the evening left off. Badly dressed laughing seniors headed into the banquet room to meet their new friend from Toronto. They found him striding about the banquet centre like the director on a Hollywood movie set. He had several rows of tables placed in an arc with chairs on one side facing the front where an easel stood beside a much smaller table. In front of each chair lay a small round hand mirror, Q tips, a small soft sponge and a pocket pack of tissues. A large zip lock plastic bag lay alongside the grouping. On the table beside the easel was a large open black carrying case, much like the kind lawyers carried into courtroom, containing row upon row of bottles, pens, and swabs. Beside this lay a king size bag of cotton balls and a mirror.

Alex met each participant with a big smile and a funny comment but close scrutiny disclosed how he was sitting people exactly where he wanted without them even noticing.

Within minutes one could see he was sitting the shortest at the front and those taller at the back. He knew what he was doing. In no time at all everyone was seated and eagerly awaiting class to begin.

"How y'all doing?" he called out as he looked over his class of students.

He was answered with a cacophony of 'fines', 'just greats' and 'not bads'.

"That's good because by the time I'm finished you're going to look like a bunch of old Indians down on their luck and badly in need of a job." He let this sink in and could plainly see the lack of understanding in their faces. "My dad thinks you look far too prosperous for his program so he called me in to make you look crummy. It's going to be a tough job, especially with some of you girls, but I'm willing to try if you are." He moved to his table for some notes amid giggles and a few good natured rude comments from the men.

"My father told me all of you have read several books by a writer who sets his stories in this area of the southwest." All heads bobbed in unison. "Good. I hope you grasped the thread of religion and spirits and ghosts running through his stories." Again all the heads bobbed.

"The spirit world is very important to these native people and you must respect it. They believe in ghosts and most would never consider living in a Hogan, or house, where someone had died. Even the idea of touching a dead person is a disturbing idea to them. Remember, they love their elders, their children and their planet and most are very stoical in their everyday manner." Alex moved about the room passing out papers as he spoke.

"These are a proud people. They have a long and colorful history full of great and brave warriors, gods, spirits, and grand events. They've been treated badly by most white people and very badly by some. Don't ever mention the name Kit Carson within earshot of any of them. It will cause a reaction. Just remember, you will be playing as a member of a proud and noble race. Think of that as you go about your duties."

Now back at the front he started their acting lessons, going through the motions as he described everyday activities.

"First a few lessons on basic body language. They're quite simple but they will help you be much more believable. First off, never carry a lot of money and never any large bills. Money is very important to poor people mainly because they have very little, and lots of people want to get what they have from them. So they must dole it out very carefully. Carry only one dollar bills, lots of coins, and never anything bigger than a five if you can help it. Keep your money in a change purse, the kind that snaps closed at the top, even you men, and roll the bills up and keep them with your coins." He saw several taking notes and all were listening closely.

"Also, when you need to get money out for a purchase, keep the purse close to you. Hold it with both hands close to your chest, and look down into it, not letting anyone see how much you have. You might not believe it but poor people are taken advantage of and victimized far more that you would think. They usually live in areas where crooks and petty thieves live and they have to be very careful. It's far easier for a thug to rob poor people rather than some well off dude because the police won't put as much effort into solving the crime. To many police, a robbery of twelve dollars, even if it's all a person has in this world, is not worth the time of two police officers and a patrol car. What the hell, at close to one hundred dollars an hour for two cops, plus the cost of the car, they're not going to spend a lot of time with it. Believe me; low income people truly get the short end of the justice stick."

Alex continued in the same vein, serious for the first time. "Poor people tend to be very cautious and wary of their surroundings. I want you be wary too because if you look and act like a poor person, you'll get the same treatment from both villains and police. So remember ladies, your purse strap over your shoulder and the purse clamped between your body and your arm. Snatchers love it when you walk along swinging your purse so they can grab it easy. Also, never go about the community alone, always in two's and preferably three's."

"The other thing is how you deal with other people. You never stick out your hand first for a handshake. Always wait for the other person to offer and when they do, hesitate before reaching out. Don't look people in the eye and don't smile often. Poor people are not very happy with their lot in life, and they have little reason to laugh and joke and walk around with a big grin on their face. Save the grins for back here and your laughs for my hilarious jokes in the evenings."

Alex then took them through lessons on how to walk (slow and shuffling) and where and when to scratch. He also asked them not to wear deodorant, perfume or after shave lotion, but to bathe or shower with a strong smelling soap, like 'lifebuoy'. He told them how they would be applying for jobs at the casino office and would have to wait in the hall and outside the building before their interviews. He kept repeating how they were poor and how they should act. "Say 'excuse me' a lot. Say 'I'm sorry' even when you're not and step out of the way of the suits. We want them to think you're members of an old impoverished band of Indians who need work and aim to get it at the new grand casino. They won't look closely at you but as long as four or five of you are around the place, our friends will think there's action in the new casino project."

After the acting lessons Alex started the makeup session. He made husbands and wives into teams so they could oversee each others application. He showed them how to apply the base material and then the color. He gave each one a color chart with the brown skin color he wanted and demonstrated how to apply it with a sponge. There were laughs and giggles throughout the room but they were taking the whole thing serious and in no time they were done their faces.

"Wonderful. You look great," Alex claimed as he moved from couple to couple. "Now everyone look at their partner and search for spots not colored. And I mean everywhere. Actually this could be a lot of fun if you feel a little rude. You'll have to go over your hands and any part of your arm that shows although most Indians wear long sleeved shirts. You women will have to do your legs and feet too 'cause we can't have you flashing a well turned ankle in different shade than your arms. Remember, check and then double check before you leave your room to go downtown."

"One last thing before we break," Alex said from the front of the room. "The only thing we can't control is other Indians. We suspect some will come around looking for jobs as well as some white people. If that happens, we will treat them the same way we treat you but talk to them as little as possible. Remember that American Native People are known for their reticence and silence. Be polite but say little. Answer as few questions as possible."

"Now before you go, here are some details about your heritage. Read them over, memorize the details if you can and keep this information to yourself. We made it all up, there's not a grain of truth in any of it, which makes you all a gang of liars, and we don't want anyone checking it out so let's not throw it around." Alex moved amongst the group, handing out sheets of paper. "Keep these papers safe. We don't want them sitting about for anyone to get a look at. Now, work on what you've learned, practice it in groups or together in your rooms and get it as right as you can. Remember, you are all actors in a play. You must be convincing. If you are, you won't get an Emmy or an Oscar, you'll get your money back. Now get going and we'll meet back here tonight for a dress rehearsal at eight thirty, after my golf game."

Nick stepped forward and put his hand on Alex's shoulder to thank him. "I have a couple announcements to make so listen up. The program starts in earnest tomorrow. We have to schedule who does what and when around the office. You know we have a receptionist, and I'd like to introduce her now." Nick turned and motioned for Jennifer to come forward to meet the crowd. She was greeted by appreciative applause, especially from the men.

"As many of you know, Jennifer is the granddaughter of Vince Strong and she's a student here in Phoenix. She has volunteered to handle the receptionist's duties at the office so most of you will be seeing her when you apply for your job at the casino. Be nice to her, but you guys, remember, not too nice."

Jennifer wandered through the group, introducing herself, shaking hands and joking with everyone. She had a smile and grace that charmed both the women and men. It was several minutes before Nick could make his next introduction but he was astute enough to notice how attentive Alex was and how close he kept to her as she made her way around the room.

"Okay, okay, enough of this love-in. We have work to do. Now that you have met our lady at the office I want to introduce you to the Chief Executive Officer of the Lasenda Nation Casino Corporation. Ladies and gentlemen, please welcome our CEO, Mr. Harold Stillwaters." Nick turned to the door as a tall, distinguished, almost noble Indian elder strode into the room. He was met with silence, possibly awe.

Mr. Stillwaters stopped beside Nick, shook hands and turned to the group. He wore well used but polished black cowboy boots and faded jeans held up by a black leather belt with a large silver buckle. His shirt was pale blue, clean and pressed, the collar held tight with a string tie and silver slide. He wore a beautifully made open buckskin jacket with fringe hanging from the sleeves. Ramrod straight, the six foot plus frame was topped with a black hat encircled by a silver hatband in the same design as the belt buckle and neck tie slide. Beneath the hat brim, piercing eyes looked out on the world from a dark weathered face that seemed to belong to an outrider on a ranch, not the CEO of a major corporation. When he turned his head, his foot long hair braid swung across the buckskin in a manner that would have unnerved most corporate lawyers trying to negotiate a casino deal. He looked like a chief; a leader.

The silence in the room was finally broken by Jorge Martinez who stood, moved toward the front and stopped a foot from Mr. Stillwaters.

“Harry? Harry Stanton? Is that you?” he asked.

“Harry Stanton? No. My name is Harold Stillwaters, a Lasenda Apache of the Bear clan.” He smiled as he said it, knowing everyone in the room would recognize his voice.

Pandemonium broke out. He was greeted by astonished exclamations of disbelief. One woman said no way and another fellow simply shook his head and muttered how he didn’t believe it. Several jumped from their seats and came closer to see for themselves, some stating their amazement. Harry had fooled everyone in the room and that’s exactly what Nick and Alex had wanted. This way everyone now believed their part in the charade would be successful.

All the effort put in that afternoon getting Harry ready for this meeting had been worth it, the test had been a grand success. They both knew now the plan was well on its way.

25

Tony and Al were lounging in Tony's office discussing the latest figures on their project. It was early evening and Tony had poured a couple drinks as they relaxed after their days work. Both were overjoyed at the numbers. Al felt it would be far better than the Sarasota project and could turn out to be the best ever of their many joint ventures. The scotch crept through them, putting them in an expansive mood, quite pleased with their business acumen and ability to make huge sums of money from a smoothly run operation. They were on a roll and ready to take on the world.

"Did you meet the big Chief?" Tony asked as he put away the list of marks already sucked into their scam, "the old one from the casino operation down the hall."

"Yea, I was in talking to the receptionist. Boy, is she something else. You were right, she's probably the best looking broad I've ever seen, Indian, white, yellow, anything, you name it. And built like a brick teepee too." Al waved his hand in front of his face to cool his imaginary heat, grinning all the while.

"The chief, Al, the chief; did you meet or talk to him?"

"I did, and he's some formidable guy, you know. Almost scary with those eyes of his and the way he looks at you. I don't think he has much love for white men but he told me all about his casino and what they were doing. He's quite proud of it and well he should be. Man, you should see the drawings. It's going to be one hell of a place you know, set back from the highway on a raising piece of land backed by a range of mountains.

"He took me in the back and gave me a walk through the project. It's huge. Why do you ask?" Al was still smiling about Jennifer.

"I was wondering if we could get a piece of the action in a place like his casino? You know, it's legitimate, and it's just starting to get under way. This may be the perfect time to jump in. I love the climate here, and this town is great. We may have lucked out with them opening down the hall. Everything seems to fit, what do you think?" He relit his cigar, waited for the match to go out then threw it into the wastebasket.

Al had known his partner for many years and knew the telltale signs when something was brewing in his devious mind. Back in the early days when they ran numbers and did some loan sharking together, Al knew the signs. Whenever Tony said he was wondering about something, a lot of thought had already gone into that wondering. He would sit and wonder out loud over a few drinks and before long, they were into another scam. Al had to admit though, each one was better than the one before.

"What do you suggest, loan them money, then take over the operation?"

"No, nothing so crass," Tony admonished. "I mean do it legit, like the good upright citizens we are. Sit down with these guys; offer a bucket of money for a bunch of their stock and a couple seats on their board of directors. Think of it, there must be a ton of dough to be made. Hell, look at what they do in Vegas or Atlantic City. Look at Trump.

"We'd become honest businessmen. I know, I know, it's a pretty novel idea and would take some getting used to, but we'd be able to attend board meetings, mix with all the big shots who want to be associated with a successful casino, contribute money to political campaigns, that kind of stuff. We'd even get a chance to rub shoulders with some of those high powered entertainment people. We'd bring 'em in for shows, or they'd just come around for some action and fun. Once it was going smoothly and all the heavy lifting was done, we'd see about buying out the whole thing." Tony paused and looked across the top of his glass to watch Al's expression, although he had a good idea what it would be.

Al had commented once or twice about retiring from the grind of seemingly endless con operations each year. He had more than enough cash stuck away in accounts all over the Caribbean to live like a king anywhere he wanted. He was fifty eight years old, loved golf, great looking women, and had mentioned more than once when they were in town how Phoenix would be a nice place to settle down. *Could there be a better way than as the executive of a large casino hotel operation?* Tony could read his thoughts.

"It would be nice my friend, I could see me spending the rest of my life here." Al grinned across the desk and added: "let's see what we can do. If we're going to do it legitimately, we'd have to put up a hell of a lot of dough but between us we could do it. Some of the other guys may want in as well in a small way. Why don't we sniff around a bit and if we can pull it off, it would be one hell of a nice way to round out our long and distinguished careers. You can sure as hell count me in."

"I figure it would take at least a million, maybe more, to get a big enough piece. There's no sense in doing it in a small way and that kind of money talks loud. Are you in for five hundred, maybe more?" Tony asked.

"I'm in," Al said with enthusiasm. "I could comfortably do a million, maybe a bit more, but count me in. Why don't I take you in to see the chief tomorrow and you can raise the issue with him. He'll show you the plans and drawings and I know you'll be impressed. If you can cut some kind of deal with him it will probably take some time to put it together but keep me posted and let me know when they'll want the money, and how much. I'll go along with whatever you come up with but it will take me a week to round up that kind of cash." He reached for the bottle on Tony's desk and poured a large splash for both his partner and himself. Picking up his glass he reached across the desk for a toast. "Here's to our new venture. May it start quickly, run smoothly and may it make us a ton of money." They touched their glasses and sipped in silence.

Drinks finished, they put the bottle and glasses away, turned off the lights, locked the door and headed for dinner at their favorite Italian restaurant. The route out took them down the hall to the stairs and the lobby. They didn't pass the casino office two doors from theirs so they couldn't see the light inside or know someone was there, working late in a back office.

Ten minutes after Tony and Al left, the light in the casino office flicked out and Nick, briefcase in hand, with his son Alex moving quietly behind him, slipped out to the parking lot and drove off.

26

Nick and Alex met in Harry's room with LJ and Bob Hardy. Two sat on the bed, Nick was propped against the quietly humming air conditioner and Harry sat at the small, round table in the corner between the door and the bed. Alex knelt by the table plugging in a power line from a tape recorder on the table. No one spoke until Alex finished the set-up. When it was ready Alex deferred to his father and moved back from the machine.

"Thanks son," Nick said and turned to the others. "I didn't mention that Alex dressed up as a phone installer the other day and had the tough job of waiting with Jennifer for the two top guys down the hall to leave. He then had to talk his way into our nasty friends' offices. He told their receptionist he was having problems with an installation down the hall and needed to check a few things. She took a shine to him and he had the run of the place.

"He crawled around for half an hour using a cooking thermometer and an old battery tester of mine, pretending he knew what he was doing." Nick waited for the laughter to fade. "He must have been convincing because a couple of the thugs working the phones in the back room helped move furniture so Alex could check a wall connection. While he was doing this so-called line check in every office in their unit, he installed a couple of voice-activated wireless bugs on the underside of the largest desks in the two most important looking offices. We hope they were the top guy's desks. This tape is our first real result of his efforts. You turn it on Alex, you earned the honors."

Grinning, Nick's son reached over and pressed the play button, filling the room with jerky but clear and distinct voices of the leaders of the confidence gang. Harry, LJ and Bob sat transfixed as the conspirator's words rolled through the room. None moved for more than twenty five minutes as the tape started and stopped every time someone spoke near either of the desks. When finished, no one spoke for several seconds. When they did find their tongues, the questions tumbled out all over Nick looking for answers.

"Isn't it illegal to tape people's conversations without them knowing?" LJ asked.

"I don't know; possibly," shrugged Nick. "Why, are you going to report us?"

Harry laughed and said: "You guys have got one hell of a lot of nerve you know. If they find those bugs we'll be in one hell of a pile of trouble."

"I don't think so." answered Nick. "If those things are found they'll think it's the local police, the FBI, or something like that; not some poverty-stricken Indians down the hall. If you listen to that tape again you'll notice they never mention their reason for being in Phoenix. These guys are smart. They may joke about going straight and getting into something legitimate but it's just that, jokes. I'll bet our tapes over the next week or two will be only about legitimate things, like an honest purchase of stock in a legal business."

"How do we use this to our best advantage?" Bob asked.

"That's why we're here tonight. To plan our response relative to the information these tapes have provided to us." Nick reached for his ever-present note pad and turned to his small audience. "They're coming to see Harry tomorrow and we know they want in and how much they're ready to offer. I think we should play it cool and not jump at any offer they make. I'm open for comments and suggestions."

LJ was first. "Nick, the longer I know you, the greater my respect. These bugs have got to be about the most brilliant thing I've seen in years. And you, Alex my boy, talk about balls of brass. Boy, do you ever have them. Of course having seen their secretary, I can understand you wanting to spend some time in their office."

Alex laughed. "She's nice, but not as nice as ours, and I'm an expert in the business of judging beautiful woman."

"Hear, hear," said Harry, raising a glass of soda in a silent toast to Jennifer, noting the glint in the boy's eyes when he mentioned their secretary.

Nick brought the discussion back and turned to Harry. "When they come, you must be gracious and show them anything they want to see. Answer all their questions about the casino, including building, financing and projected revenues. I know you'll be able to convince them, and if they want, tell them you'll arrange a trip out to the site. When they broach the matter of investing we have to figure a way for you to handle it without raising suspicions."

"I've got an idea," Bob Hardy chipped in. "What if we tell them state law will not allow non-Indians to own stock in an Indian casino. Tell them a non-Indian can buy into the hotel complex or loan the band money, but not be shareholders in thc company that gets the license. Knowing the way these guys work, a little thing like a State law won't stop them. They'll come back to see if some way can't be found to let them in."

LJ wanted to know if anyone had a suggestion to get around the problem. There was silence for a few moments before Alex jumped in. "Since the law says they can't buy shares in the casino, how about a share in one of our other companies that could invest in the casino."

"You're losing me," Nick said.

"It's easy. Tell them the tribe owns a company, any kind of company, somewhere else in the country, maybe Cleveland, or Buffalo, that can invest in the casino because it's an Indian-owned company. There will be a corporate veil between them and the casino caused by the other company which has no regulations on who can buy shares in it. We sell them a part of this other operation and the funds are transferred to the casino by way of an equity purchase. Therefore the state laws are complied with because it's an Indian company investing in an Indian casino." Alex was on a roll now.

"There is no law about who can be on the casino board of directors, we can get anyone we think will help advance the operation so we can appoint these guys. We can then pass profits on to the shareholders, including the outside company, and they can pay a fat dividend to our friends." He finished, quite pleased with himself.

Nick got up and started to pace the small motel room. "Alex, that is brilliant. Now I'm sure you're my son. We'll put them off tomorrow, telling them we'll look into the situation, check with the Elders, that sort of thing. It will give us time, several days, to refine Alex's story, decide what kind of company and where it's located and work out any kinks. Then we'll come back with the plan as a solution to the problem. The fact it's a little nefarious will make it all the more believable."

Nick was getting excited. "This will fly, I know this will fly. Alex, can you set up something just over the border that looks legit? Like an office, or something? We'll offer to let them visit and see the place if they want. In fact, to make it seem legal, maybe they should ask them to take their money there to turn it over."

Nick was wound up now and he started making lists and working out the details of the plan. He shot questions at Alex about a setup over the border and how much money he might need to cover it.

He then turned to Bob to see how much lead time he needed to set up his sign. They knew a visit to the casino site was mandatory and the sign could be the clincher.

"Two hours. I just need to get two or three guys and depending on the time of day we can get out there in about forty five minutes to an hour. If you want to be really sure, we can take out one of the motor homes early and you can phone us. We'll just sit out in air conditioned luxury waiting for you."

"Great idea" said Nick. "You'll get enough warning, but keep close. When they want to go out you'll have at least an hour to set up before they arrive." He turned to Alex. "Get on the phone first thing tomorrow and see if some of your buddies can find us a business. Also, call the airline and get a seat. We need you back up north rightaway."

Harry raised his hand to get Nick's attention. "Listen, Nick, there seems to be a lot more to this than I expected. I'm not sure I can keep everything in place while I'm conning these guys. I might need some help."

"Not to worry. I plan on parking a couple blocks away tomorrow morning. Have Jennifer call me as soon as the villains arrive. I'll wait a little bit and then come in. Introduce me as the tribe's legal advisor and business consultant on casino matters. I'll step in and help out if you need it, even though I doubt you will. All the time we'll have people coming in for job applications." A look of relief swept across Harry's face at the plan.

The next hour was spent sorting out details and timelines. Alex would help with early morning makeup before calling his pals and the airline. Bob would set up for the sign while Harry got his chiefs outfit ready. LJ would organize the job seekers and assorted extras at the casino office. Alex volunteered to call Jennifer first thing in the morning before she left for work to give her a heads-up on what was going on. All considered him a good choice for that little job. Everything seemed to be fitting together.

When all of them were comfortable with the arrangements, Nick looked around the room. "Tomorrow is going to be important. If we can get through the day and these guys are still onside, we will succeed in this venture. Tomorrow is our big day so let's all get a good night's rest and meet back here at seven." He got up, gave Harry a pat on the shoulder, shook hands with the other two and left with his son. He felt good, really good, for the first time in a long time.

27

Nick awoke with a start at 5:30 a.m. and it took him several seconds to fully get his brain in gear. In moments he realized it was flashing red and blue lights and multiple car doors slamming that disturbed his deep sleep. Within minutes he was dressed and outside, finding two police cars, an ambulance and a fire emergency vehicle parked three spots down from his unit. Bob Hardy was standing just outside the motel door talking to a Police Officer and it didn't look good. It was the Browns' room.

"What's going on?" Nick asked, interrupting the two.

"Who are you, sir?" the officer politely inquired while taking out a pen and notebook.

"I'm Nick Archer, the tour organizer for a group of seniors staying here. This is Bella and Richard Brown's room, two of our tour members. What's happened?"

"Well Mr. Archer, I'm sorry to have to tell you, but it appears Mr. Brown passed away during the night while sleeping. His wife called us about twenty minutes ago. Can I have your room extension number and your home address, please?" he asked while jotting Nick's name in the notebook. Nick gave the information asked for. The officer also wanted details of their tour so Nick explained its premise and what they were doing in the Phoenix area. He described themselves as a group of seniors deeply interested in Native American culture. All in the group had been briefed on their cover story and how they were on a visit to the Four Corners region and its many Navajo, Hopi, and Apache reservations. Their itinerary included side trips up to Window Rock, Ship Rock, and the pawnshops and souvenir stores of Gallop, plus a visit to the cliff houses of the Hopi. The clinching piece of information was saved for the last. Nick told the officer most members of the tour were Tony Hillerman fans and they wanted to visit the places described in his novels. The officer naturally knew who the writer was, himself being a Native American and living in the same general area of those stories. He nodded acknowledgement and closed his book with a sad smile.

"I understand," he said. "Mrs. Brown is in the office with Mr. Hardy's wife and a few other women of your group. We're getting the remains ready for the coroner's office. You understand, procedures require we treat this as a crime scene until the coroner declares it natural causes. That should take a day or two and then the body will be released to a funeral home of the widow's choice." He turned back to Bob and asked him if he could arrange another room for Mrs. Brown, then gave both men his card with the station phone number on the front and an incident number written on the back. Politely excusing himself, he moved back into the motel room.

Most members of the group were dressed, standing around outside quietly watching the activities, knowing how inevitable it was for all of them. Almost all held the hand of their spouse or had an arm around a shoulder as though it would fend off this eventuality. The ambulance attendants brought the gurney out with the covered body of their likeable friend and wordlessly slid it through the ambulance doors for the ride to the coroner's office. They seemed to sense the moment, carrying out their duties with quiet and restrained dignity.

Harry had talked to Nick about this very thing several times, discussing how he and Kitty planned their funerals, wrote and rewrote their wills, picked out their cemetery plot and prepaid everything. He said the closer he got to his final day the more he thought about it. Nick remembered those chats as he watched the group around the door of the Browns' room.

There were no tears or inappropriate display of anguish. These were people of a generation that considered public tears and an open display of grief as unseemly. Quiet sadness would best describe the scene as they stood by, supporting each other with their presence. Richard Brown lived ninety-four years, seventy of them married to a fine supportive lady. He had watched his children mature, attended his grandchildren's weddings and once or twice was allowed to bounce one of his four great grandchildren on his boney old knee while anxious parents hovered near to catch the child should it fall. To die quietly in his sleep, beside the woman he loved, while on this great adventure, was about as good as it could get. All his friends, these fellow conspirators standing like a guard of honor behind the ambulance, knew it. They were just sad he hadn't lived to see the job finished.

Soon there was quiet. The fire emergency vehicle was first to leave. The others shut off their flashing lights and one by onc slipped off the property leaving nothing but the silence of the desert night and a strip of yellow tape pinned across one motel room door. The officer said someone would be back about 10 a.m. to supervise Mrs. Brown's removal of some of her personal belongings to another room. He told Nick and Bob he was very sorry and they believed him.

The crowd dispersed and moved back to their rooms to get ready for a busy day. Nick and Bob headed for the office dreading the coming scene. When they stepped through the office into the living quarters it wasn't quite what they had expected.

Bella Brown sat surrounded by five or six women with LJ and Harry hovering in the background, ready to give assistance. It neither looked nor sounded like it was needed. The laughter in the room was genuine, robust and irreverent. Bella was entertaining all with funny stories of her seventy years as Richard's lady.

"Come in boys," she called as they opened the door. "I was just telling them of the first time I left Richard to mind our first youngster while I took horse and buggy to visit a sick aunt down the road. I was only gone three or four hours but that was enough. He had some trouble keeping a clean diaper on the toddler so after several failed attempts he decided just to let the child wander about bare backside. Within fifteen minutes he knew that wouldn't work so after cleaning up the mess, he set about designing a better way to hold up the diaper." She paused here to sip her tea, chuckling at the long ago scene.

"He took one, laid it out and decided to sew a loop at each of the three corners. This done, he sat the child down with one corner pointing straight out in front and the other two behind and to each side. Then he pulled them up and ran a rope, can you imagine, a rope, through each loop and crossed them over the poor child's shoulders. Mind you it worked, but mercy me, it was the most god awful contraption I'd ever seen. I feared the child would choke himself, I truly did." She laughed at the memory and took another sip of her tea.

"Don't look so sad, fellows." She said to the two new arrivals. "Richard and I knew this would happen someday. We've often talked about it and just hoped there would be no pain or fussin' or burden on our family or friends. When I go to join him I hope it's the same way, in my sleep, hopefully after a few good drinks." Everyone laughed at this.

"We had a good life. It was full of laughter and tears and wins and losses but I remember the laughter and the wins more than anything else. I'm just glad we were on this grand adventure and surrounded by so many old and new friends. Don't you men worry about me any, I'll be just fine."

Nick was sure she would be and knelt down beside her to say so. She took his hand and patted it comfortingly, offering some advice and encouragement. "Richard liked you. He said you were a bright young man who could be trusted and if anyone could get our money back, it would be you. Now you've got a lot to do and so do the rest of you, so get on with it and don't let my Richard or the rest of us down. We girls have a great deal of arranging to take care of so we'll be busy. Just remember something; my husband was enjoying himself more on this trip than I've seen for many years, he felt needed and useful. So don't feel bad. You've got a big day dawning so best you get started." With that she gave him a small shove to help him on his way. Nick motioned to Harry and LJ, and, with a wave, left the widow and her friends to plan Richard Brown's big day.

28

Jennifer had the office open and humming when Harry arrived at five after nine. This could be the pivotal day of the project and the cloud of Richard's death would make it a tougher day than Harry had anticipated. His first job was to take Jennifer into his office and explain the events of the morning. Alex had mentioned it in his early call but he didn't have the details Harry brought. She didn't remember the Browns from her introduction to the group but she felt badly and was quite sorry. Harry told her how Mrs. Brown was handling the event and suggested she might want to visit with Bella. The idea brightened Jennifer and got her planning to pick up some flowers for the widow Brown.

In the meantime she helped Harry sort out a bundle of supplies delivered the day before from the Livingston Printing Company of Camden, New Jersey. This was LJ's old firm now owned and operated by his two sons. Every time the group needed something printed, LJ would simply find Amanda, smile and ask her to fax the details to his boys. Within one or two days a courier truck arrived with the goods. These included business cards for several of them, letterheads and envelopes, posters, and signs for the office. They outdid themselves early in the venture with a beautifully illustrated twenty-four-foot by eight-foot canvas sign put together like a giant bag to fit over the small billboard erected out at the project site on I-17.

It was during their sorting job that the door swung open and Tony DiAngelo walked in with Al Silvestro. The hair on the back of Harry's neck stood on end as he turned, with a smile, to meet them. Now he was facing the leader of the bastards who stole his money.

Jennifer, who knew the details behind her job and why she was there, sensed Harry's momentary hesitation and stepped toward Al with her sweetest smile, holding out her hand, "How nice to see you Mr. Silvestro, I'm so glad you could drop in again." She warmly shook his hand and guided the two of them over to Harry. "You remember Mr. Stillwaters?"

"Of course I do, I remember how much of his valuable time he spent showing me the layout of the casino. I was so impressed I brought my partner, Tony DiAngelo along and wondered if he could see your setup." As Al spoke Tony stepped forward and put his hand out to Harry.

"Nice to meet you Mr. Stillwaters, I hear you have one hell of a project about to get underway here in Phoenix and Al said I should take a look at it." As he shook Harry's hand he gave him a good look and understood what Al had said about his eyes. This Indian only tolerated those white men he needed.

Harry was the epitome of a host with class, dignity and grace. He gave Tony a brief rundown on the project and while Al hung back to drool over Jennifer, the chief guided his guest into the boardroom where maps, drawings and blueprints adorned the walls. It was an impressive display.

Harry started with the site plan and described how they would use the natural slope of the land up and away from the highway to showcase the buildings. Closest to the road would be the casino with the hotel complex behind and much higher up the hill. Between the two were several restaurants, the spa and two huge swimming pools. This would make almost the entire complex visible from the interstate. These details and all the answers Tony got to the many questions he fired at Harry left no doubt the project was something he definitely wanted to be in on.

"Who can buy into this venture?" Tony asked abruptly

as they sat at the boardroom table sipping coffee brought in by Jennifer.

"Well it's a little complex but it all basically revolves around the State rules applicable to the casino license. The hotel and spa, in fact everything but the casino, will be owned and operated by a separate company we've set up, a company anyone can purchase shares in. We could sell the whole thing but it's in our interest to keep control. The casino is different. It must be a separate entity because State law stipulates only accredited Native people can hold equity." Harry slid a folder titled 'Lasenda Holiday Condo Complex' across the table for Tony to peruse. It was another of the Livingston Printing Company's efforts and it looked good. "This will give you some idea on how you can participate."

Tony casually laid his hand on the folder without looking down and staring straight into Harry's eyes asked: "How can we get a piece of the casino?" and sat silently with Harry in his crosshairs.

"I'm sorry Mr. DiAngelo, but the rules won't allow that."

"My friend," Tony said casually as he picked up the folder and stood to leave. "I have never seen a rule one couldn't get around if one really wanted. My partner and I would love to be part of this great project. We're both well off, considering semi retirement and Phoenix sure looks good to a couple of east coast boys. We have substantial funds available for a quality investment, I'm talking in the seven figure range, so please understand we're serious. Give it some thought and see if there's some way we can work together on the casino part of your project. Let me know if you can come up with something. It's the casino we're interested in." With that he walked to the boardroom door, stopped and turned. "You and your people have put a lot of work into this and I respect that. We would like to be part of it. Thank you for taking the time to show me the details. Please think over what I said." Turning, he walked out to the lobby and motioned for Al to come along. Tony was a man accustomed to getting his way and he expected nothing to be any different this time.

Harry sat quiet and motionless for so long Jennifer came in to see if he was alright. He smiled as she entered and invited her to sit down. "How do you think we did?" he asked.

"Hook line and sinker, as Grampa Strong would say. They hit, bit and swallowed it all." She reached over and patted Harry on the hand and grinned like a cat that had figured out how to open the birdcage. "While you were with Tony, the other jerk, Al, who thinks his Latin charm has me halfway into his bed, did what most men do when they have the hots for someone, he talked too much. He told me about their connections and how much money they have and how much travel he does and on and on and on. The guy had verbal diarrhea. Don't worry, they're dying to buy in."

The entrance door to the lobby swung open and an elderly Indian in hat and jeans stepped in and asked for a job application. Jennifer opened a filing cabinet and pulled out some papers and handed them to the man. Harry suddenly recognized him as Edward Fisher, the Bradenton restaurant owner. Without blinking an eye he thanked Jennifer for her help and continued on to his office without looking at the man standing in the foyer holding his wide brimmed hat in his hands. At the moment he closed his door Harry realized Nick hadn't arrived and he had handled the whole interview on his own. He hadn't been nervous and best of all, he had been convincing. It had been a long time since he had felt as good as he did that moment.

29

Harry was tired but exhilarated as he slipped the old cassette out of the recorder, dated it, tossed it into his briefcase and slid a new tape in for the next day. He wanted to hear it before leaving but decided to hold off until Nick and LJ were present for the playing and the next day's strategy session.

Jennifer had already left for the evening, wanting to stop at a flower store to pick up something special for Mrs. Brown. Harry thought how nice a girl she was, refusing to take any money from him for the flowers, sniffing that she had cash of her own. Before she left though, she came over and gave him a peck on the cheek, saying how good he had done that morning, then cheerily swung out of the office. Harry couldn't help think but how nice a pair she and Alex would make. He shut off the lights, locked up and headed out, tired but very pleased with himself.

As Nick opened the door to his room he knew the day had gone well simply from the look on Harry's face. The drive out to Apache Junction in heavy traffic hadn't dampened the chief's feeling the project was going according to plan and he showed it.

Nick grabbed Harry's hand and shook it vigorously, thanking him profusely and dragging him into the room where the others sat. "I'm sorry I couldn't make it into town this morning Harry. There was so much going on. I just forgot. By the time I remembered what I had said I would do, it was noon. I called, but Jennifer told me all was well and not to worry. She said you were great and she's nominating you for an Academy Award. I'm sorry Harry; I wasn't there in case you needed me." He was truly upset with himself.

"Not to worry." Harry said and put his arm around Nick's shoulders. "We've been friends long enough for me to know you must have had some heavy lifting to do. Besides, everything went very well and I think these chickens are just about ready for plucking. I brought the tape. I don't know what's on it but let's run it now and hear if they gave anything up." He waved at Bob in the corner and handed the tape to LJ. "Where's Alex, by the way?"

Nick glanced at his watch "Should be in Toronto by now, hopefully getting his team together."

LJ motioned for quiet and hit the play button on the recorder. Within seconds the voices of their targets swept over them. They listen closely as the voice-operated mike hidden in the room started and stopped. It was a little jerky but you could understand everything.

It began with a door slamming and a voice saying: 'What do ya think Tony?'

'Damn fantastic. Their designer has done a tremendous job. It's a beautiful setup. I love the way the towers rise up behind the casino and entertainment complex. You can stand on your balcony and look down on the pools. You were right, we have to get involved,' as the voice was replayed you could hear the clink of ice in glasses and liquid being poured in the background.

'Well, I can just see it full of people, thousands of people, all begging to drop money in the slots and on the tables. I'm telling you, it would be like owning part of the mint.' The first speaker almost panted.

'I agree,' the one referred to as Tony said. 'We have to get a share of it. Do me a favor will you? Drop in and see the chief tomorrow and arrange a visit to the site. Try to get him to take us out personally; it'll give us a chance to work on him. I'm telling you, this is the big one and it's legit. I think you'd better start arranging your part of the money. I'll bet you a weekend with Malita they'll find a way to let us in. You watch, money talks.'

They tape went on in the same manner for several minutes more, before moving on to other matters, mainly their gemstone business and how well the investment program was going. The small group in the motel room sat transfixed as the voices went through long lists of marks, how much they were in for, and almost every detail of their operation. It seemed to be enough to put them both behind bars for a long time if you knew what their project was. As it was, they sounded like businessmen discussing investors trying to buy into their manufacturing operation. The tapes had to be kept a secret. If anyone got hold of them, Nick's group of friends wouldn't get a penny. When the sound ended LJ took the cassette from the recorder. "What should we do with this?"

"Can you make a copy or two?" Nick asked and LJ nodded yes. "Good, make a couple copies, keep one yourself, give Harry one and I'll take the original. When we finish with Tony and his bunch they may be a form of insurance in case we need it. You never know about guys like these." All in the little room nodded in agreement.

"Now let's go over tomorrow and the visit to the site." Nick pulled up a chair. "First off, I think we owe Harry a big thank-you for today's work. From what we heard on the tape you did a tremendous job on those two jerks and we owe you." LJ and Bob, sitting on the bed with Harry between them, turned at the same time and gave him a friendly punch in each shoulder. Everyone laughed at the spontaneity of their actions and Harry, a little embarrassed by the attention said something like "aw shucks" and waved them away. Nick carried on.

"Harry, let them talk you into going. In fact, before they show up, get Jennifer to draw a map to the site, make several copies and put them away in your desk. When they ask about going out there, pull one out and hand it over. When they ask you to go, be a little hesitant, tell them you're busy, you know what I mean, important meetings and all that crap, then finally give in and get Jennifer to call and change your appointments.

"As they said on the tape, they're going to lean on you to find a way for them to buy in." Nick continued. "Tell them you talked to the lawyer and say he considers it risky but you're still willing to try. Let them think you're not really opposed to them investing but you won't do anything to jeopardize the project. Tell them there may be a way of doing it but you're not sure. Say you'll have an answer in a day or two because no matter what you do, it has to be approved by the band's elders."

The four of them discussed the next day's activities for almost an hour and it was decided Harry try to get them to go out as early as possible. Bob would be on site with his gang and Jennifer would call him on his cell as Harry left the office, giving lots of time to pull the sign up. They discussed Bob's engineering skill and joked about the sign. Their billboard, designed to lay flat on its back out of sight when not in use and pulled upright in minutes was a wonder to behold.

Bob and his crew had sunk seven twelve-foot-long four-by-four posts into holes filled with fast-set concrete in the desert, then attached six four by eight sheets of plywood to them to make a twenty-four-foot by eight-foot sign. Once in place and solid, Bob cut the posts eight inches above the ground and affixed heavy steel hinges to connect the cut pieces. On top of the sign he screwed in three large iron rings that long ropes were tied to. When Nick wanted the sign up, Bob and some of his crew took hold of the ropes from the rings, four or five others picked the sign up and the rope crew pulled from the front of the sign while the picker uppers shoved from the back. Everyone agreed it was a little primitive but it only took a couple minutes to get it up or put it back down and best of all it worked.

On the back of the posts in the ground and on the upper hinged pieces, Bob had screwed more iron rings and when the sign was up, he slid a piece of pipe down the back through the rings. It held the whole thing in place beautifully. To cap it off was the Livingston canvas sign with great sweeping letters in red proclaiming it to be the future site of the Lasenda Casino/Hotel. All in all it was a damn good installation and from 200 feet looked professional and permanent. Bob was proud of it and took all the ribbing good naturedly.

They broke up after going over the details of where Harry was to stand with the guys in the scrub brush in front of the sign near the road. It was very rough between where the car would be parked and the sign site so there was no fear Tony and Al would want to walk any closer through the dirt and rocks in their Gucci's. These were city boys and if they did want to get any closer, all Harry would have to do is say: "Okay, but keep an eye open for rattlesnakes."

It had been a good day and they all went to their respective rooms feeling quite pleased with themselves.

30

Tony and Al met early to discuss their trip to the casino site and how to go after Chief Stillwaters on their drive out and back. Both agreed Al should play good cop to Tony's bad, swinging the old Indian back and forth between them. It was an old and well used method they often employed on marks in order to get their way. Neither saw any reason why it wouldn't work today. At 9:30 a.m., Al finished his coffee, sauntered down the hallway to the casino office, stuck his head in the door and asked Jennifer if the chief was in. The chief was, of course, sitting in his office, with a tiny piece of plastic connected to the recorder stuck in his ear, listening to every word of their conversation.

"I'll get him," Jennifer smiled, and stood up, smoothing her blouse and turning toward the inner offices. She almost heard Al's heart skip a beat and stifled a giggle.

Harry came out immediately and shook Al's hand, inviting him into his office. Wanting to keep Jennifer in his sights Al demurred and asked about a trip to the site that morning. As discussed the night before, Harry instructed Jennifer to get a map. She made a big production of looking in the filing cabinet, finally pulling one from the bottom drawer, which meant she had to bend over to get it. Smiling sweetly, she handed it to an almost breathless Al. She could have handed him a pound of toad poop for all he seemed to care, the way his eyes were glued to her chest. *What a pig,* she thought, and kept right on smiling sweetly. She was a good actress and was getting some good experience.

"I can't possibly go with you," Harry said to Al's insistence on his accompanying them to the site. He explained how his morning was all tied up and the afternoon was shot as well. Waving to Jennifer to bring over his schedule, he showed the list of appointments he had lined up, including a 10 a.m. meeting with the lawyer, 11 a.m. conference call with the architect and a prospective construction manager and then a noon luncheon with the band elders. The afternoon looked the same.

Jennifer was perfect. As the three of them went over the list she suggested the lawyer could be put off until later in the day, maybe even the next day. She thought she could call the architect and reschedule the phone meeting and if Harry wanted, she could call the elders and delay the lunch by half an hour. All this while Al was trying to look down the front of her blouse and Harry was trying to say no, he had no time and couldn't go. In the end, Harry said "yes," he'd go with them. Al looked victorious and infatuated, and Jennifer smiled humbly, as though accepting her Academy Award for best performance of the year in a French farce. Harry half expected her to give a thank you speech.

Ten minutes later the three men pulled out of the parking lot and headed toward Phoenix and the site beyond while Jennifer worked the phone lines to Bob.

Al drove, Harry sat up front beside him, and Tony was in the middle of the back seat, like a honcho being chauffeured by his minions. Harry silently thanked Kitty for remembering to give special attention that morning to the back of his neck and head when applying his colored makeup. He smiled, thinking how she wasn't just another pretty face. A moment later they were on the freeway.

"How'd you pick your site?" Al asked.

"It's our land, to begin with," Harry answered. "It's a piece of a much larger holding, but most of the holding is sacred. You know, special to the band, and can't be used for any commercial purpose. It would disturb our ancestors to have strangers, white-eyes like you, no offense meant, wandering about our sacred areas. Our elders spent much time with shamans, they're the ones who know the old and sacred ways, and with their help, picked out three places we could use for a casino. This site we're going to is by far the best of those three."

Tony called from the back, "What about the other sites that aren't so holy?"

Harry mentally winced. "One site is very close and could be used for another, maybe less expensive hotel, to compliment the main operation. The other is a good distance away and could some day be used for a whole different casino complex if this first one was to go real well." Harry threw out more hooks for the fish. "We don't want to live in a dream world but keeping an eye open for the future just makes sense to us and if this venture is successful, well, who knows, we may just go forty miles to the east and do it all again." He turned to Tony and gave him his best *whatever will be, will be* look.

Tony tried hard not to look too eager but the avarice and villainy shone through from the back like the high beams of an SUV following too close. It took him several seconds to settle down and ask as casually as he could, how Harry was doing about getting Tony and Al in on the casino deal.

"I talked to our lawyer on the phone and he thought it may be risky but he would look into the possibilities. That was one of the things we were going to discuss this morning. I personally think there may be a way, but it could be a little involved. I'm not sure but we could certainly use the investment." Harry directed this to Tony, then tapped Al on the arm, directing him to turn off at the next Exit.

"See all this; this great farm land all around you?" Harry waved his hand in a wide swath on both sides of the car. "These are the lands given by your government to the Indians to live on. You'll notice not much is growing except some rocks, dust, and the occasional cactus. It's not much, I think you'll agree. Now maybe, we've found something that will truly grow well here and produce a better life for our people. No more stunted corn, skinny cows and hungry children. Now maybe we'll have better housing, better schools, and no empty bellies for children to sleep on." He stopped talking and looked straight ahead in as stoic a manner as he could. He thought as he stared out the windshield that Jennifer wasn't the only one who could act.

Al slowed down after exiting the highway and turned to the old Indian for directions. They were approaching a 'T' junction and he wasn't sure which way to go. Harry knew this was coming and slipped out of his 'injured Indian quiet mode' turned to Al and pointed to his left.

"I'm sorry," Harry said. "I know it's not your fault. In fact, you want to help us improve the situation and it's appreciated. That's why we're trying to find a way for you to join in with us." Harry smiled and indicated where Al could pull over and park.

The spot Harry picked was about 100 yards from the sign but a high bank just beyond the ditch blocked it from view. Although visible from the Interstate a couple thousand yards behind them, the three would have to climb if they wanted to see where $75-million would be spent in the next couple years. Excited, Tony and Al left the air-conditioned car and followed Harry up the embankment.

Taking slow strides, Harry was able to reach the top with little effort and unlike his two struggling followers, stood facing the sign without a drop of sweat on his brow.

"This is it." He said to the two sweating and panting thugs. He stood, holding both arms out and up like a preacher at a revival and dove into his pitch. "Imagine it. The two hotel towers will be farthest from here, blocking that ugly cut in the side of those far hills." He pointed at a spot half way up the far mountainside where some mining organization had blasted out a great cut long ago.

"Every room will face this way, toward Phoenix, overlooking the huge pool area and massed palms and tropical flowers nearest their base. Next will be the large convention hall and theatre complex with a roof garden and outdoor restaurant. Finally, at the front, the casino itself, stretching out in a great crescent, encircling the whole front of the complex. All of this, flowing in steps down the slope toward the highway and the city." Harry was on a roll now, arms wide open, head held high, like Moses showing the Promised Land to his followers. "You're standing not far from where the entranceway will be, surrounded by palms, flowers and fountains. It will take your breath away just to lean on your balcony railing of your hotel room to look out at it all." Harry paused for breath and looked at the two of them to gauge the effect his words had. He need not have had any doubt. They could see the picture he was painting because that's what they wanted to see.

Harry moved forward through the brush toward the sign and motioned for Tony and Al to follow. They waved him off. "It's OK, Mr. Stillwaters, there's no need for us to go any further." Tony said. "We can see the layout, your vision and the architect's plans. You're right. It is breathtaking. I can see it now and I love it." If Tony had doubts before the ride out, he had none now. He was determined to get in on this deal and to someday control it all. The decision was made. The how-to-do-it part was all there was to consider.

During the drive back to the office both Al and Tony made it clear to Harry they expected him to figure out a way to get them in. Tony hinted at some cash commission for extra efforts on Harry's part with the proviso no one else knew about it. Harry had trouble hiding his smile at this bit. In all his years, he'd never been offered a bribe.

As he parked the car at their office building, Tony reached from the back and tapped Harry on the shoulder. "We have the money and the desire. Talk to that lawyer of yours and get him onside. There's an old saying 'if it's done well, it's done quickly' and I think that rule applies here. I'll be waiting for your call." He gave Harry a friendly pat on the back and got out of the car.

31

Nick waved from the motel office door and headed across the lot to Harry's his car as the Grand Chief of the Lasenda Tribe parked.

"What's up?" Harry called, climbing out into the fading sunlight.

"Just a couple things you should know about Bella Brown in case you run into her in the lounge after dinner," Nick advised. "She's got problems with her family up north."

Harry was a little surprised. "What the hell kind of problems could she have? Her husband is barely cold and the will hasn't been read yet."

"Well, last night she called her son and two daughters to tell them their father had died and they jumped right in without hesitation saying they'd start making all the funeral arrangements right away. The son wanted to know which airline and flight they'd be arriving on and said he'd make sure someone picked her up; I guess he'll be too busy, and he'd arrange for the funeral home to pick up Richard." Nick filled in several more details about the children's plans on what should be done and how it would be done. They seemed to have given this eventuality a lot of thought, even down to which funeral home they'd use, who would give the eulogy, and how the obituary would read.

"So what's the problem?" Harry was still perplexed.

"She told them to cool their jets." Nick said with a smile. "She said she's already contacted a funeral home here in Phoenix and made arrangements for cremation, and a small service, as their father wanted. She said all of their many friends were with her in Phoenix on this senior's vacation trip and it would be best to do everything here. She said she had already picked out a nice brass urn for Richard's ashes which she was sure they would love and she told them she'd let them know when she was bringing their father home for internment so a nice memorial service could be held." He stopped for affect, loving every moment of the story.

Harry was now showing a little impatience. "Nick, where the hell is this going?"

"My friend, the kids went crazy. When she told them what she had done they just went ballistic. In fact, one of them must have caller ID because so far Bob has had calls from the son, the daughter, a friend of the family and even a lawyer. The lawyer, some two bit ambulance chaser, had the cheek to lean on Bob, suggesting Mrs. Brown could very well could be declared incompetent and someone would have to come down to Phoenix to take charge. He insinuated Bob had better not do anything to impede the Brown family's wishes or he would be liable for action. Amanda said her dad shouted some rude words over the phone. She giggled as though she'd never heard them before."

"Have you talked to Bella?" Harry asked. "What has she got to say about all this?"

"She told me the lawyer could go to hell. It's the first time I've ever heard her say anything stronger than darn. She called them all the same thing Sylvia Brenner called her family, 'beneficiaries in waiting'.

"I spent some time with her this afternoon and as you know, there is nothing incompetent or strange about her. She tells me she wants to stay with the group through to the end. She feels Richard would have wanted that because he always worried she wouldn't have enough after he was gone. He always said he would go first, she said." Nick turned to Harry and put his hand on his arm.

"Harry, she considers us her closest family. I asked her about the kid's wishes and she blew that away in a heartbeat. She said the kids never bothered with the old man while he was alive and they either feel guilty about it, or see this as an opportunity to show all their friends what devoted children they are. She actually said they make her sick."

"I think I'll go see her. Is she in her room?" Harry asked.

Nick grinned. "No, she's over in the banquet hall, holding court. Go on over and have fun, except, don't go up against her wishes. She may be only five feet tall but she's one feisty old doll and you'll get an earful if you hassle her. Bob suggested she chat with his lawyer but she said no, there was no need."

Harry nodded and moved off toward the hall. He had an idea what she was thinking. It was a common complaint he heard from fellow seniors all the time. It made him almost glad he had no kids of his own. All he heard about was grown children always too busy to bother with retired parents, especially those who lived some distance away. There were forgotten birthdays, grandchildren never sending thank you notes for gifts, and always some excuse for not visiting. These were the basis of most of the grievances Harry had heard for years. He had an idea how Bella felt.

He found her sitting with several other members of their group, including Kitty, cheerily discussing the details of the service for Richard in two or three days. They all had paper, pencils and lists upon lists of things to arrange. One would think they were planning a charity tea.

"May I interrupt?" Harry asked, politely standing to one side. "Mrs. Brown, how are you doing?"

"Quite fine, Mr. Stanton, quite fine, and how are you?" She smiled sweetly up at him.

"Oh, I'm OK, it's been a long day and I was out at the site so I'm a little tired." He found himself saying. She had a way about her, drawing things from people who normally kept their feelings to themselves. He looked down at her and the sweet smile continued to glow on her face. He decided on a different approach.

"How are the arrangements for the service going? Is there anything I can do to help?"

"Oh no Mr. Stanton, you're much too busy, and I have all these friends here to carry much of the burden for me. They're all so kind. And you, Mr. Stanton, you're so kind to ask." The same sweet smile, the same serenity, Harry wondered how she did it.

"Well, you just let me know, and the chapel service, if you need me to pick up anyone at the airport, members of your family perhaps, friends, maybe, I'd be happy to provide a shuttle service." He could smile almost as nicely as the widow Brown.

"Oh that's all right, Mr. Stanton. You see, all Richard's and my friends are here with us. These are the people who are important to us." She waved her hand to include everyone in the room. "As for family, well, they never bothered with him while he was alive so I see no reason to worry about them now that my darling is gone. Richard and I have lived in Florida for twenty-three years. I can count on one hand the number of times any of our children have visited us. Our youngest great grandchild is seven years old and we have never seen him. They have no right to any say in how my Richard is taken care of." Her steel backbone was showing, thought Harry, and he didn't envy the position her kids were in.

"Well be sure to call me if you need anything, anything at all. I'll be there to help."

"Thank you; both you and your wife have been very kind. You're just like the rest of our friends here. You stand beside us when we need you. You support us in our time of troubles and none of you has to. You're more than family, you're friends. Please don't worry about my relatives or what they think. I don't care, and neither should you."

Harry knew a dismissal when he heard one so he simply smiled, winked at his wife, and backed away from the widow's group. There was nothing more to be gained here and if he had any more questions, either Nick, or his wife could help. In the meantime he would prepare for the service and get on with the main job he was here for.

Nick was outside, enjoying the night air, looking up at what seemed like millions of stars overhead. Not far from him LJ stood quietly chatting with Bob. It was a beautiful night, warm, a light breeze, the kind the Chamber of Commerce brags about in their commercials and actually occurs once in a while. The four stood in silence for several minutes; no words necessary.

Finally, Nick turned and broke the spell by inviting them back to his room for a beer and some discussion on the day's events and future steps in their plan. All seemed a little reluctant to come back to the job at hand. With a sigh Harry turned to join the others for the short walk to Nick's room.

32

Harry waited until three in the afternoon two days after the site visit to call Tony about their possible involvement. He had wanted to keep them waiting for a while, but not too long. When he did call, Tony must have been waiting and jumped at the chance to come down the hall for a visit. He said he'd call Al and they would be there in fifteen minutes. Harry opened his desk drawer and checked the small tape recorder for at least the third time that day, making sure it was working. He was nervous and wanted to catch Tony's phone call and make sure he missed nothing. This was the big day, the biggest as far as Nick was concerned, and there could be no screw-ups.

Jennifer swept into his office with fresh coffee and Harry marveled at how good she looked. They had called her about nine the night before and told her they planned to pitch Tony and Al the next afternoon so she should be ready for them. Jennifer promised to get gussied up and she sure as hell kept her word. Harry thought the two thugs from down the hall didn't stand a chance.

Jennifer set her alarm much earlier than usual to prepare for this special day. She knew how important the pitch would be and she would do anything she could, within reason, to help.

First, she carefully picked out her favorite white cotton summer dress. Although sleeveless, it had a modest square cut bodice with wide straps over her tanned shoulders, revealing little of the wonders beneath. The stunning part was how it fitted snuggly, but not too tight, through the full length of her body, sweeping down, following closely to her slim torso to the mid point of her hips. Here it simply hung almost to her knees as a pleated skirt, full, and ready to sensuously swing with every step.

Her feet were in very high white stilettos held with small white bows tied around her ankles. She wore no jewelry save small turquoise earrings, almost invisible behind her long dark hair. On her right hand was a matching turquoise ring. She was a beautiful woman to begin with, one with an astounding figure and a style no one could miss; but when she wanted to dominate a room, putting thought and effort into her appearance, she was simply stunning.

The night before, Nick, Harry and LJ had sat with Bob outside Nick's room going over the day's events and tossing the next day's possible activities back and forth. They had argued over when to call Tony for a discussion regarding investing. LJ was thinking they should wait more than a day or two and Nick and Harry were wanting to move faster. LJ finally gave in and agreed to the need to get on with it so they decided to do it the next afternoon. They also called back to Alex for an update on the northern project. It was late evening in Toronto but Nick hoped his son might be home. He was.

"Hi son, how ya doing?" he asked when the receiver was picked up. Nick was surprised by the answer.

"I'm doing fine, in fact, really fine; but I think you want Alex, hang on a moment." The female had more than a little laughter in her voice. Nick, somewhat bemused, waited while music was turned down and the same voice called Alex to the phone.

Finally, Alex picked up the phone. "Hi dad, how goes the battle?"

"The usual, two steps forward and three back. How are you doing up there? And by the way, when did secretaries answer phones at eleven-thirty at night?" Nick asked with a chuckle.

"Now Dad, you know I'm working late on this thing

of yours. And no, I'm not getting married soon and there aren't any grandchildren on the horizon. Or is that 'in the horizon'?" It was obvious Nick had interrupted something.

"That's not why I'm calling, and you know it," Nick said. "I want to know how you're doing with the place up there and when will it be ready?"

"Oh *that*. Oh hell, everything's in place. I was going to call you tomorrow morning 'cause we just finalized everything a couple hours ago." He said it as though it was some minor deal. "We have the location. A factory called Hyde Park Pipe, in Niagara Falls. It's on Hyde Park Road, just a few hundred yards south of Witmer. It's perfect, even if I do say so myself. Let me know when you're ready to move 'cause we'll need at least two or three days notice to get things set, so keep that in mind."

"Would Monday or Tuesday be alright?" Nick asked.

"Sure. You think it'll be that soon?"

"We're going to pitch them tomorrow and they'll have to fly up there to close the deal. I'm coming as well to work it but they're hot to get it done, so I expect they'll want to be on a plane as soon as they can book seats."

Alex was silent for a moment then said: "It would be better Tuesday, if possible. We can do Monday but Tuesday would be perfect. That gives me four full days to set up and then Monday to move in the cameras and equipment. Tuesday would be the dress rehearsal."

The time constraints of the last several days plus the need for Alex to get back north had left Nick short on details of the Niagara Falls operation. He needed them now so there would be no slip ups with the pitch and the directions given to Tony and Al. He asked his son if he had time to fill him in, or if he'd prefer to wait till the morning.

"Now's fine," said Alex. "It'll take some time because I am your son, a stickler for details, and my part is as good as yours," he said with a touch of pride.

"First, you have to realize we're doing this as a scene

from a movie," Alex explained. "I had to prepare a script, put together my director's shot list and had my crew create a story board. This scene we're shooting is part of a full drama feature. It involves some very important businessmen visiting an industrial site they plan on buying as cover for a smuggling scam they're going to run across the border. You would be proud of how I've set this up. Let me give you the details."

He then went on to tell Nick how he had fake business cards made for their film production company when he got back in Toronto and took two of his friends to the Buffalo area. One, a fine looking young woman – on meeting her, most men had trouble seeing anything more than her sweater – was a location scout for a major Toronto studio. Alex had explained to her what he needed and within hours they were sitting in the foyer of the new executive offices of Hyde Park Pipe, Inc., a legitimate steel pipe-making operation across the river in Niagara Falls, New York.

Alex met the President and three of his underlings with the director's shot list and story board in hand, explaining how his film company needed an industrial site with offices for a major scene in a movie they were producing. While he talked, Lisa, the location scout, sat with legs crossed, taking notes on a clipboard she held strategically low on her lap so the four executives could properly take in her fine secretarial abilities. She sure knew what she was doing.

They accepted Alex's offer of a five thousand base fee for the first three days plus a thousand a day for each additional day. They weren't overly concerned about the insurance details and suggested they would accept industry standards. Inside fifteen minutes the deal was set and they had the run of the place.

He explained to Nick that Hyde Park had just moved into new corporate offices detached from the main warehouse, unlike the original ones. The old ones were still standing; a one story section attached to the huge factory some distance from the new building. Management wanted a whole new image so they outfitted their new place with all new fittings and furniture. They just moved their people and paper over one afternoon and left the old offices sitting there, complete with desks, filing cabinets, even the old phone system, non operating, but sitting on all the desks. They said management hadn't decided what to do with the old place, considering either an auction or a sale to staff who may want some of the stuff. In the meantime they would just sit waiting until a decision was reached. It was more than perfect. It was a dream come true.

He told Hyde Park's President they would be back in a few days to start cleaning up and received an offer of help from the plant staff. Everyone wanted to be part of making a movie. Alex took him up on it and made the place as good as new. Over the next three days Alex would bring in some extras to staff and fine tune the set-up, getting their places set and learning where everything was. It wouldn't do having one of the thugs ask for the washroom if no one knew where it was.

They would inform their hosts there would be a dress rehearsal on Tuesday and they didn't want anyone around to disturb this practice run. He explained they would all be invited to the actual filming but they had to stay away from the rehearsal.

"You sound like you've been busy," Nick said with some pride. "I like the set up. I'll get there on Sunday and be waiting for our friends on Tuesday. I'm going to get Jennifer to arrange their flight, hotel and car rental so we'll have their schedule. I'll have her call you. You don't mind do you?" This provoked a chuckle. "They should arrive in the afternoon, rent a car, check into their hotel and then come straight to the warehouse. After we get their money, I'll take them for dinner, get them a little drunk and send them on their way. After that, I don't care what they do."

"Well, we already have our signs, letterhead and

envelopes courtesy your friend from New Jersey. It's called Frontier Pipes and those guys did a heck of a job on the signs. They even sent us one with an arrow pointing to Frontier Pipe Employee Parking. I couldn't believe it. I'll fax you directions to the place. That way your buddies can find it easy on Tuesday. It'll be on our letterhead so that should impress them. I'll address it to Mr. Stillwaters. By the way, if you want a good laugh, go to FrontierPipes.com. I'm sure they will and if they're still not sure, they will be after a visit to our website. It's the greatest piece of fabrication you'll ever see." Alex laughed and told his dad how much fun he was having.

They talked a few more minutes and Nick promised to call late the next day to confirm all their plans. He hung up quite proud of the work his son had done in such a short time.

When he told his three co conspirators of the plans they either whistled or shook their head. LJ suggested the apple hadn't fallen far from the tree and they all had a good laugh.

33

Tony and Al took fourteen minutes to enter the Lasenda Casino offices and ask Jennifer to tell her boss they had arrived. She smiled, said sure, and stood, stepping from behind her desk to sweep across the office foyer toward Harry's office. She didn't have to look to know what effect she was having on the two standing men.

Harry immediately came out of his office and welcomed them with warmth and sincerity. As he did it he wondered how he had become such a good actor. They all shook hands, made small talk, and Harry asked Jennifer to get some coffee for the boardroom. As they moved toward their meeting Harry noticed how his guest's eyes had trouble staying off Jennifer's backside. *Nick was right,* he thought.

Almost nothing was said as the three men entered the boardroom, pulled chairs out and sat down while Jennifer set out mugs, cream, sugar, and a large carafe of coffee alongside a plate of cookies. Harry watched his guests closely and knew they were simply waiting for the deal.

"How are you fellows doing?" Harry asked.

"Fine," said Tony. "What have you got for us?"

"A solution, I think. Our lawyer has come up with a way to let you own a piece of the casino and I think he's done a pretty good job." He opened a manila folder on his left and pulled out some papers, passing each a copy and keeping one for himself. "This is just the outline so just hang on to it. Because of the sensitivity of this matter I'll need all those papers back. If the Arizona Gaming Commission ever got hold of them, there would be hell to pay."

Harry leaned forward over a yellow legal pad on the

desk and with a pencil wrote a name in capital letters across the top. It was FRONTIER PIPES INC. "This is a company our band owns. It will be the vehicle that brings you in. I'll explain how."

"A few years ago," Harry began, "the federal government came up with a bundle of money, millions, actually, for new drinking water services to be installed on all the reservations in the four corners region. It's a huge area and the distances between settlements can be as much as twenty five miles. A small typhoid outbreak a few years before scared the hell out of everyone and the politicians wanted to look like they were doing something. They gave us plenty of say in the planning, design and especially tendering of the work being done. Again, they wanted to look good, and letting us employ locals did just that. We learned there was an incredible amount of pipe needed to complete the job and it didn't take a rocket scientist to figure if the feds were paying, and we controlled tendering, we could score big if we owned the pipe supplier. So we bought a company that sold pipe."

Tony stared at Harry with a new look of respect on his face. "Isn't there a bit of a conflict involved here?" Tony asked with a grin, thinking these damn Indians were no different than him and his fellow Sicilians.

"No one knows we own the company, just a few of us and our lawyer. Let's just say it's buried under a couple obscure layers of ownership but in the end, believe me, we own the whole thing. We figure you may be able to acquire a piece of the casino through the pipe company if you're still interested."

Tony was more than interested. He was panting. He looked at Al, winked, and turned back to Harry. "How do we do it and how long will it take?"

"First you buy a twenty five percent share of Frontier Pipes of Niagara Falls, New York and get two seats on their board of directors. Frontier is owned by a holding company which will 'okay' the sale of the shares. The holding company in turn is owned by a venture capital company that is supplying most of the money for the casino. Our band owns the venture company. The hotel and banquet centre is financed separately by a mortgage and investors from all walks of life and plays no part in this deal. We may sell suites in the towers as condominium hotel units but nobody cares as long as the casino is entirely in our hands." Harry stopped to fill his coffee cup and take a cookie.

The pause also gave him a chance to see how his story was going. Harry had told a few real whoppers over his years; like the time he was caught doing 115 in a 65 zone. The traffic court judge said his story was so good he would give him an entertainment discount and cut the fine in half. The old fossil said it was the best fairy tale he had heard in 42 years on the bench. Harry must have gotten better because this story he was into now made the tale for the judge sound like the first three books of the Bible. These two guys seemed to be buying the whole story, likely because they had never read the Bible.

Tony took a sip of coffee. "How do we get our piece of the casino? I'm sure the pipe company is profitable, the way you've got this water thing fiddled, but we'd like a gambling spot in a nice climate, not a steel mill in the rust belt."

"Well, Frontier is going to lend all the money you give them to the venture capital company. They in turn will secure this large loan with ten per cent of the casino stock, so Frontier, and its board, will control ten per cent of the casino's voting stock, get two seats on the casino board, and Frontier will appoint you two as their representatives on that board. The actual ownership of the stock stays with the band, they've just assigned them as collateral. We believe the State Gaming Commission will be satisfied with the arrangement, at least our man on the inside says so. You can rest assured that everyone involved, the boards of all companies, will approve these transactions. The loan interest will be ten percent."

Harry stopped again for questions.

Al asked about their contact in the gaming commission and Harry was very vague about it. He wanted it to look a little dishonest, making them all kindred spirits. Tony wanted to know how they would get their return. They were in, hook, line and sinker, as Jennifer had said and now were thinking like they had already invested.

Harry told how Frontier Pipe made a profit of six hundred thousand last year and Tony and Al's share of that alone was one hundred and fifty grand. This profit should continue for at least ten years because there were still hundreds of more miles of pipe to be put in the ground so profits would go on at least that long. There was also the interest on the loan, ten percent. Their share was twenty five percent of that amount, or about fifty thousand. So if it took two years to get the casino open, they would at least have a decent return of around ten percent for the first couple years.

Harry advised that when the casino opened, they were in for a straight 2.5 per cent of all profits, which a consulting firm conservatively estimated at ten-million dollars to start and increasing to a possible fifty-million a year. That would give them an amount of somewhere between $250,000 and $1.25-million each year. He was writing all this down as he talked and ended by circling the high number and setting the pencil gently down on the table. The number was $1.45-million a year.

Tony sat stunned. Al had stood to get a better view of the paper Harry had written on and whistled at the numbers. They both had trouble finding their tongue.

Harry knew it was time for the knock out punch. He reached over, picked up the pencil and wrote ten years just below the largest number. Both men jerked their head up and stared at him.

"What's that?" both said at the same time.

"Our elders have one condition they believe is necessary and it's not negotiable. You must agree to a buy-back clause that can be triggered ten years from the day the casino opens for business. The buy back is for fair market value of the ten percent of stock used as collateral. It is not mandatory and may not happen, but the elders insist on the right to exercise the clause if they want. I don't think it's unreasonable." Harry sat back and waited.

"Why the hell would they want a buy-back clause. I think it's damned unreasonable. I mean, we get in on such a good deal, why would we give it up?" Tony huffed.

"It's simple my friends." Harry almost choked on *friends*. "Ever since the white eyes came to this land they have taken and taken and taken from our people. Five hundred years of being shoved around, moved off our lands and onto reservations, even killed, has made many of us a little wary. Everything of value has been stolen, our food supplies killed for sport and profit, our families decimated with disease. If you sat with the elders you wouldn't find them bitter or bad tempered, just resolute in their efforts to protect the interest of their people. On this buy-back thing, they are adamant."

Harry continued: "Listen, you invest two million, you get an absolute minimum of four million eight hundred thousand over twelve years. It is more likely your return would be in the range of twelve to fourteen million. Then, if the elders decide to activate the clause, we give you back the fair market value of the stock plus your original investment. I'd say it's not unreasonable at all."

He sat and waited. It didn't take long.

"How do we put it together?" Tony asked and Al just shook his head up and down.

"I'll have the papers drawn up and you'll meet with our lawyer in Niagara Falls at the plant. It will give you guys a chance to look the operation over and meet some of the key players. After all, you're going to be on their board of directors and even if you don't want to bother much, you'll still want to visit each year for the annual meeting and booze up. When do you want to go?"

"Right away" Al said. Tony agreed.

"Let me call the lawyer and see how his schedule is. If you like I'll have Jennifer round up plane reservations. Today's Wednesday, it may be hard to get everything done by Friday so why don't we aim for Monday or Tuesday. I know the elders will want to look over the contract before it goes north. How does Tuesday sound?"

Tony and Al consulted each other's day planners as though they were very busy people with important meetings all over the place but in a moment turned to Harry and said Tuesday was fine. The three stood and shook hands.

"I'll have Jennifer put a package together for you. You'll need a map from the airport to the plant, phone numbers if there's any problem. I know there's some information about them on Frontier's website so you can check that out and anything else you may need. Leave it to us, she can arrange the flight and a car rental and she'll drop all the stuff on your desk tomorrow." They seemed to like the way Harry was handling things so they agreed and left smiling.

As the glass door closed he called Jennifer to tell her the news and get her started on the travel arrangements. All the time he couldn't get the old Sherlock Holmes expression out of his mind. Over and over, it rolled through his head: 'the games afoot, Watson'.

34

The funeral service for Richard Brown was held at 10 a.m. the next morning at Hemstreet and Sons Funeral Parlor in Mesa, another suburb of Phoenix just west of Apache Junction. Mr. Hemstreet, the funeral director and owner, later admitted to friends it was the cheeriest and best natured group of mourners he'd ever seen in his 23 years of sending people into the great beyond.

Mrs. Isabel Brown, the grieving widow, had called him several days before the service and told him she wanted a cremation, a nice but not too expensive container for the ashes, and she wanted it done as soon as possible. He had suggested she might send a friend around with all the details and he would start work making preparations in this hour of her grief. She told him to cut the fiddle faddle – can you imagine anyone saying *fiddle faddle* these days? – and ordered him to stay put because she would be there in an hour.

Almost to the minute Mrs. Brown, Kitty Stanton, and two other friends entered the funeral home, ordered a somber young fellow in black who met them at the door to get the boss and then proceeded to look the place over. It took only minutes for the senior Mr. Hemstreet to arrive on the scene.

"Can I help you ladies?" he asked, solemn of face with hands crossed in front of his stomach the way he was taught in undertaker's school.

"I'm Bella Brown. I called you an hour ago about my husband Richard and I'm here to get things in place," said the shortest and by far the oldest of the four women. She stood straight, although she wasn't more than five feet tall, and moved better than some half her age. "Where can we sit down to get this done?"

"Right this way," Hemstreet said, ushering them into a boardroom. Within half an hour all was done and the date set for the service. She had asked for an Episcopalian minister but said she didn't want him giving the eulogy. She told him she didn't want some twit who never met Richard up at the podium telling everyone what a fine fellow he was. The eulogy had been arranged by her husband a long time ago and the person giving it was in town and ready to go.

She gave him her fax number; she was in her nineties and had a fax number, and told him to send a draft of the service details when it was done. Then she stood, told her three friends it was time to go, and without another word, left.

The service was one of the nicest, and funniest, Nick had ever been to. He had expected to be the youngest in attendance but Bob and his wife closed the motel office to attend with their daughter and to everyone's surprise and delight, including Nick's, Jennifer showed up with a smartly dressed and beaming Alex on her arm.

The minister brought in by Mr. Hemstreet was exactly what one would expect. Father Cook, who seemed hardly old enough to be a real father, was probably the youngest assistant at the local church. To him fell the duty of serving at itinerant funerals because, being too young to shave, and low man on the seniority list, the head Pastor told him he needed the experience.

Father Cook was very nice though, trying hard to be properly solemn and comforting, all the while not knowing a thing about what he was into. The old ladies loved him and giggled at his only major problem. The good reverend had an inability to keep from laughing out loud every time one of his temporary congregation said something funny, which was quite often.

After prayers there was a hymn sung in Spanish by

a pretty young Mexican girl who accompanied herself on guitar. Most in the chapel figured she likely sneaked north across the border only a few weeks before to find a new voice teacher. When she finished her rendition of a beautiful Mexican religious song, most were sure she hadn't been too successful in her search. All were relieved as Father Cook called upon Harold Evans to come forward and give the eulogy.

Harold, five-foot-two and 195 pounds creaked up out of his chair next to Bella and slowly made his was to the podium. When he turned his round full face to the group, beads of sweat were evident on his brow. It took him a few minutes to mop it dry.

In his early eighties and a little slowed by arthritis, Harold had been a member of the group from day one. A retired schoolteacher from Moore, Oklahoma, he had lost $21,000 to the villains and was a staunch supporter of the recovery efforts since the very beginning. Harold and his wife Bess lived directly across the street from the Browns in Florida for almost twenty years and were close friends. Many thought this was the reason Bella asked Harold to give the eulogy. It wasn't. Richard and he had set up this arrangement long before the service was needed.

The eulogizer started off by looking over the band of expectant mourners for so many minutes, most thought he had fallen asleep standing up with his eyes open. When he finally made a sound it was to clear his throat. He did this with such vigor Nick half expected him to turn and spit into the baptismal font on his right, but he didn't. He started a well thought out speech that must have been a long time in the planning.

"You must all be wondering why I was chosen to give the eulogy over so many others who could probably do a much better job. It's quite simple so I'll tell you. Over the past several years, Richard Brown and I spent long hours chatting about our deaths and our funerals while partaking of the occasional adult beverage. These in-depth discussions usually occurred in the gardens of our homes back in Florida after a hard day of being retired. It was actually a great excuse to pop open a beer or three without getting you know what from our wives." This brought a chuckle or two from the gathering because all knew Richard Brown and a long neck Coors beer had a special relationship.

"Richard and I had an agreement. I would write my eulogy and he would write his and we would exchange them and keep them in a safe place. Neither of us read the others words but both of us had some idea of the contents of the envelopes. Once in a while we would get together, get back our eulogy and look them over to make some changes or updates. We did that just before we came out here to Arizona. Our agreement was; if I went first, he would read what I had written. If he went first, I would read his words. We both believed if someone was going to stand up at our funeral and tell lies about us, they were going to be our lies, no one else's, and they would be told the way we wanted. I'm not happy standing here, as you may well understand, but then again, if Richard was before you, I wouldn't be very happy either, I'd be dead.

"Anyway, I'll miss those long afternoons and warm evenings we spent together. We solved most of the world's problems and argued everything from politics, which we both had a passing interest in, to sex, which we both vaguely remembered." He had to wait here for the laughter to die down. "Here are his words, exactly as he wrote them."

Harold paused, cleared his throat again, and started reading the paper he pulled from his pocket. 'Well my friends, if you're listening to these words I guess I'm dead; or, there's been one hell of a mistake and you're all wasting a perfectly good funeral." More laughter. "Assuming there's no mistake, I just hope my good friend Harold

Evans is reading this note and my dear Bella is sitting out there listening. Don't worry dear, I've written nothing rude about anyone except maybe a couple Democrats.'

Harold stopped for breath while Mrs. Brown smiled and wiped away a tear as several chuckled quietly over the last few words. Richard's favorite and oft used phrase was 'damn Democrats'. The eulogy continued.

'I have lived more than ninety years, blessed with good health most of that time and the great fortune of being married for seventy years to the finest lady in the world. I often said it was the best day's work I ever did, marrying her, and I could never understand why she didn't chuck me out on my ear at least a thousand times during those years. This singular lack of good judgment was her only weakness but one I'm thankful for. A friend at our sixty-fifth anniversary party asked her if she ever considered divorce over all the years of our marriage and she said no, never. She went on to say she had considered murder more than once, but never divorce.' This caused a lot of outright laughter.

'I updated this missive just before we left on our great adventure to Arizona and it can't be over if you're hearing this so please, for my sake, my wife's sake, and for all my friends involved in this project, carry on and complete it successfully. It has been a wonderful way to cap the life of an old codger and I thank every one of you for including me. I know I was a bit slower than most but with the help of my Bella, I think I made a contribution. I also made many new friends and had a lot of laughs and if it weren't for a few damn Democrats in the group it would have been perfect.' This last prompted loud laughing and much shuffling and head bobbing. Mr. Hemstreet looked around the room and marveled at the good humor and high spirits of the crowd.

'I won't go into details of the events in my life because you'd grow tired of hearing such a litany of great deeds and fabulous accomplishments. Just let it be known that I never cheated on my taxes when the Republicans were in office and I never lied to my wife except when I thought it was for her own good, or, in most cases, mine.' More laughter rolled through the room.

'I have no advice or grand wisdom to pass on other than to say how important all you, my friends, are, being around me to the end. It is you who have made it worthwhile, a pleasure. People like Harold, who, even though he couldn't keep up to me in the beer drinking department, spent many long hours figuring out solutions with me for the worlds problems. I hope he remembers those hours as being as enjoyable as I found them.

'The new friends, like Harry, LJ, and Nick, whom I've known just a short while compared to the time I've spent on earth, are great friends non the less. I encourage you to get the job done. These villains need to be taught a lesson and I know you're just the bunch to do it.

"I would suggest one thing for your consideration. You should try to hold annual reunions so a toast can be raised in memory of those who have come to join me, and a few drinks and laughs with those left behind. It's a great venture you're on, one which should provide many hours of reminiscence.

'Lastly, to Bella, my love; I asked Harold to do two things for me when this day arrived. One was to give you an envelope containing the map of where I hid the treasure in taxes I kept back when those damn Democrats were in power.' More laughing and knee slapping resulted from this last bit of information.

'The other was to arrange a good old fashioned wake at a place of Harold's choosing, paid for with some money I gave him years ago when we first set up this eulogy arrangement. Everyone's invited to have a drink or two or more on me so please, join Bella at the spot Harold has chosen and don't be afraid to tell her what a fine fellow I was; I'm sure she'll forgive you for your little lie.

'Well, my friends, that's all I can think of to say and besides, my arthritis is acting up and I can't write anymore. Please, enjoy my funeral, because my life has been a slice."

Harold stopped talking and stood quietly, looking out at the group of mourners. It didn't surprise him when some of them started to applaud. In seconds most everyone joined in, all standing, some even calling bravo. It was an ovation that was hearty and happy and Richard would have loved it.

Harold spoke when the applause finally died down. "The party Richard wanted is now set up in the banquet room back at the motel. Ed Fisher, our intrepid restaurateur, helped me choose the menu and arrange the catering so if any of you have a complaint, blame him. I'll turn this service back to Father Cook and then we'll head back." He stepped from the podium, ambling back to his spot next to Bella, who patted his hand and smiled up at him with tears in her eyes. She seemed surprised when he slipped her an envelope.

The minister had the good sense to keep his benediction light, upbeat, and short. He then thanked all present for coming and won them to his side when he shyly asked if he and Mr. Hemstreet could join them at the party because it sounded like one not to be missed. To much laughter and good natured ribbing they were both welcomed and encouraged to join in.

35

It was just as well Nick's Sunday flight back to Toronto was uneventful because he was nervous, on edge, and a little irritable. At the airport check-in he was handled by an agent who chatted to a friend on his cell phone while doing the check in. This irritated Nick so much, when the agent set the phone down to do something, he reached over the counter and flipped it closed, ending the call. The agent was stunned and started to say something but thought better of it when he noted the dark look on his passenger's face. The check-in was completed in total silence and Nick, with a pointed 'thank you' took his boarding pass and headed for the gate. He didn't look back and had no idea what the agent was doing but on inspection of his pass he notice the agent had seated him in business class, an isle seat, which somewhat made up for his rudeness.

Alex met him at the airport and Nick was in a much better mood, due in large part to the liberal application of free business class booze and the attentive care of a charming Flight Attendant. During the drive to his home in Mississauga, his son commented on the funeral and how he almost missed his flight home the next morning. Nick mentioned he didn't know he was coming but it was a pleasant surprise to see him. He also said he didn't see him leave, stopping short of asking which hotel he stayed at.

Alex also gave him an overview of what he had set up in Niagara Falls and it seemed he had touched all bases. He explained it was about the same as making a movie except for the field of vision you had to work with. He said what they did for film was create a scene within the confines of the camera lens because that's all a movie or TV viewer would see. What they were doing at the pipe plant was more like a stage play, where you not only saw the play but everything around it. They had to walk through their scenes several times to determine what a person who was there would see and include that view into the overall vision. It had been a challenge but he was sure they accomplished what they wanted. He also mentioned his crew of volunteers numbered around twenty five and they all expected a big wild drunken party when this was finished. Nick grinned, knowing this was coming, and told Alex to start planning the party and not worry about the cost. He immediately regretted his magnanimous offer. Knowing Alex caused him to worry about the bill as soon as he gave the go ahead but, with a sigh, put it out of his head.

The next two days passed in a constant flow of phone calls between Nick and his crew in Phoenix. Harry and LJ had worked out a minutely detailed withdrawal plan for the Arizona operation because the timing of its activation was critical. An hour too early and the thugs still working in the Emerald Company's office might notice something odd and warn Tony and Al in New York of strange happenings at the casino office. An hour too late and Tony and Al could discover they had been scammed and warn these same thugs, ordering them to march down the hall and grab whoever was in the Lasenda office. The strategic withdrawal, as LJ called it, was put together with the planning and precision of the raid on Entebbe. The only things LJ didn't have were planes and guns. At least Nick hadn't seen any before he flew out and didn't think LJ had commandeered any, yet.

Tuesday rolled around with Alex and Nick meeting early for coffee and donuts at the crew rendezvous spot, a Tim Horton's in Beamsville, Ontario, on the way to Lewiston, New York. Within minutes their gang of volunteers rolled up, parked, and piled out of a fifteen passenger van and a large rental cube van. Within a minute two more cars arrived. One a large, spotless black Mercedes sedan; the other, a silver Lexus. Father and son stood to meet everyone as they noisily poured into the coffee shop, and Alex, with a big grin, began to introduce what he affectionately called his motley crew.

He rattled through their names and Nick shook hand after hand and said over and over 'nice to meet you' to a blur of faces. Some were young, some middle aged, a couple quite distinguished looking and several more like factory workers or truck drivers. All were in a good mood and eager to get at the promised free coffee and donuts. Quickly the scrum around Nick moved across the room to the shop counter where the three young servers working the morning shift had their hands full catching all the good natured orders flying in from the group. Slowly each got their preferred drink and multiple sticky sweet donuts and found seats in the general area of Alex and Nick's table.

One of them, a well dressed gentleman in his late forties or early fifties sat near Nick and called out how he thought Nick was doing a fabulous, even a noble thing. Many of those near who heard him nodded between bites and sips. All of them were treating Nick with a great deal of respect, even deference. Alex jumped in to explain.

"Everyone here knows what's going on, Dad." He said. "I thought it was only fair they be aware of the plan since I was asking them to do all this work buckshee. Once they knew about Florida, Phoenix, and this gang of dastardly villains you're dealing with, well everyone just said count me in. I don't think you could keep them away with gunfire."

One from the back called out how villains had nothing to do with it. Most present would sell their granny for free coffee and donuts, that's why they were there. His comment brought boos, catcalls and a few well directed napkin balls amid the gales of laughter.

The well dressed gentleman leaned forward and offered some advice. “When this is all over you should write the whole story down and protect it. This would truly make a wonderful movie. Can you imagine some of those old pros around Hollywood who haven’t made a movie in years because no one writes scripts for old people? Wow, they would jump at the chance for one last shot at a good story. Mark my words” he said with great emphasis, “you’d have a hit on your hands when this is all done.”

Everyone agreed; some tossing out suggestions, others offering assistance, all of them wanting to be a part of the event.

“I’ll tell you what” Nick said loud enough for all to hear, “when this is over and I get a chance to catch my breath, I’ll talk to Alex and maybe we can look into this idea. I never thought of it, but you’re right, it would make a great movie. I will promise you one other thing. If we complete this deal as scheduled and we do move ahead with your idea of a movie, I’ll demand that every one of you go to the top of the list. I’ll simply tell whoever does the film, it will include the motley crew, or it won’t get made.” This was greeted by loud cheers and much joking but Nick knew this group was as good and dedicated as the one in Phoenix and he was wondering how they could miss.

Alex stood, called everyone to order and started to herd them out of the coffee shop to their vehicles. “Let’s get going,” he shouted, “we have a long day in front of us. And get your Passports out and ready.” He handed out the special customs papers for all the equipment in the cube van, telling the driver they would go ahead if he was delayed at the border. With almost military precision the small convoy assembled and was on its way to the Lewiston border crossing and the pipe plant in Niagara Falls, NY.

For the next five hours Alex and his crew worked on their 'set'. Without a break they set about cleaning windows, polishing floors and generally making the place shine. With hardly any direction and in almost complete silence, they installed large 'Frontier Pipe' signs on both sides of the cube van and stuck smaller ones on the front doors of the fifteen passenger van. Two of the crew pulled a sledge hammer from the truck and pounded three steel signs into the parking area near the front door painted 'President', 'General Manager' and 'Visitors'. The employee parking sign was set aside for later installation. Next, two burly young men pulled a line marking machine out of the back of the cube van and started painting fresh white stripes on the tarmac. Nick was impressed with the detail they were going into but was even more impressed when he watched a young fellow drive the van back and forth over the new painted lines, sometimes spinning his wheels. He grinned and told Nick his boss, 'Alex', didn't want the lines to look too new. They didn't when he was finished.

At lunch time several of the regular plant workers retrieved their own cars from the regular company parking area and moved them to the front of the offices between the new old lines. They all wanted to be part of a big Hollywood production and had jumped at Alex's request for cars to make the lot look used. Nick stood back and could not believe the transformation. One would be hard pressed to believe this was anything other than the corporate offices of Frontier Pipes Inc., a busy and prosperous industry.

With a couple hours to go before the guests arrived, Alex found Nick, requesting he go inside for a run through of the scene with the 'President' and some of his executives. The plan was to have the receptionist take the guests to the President who would meet them at the door of his office. The President was the well dressed gentleman from the donut shop and he looked more like a President here, than there. Alex mentioned he was a much-sought-after actor for this type of role.

Vince, 'the pres', as everyone called him, would spent a little time with Tony and Al and then take them to the boardroom to meet two other senior executives and Nick, the lawyer from the Lasendas in Phoenix. He would invite them to take a tour of the plant and if they said yes, white hard hats with the company name and 'Visitor' on the front along with safety glasses would be handed out. The President and his executives had their own personalized yellow safety hats.

Because the visitors wore Gucci's instead of steel toed work boots, Alex even had a legal waiver ready for them to sign. The tour would take about half an hour and everyone in the plant knew this was a dress rehearsal without cameras or lights so they would just keep on working and not interfere. During the afternoon the director had instructed them on being 'extras' in a movie and retrieved the signed documents required for their part in the film. After the tour it was back to the office.

Alex told Nick the place would work and look like a real office with phones ringing, people moving from here to there and employees in safety shoes, hard hats and work clothes coming in from the plant floor with problems and needs. All were members of the motley crew.

The phone ringing was phony, Alex said; just a recording with a wireless connection beaming to speakers in desks around the office. Their electronic wizard had even hooked up a couple cell phones to desk top models in case the guests needed to make a call so if that happened he pointed out the ones to be used. They were working with two scripts at the same time; one for the office and plant operation and the other for the two guests interacting with the executives. Nick was enthralled by the smooth professionalism. Everyone moved and worked as though they were in a dance routine staged by some world class choreographer. The only thing missing was the music.

At a couple minutes before 2 p.m., a young girl stepped out of an office and with a grin, handed Alex a sheet of paper. It had details of the US Airways flight from Charlotte carrying the 'gruesome twosome', as she called them. They would be on the ground in 12 minutes and their contact at the airport would update Alex as things moved along.

"While I was in Phoenix I took a couple photos of our friends with my telephoto lens when they visited the hotel site," he told his dad. "I'll give them to you later. In fact we should have one of your old buddy Harry with his arms stretched out to the sky. He looks like Geronimo talking to the Spirits and the other two look so out of place you'll fall over laughing. I might have it blown up and framed."

"Our lady at the airport has the pictures and a cell phone. She'll spot them, follow them, and keep us informed of their progress. We'll know when they park outside within thirty seconds of them entering this building. Don't look so surprised Dad; we don't leave these things to chance you know." Nick just shook his head in wonder, and respect.

A tall, well dressed man stepped into the middle of the office foyer and raised a bullhorn. "Twenty minutes, please, twenty minutes to places." No one seemed to take notice and what appeared to Nick to be organized chaos just continued.

Alex waved over a short young fellow with a clipboard and introduced him to his father. "Dad, this is Bill, our script man; you should go with him to a quiet spot and listen to him. He's the best in the business but we don't tell him that 'cause he'll want a raise." Nick shook hands and the two moved away through the organized confusion laughing.

Bill went over the plan for the meeting between Nick and the two investors. He suggested where Nick's briefcase should lie, whether the papers were laid out or kept from sight and how the seats be arranged. He also suggested talking points, things to steer away from and how to handle problems should they arise. He told Nick the room was bugged and they would be outside listening to every word. If he got into trouble Bill would send in someone, probably one of their better looking girls, to interrupt with some piece of business. It would give Nick a chance to think his way out.

He also told him to use the intercom unit on the boardroom table should he require an answer to anything. He said two of his people were sitting at computers, one on Google, and the other on Dogpile, both set to find out anything that may arise. "If you run into something you're unsure of, don't fake it, just tell them you'll get the answer, take your time reaching to the intercom and within seconds we'll send in the girl with the answer. We'll be working on it before you even ask us. It's easy, so just relax and leave the hard stuff to us." With these calming words he got up from his seat at the table and left the room. Nick just sat there, not realizing the fingers on his right hand were tightly crossed.

Alex stuck his head into the boardroom and informed Nick the target just passed over the Grand Island Bridge and were headed up I-190 toward Witmar Road and the plant. He estimated their time of arrival to be about six minutes hence. The tall man with the bullhorn was at it again, calling all to order. Within minutes everyone was in their place and The Frontier Pipe Company was in business.

36

Al parked the rental car in the visitors spot and hopped out to look around while Tony got two briefcases from the trunk. He watched as a truck loaded with pipes about six inches in diameter groaned slowly from the loading dock at the end of the building; the great diesel engine straining as it pulled the long trailer up the slope toward Hyde Park Road. He wondered if the load was headed for an Indian village near Phoenix.

"What do you think?" he asked, as Tony joined him near the entranceway to the office.

"Well, someone sure has good taste," he said, pointing to the Mercedes and the Lexus. "It looks like a going concern. The place is probably worth investing in on a stand-alone basis. I think we have a winner here, Al." He slapped his partner on the back and they strode up the walkway to the entrance and the glistening main door, complete with large gold letters, 'Frontier Pipe Incorporated, Established 1959.'

Tony and Al were met by the receptionist and as usual, they quietly rated her. Both agreed she wasn't as good as Jennifer but no better than Malita, their own secretary. They also agreed her best side was her backside as she led them down the hall to the President's office and handed them over to the big boss himself. They watched her walk away and nodded to each other; her backside was indeed her best side.

"Come in gentlemen, I'm Vince Armstrong, we spoke on the phone." He stuck out his hand, shook theirs, and held his office door open for them. "How was your flight?" he asked. "Would you like a drink?"

The office was well appointed but not ostentatious. It

was the private place of a careful man who liked quality things around him. Good paintings hung on every wall, mostly landscapes and seascapes. The carpet on the floor looked oriental and expensive. These accessories caught one's eye but what dominated the room was the desk sitting two-thirds across the floor from the office's entrance. It was a desk any businessman would love to sit behind. Large, solid, and very old, with a patina earned by decades of care and cleaning by staff who knew grand furniture when they saw it; Vince Armstrong's desk was a treasure to behold. Tony stepped to it and ran his hand reverently along the intricately hand carved wood surrounding the green leather work surface.

"Beautiful, isn't it?" Vince asked as he stepped up beside Tony. "I'm the third generation of Armstrong's to have worked at this desk and someday my son will be the fourth. It's nice to meet someone who appreciates a piece of quality furniture."

"Yes it is beautiful. One of the nicest I've ever seen. Third generation, you say. That's a long time. It sure has aged well."

"My grandfather ran a small casting foundry in Tonawanda at the turn of the century and he bought it used from the estate of a local banker. We have no idea how old it is, more than a hundred years I'd suspect, but it's beautiful and I love it. Grandpa left it to my dad, who was in insurance, and when he retired, I got it. When I leave here in a few years, my son gets it. By the way, what would you like to drink?" Vince walked back to the small bar against the wall and picked up a glass.

The balance of the visit went as planned. They sat and chatted about furniture, especially old furniture lovingly made by craftsmen now long gone. They discussed expensive scotch, the good taste of their host, and business, which seemed to be going along very well. When the three finally stepped from the office to move to the boardroom the effects of half a bottle of 24-year-old single malt hardly showed. They were laughing about some comment made and anyone seeing them would think they were old golfing buddies setting up their next round. As they slowly moved along the hall Vince asked his guests if they would like to see the plant. Both said sure and within minutes were handed plastic safety glasses and white hard hats.

The tour took about 30 minutes and their host had them mesmerized by the time the three got back to the office. They now knew more than they ever wanted to know about pipes, pipe shipments and pipe storage. Both Al and Tony had a glazed look in their eyes as they took off their hats and safety glasses and jumped at the chance to get back to the bottle of Scotch in Vince's office. They all knew it was time for a stiff drink and then get down to business.

Vince poured those stiff drinks into them and then all marched down the hall to the boardroom where Nick and two of Alex's best men were waiting to complete the deal.

"Gentlemen, I'd like you to meet Don Askew, chief financial officer for the company and Stan Cook, vice president of operations and our general manager." He waited for the hand shaking and greetings to end and moved the two over to Nick. "I think you've met this fellow down in Phoenix. Nick Evans, you know Tony and Al."

Nick got to his feet and stuck out his hand. "Of course I know them both. It's so nice to see you again." He stood, smiled and greeted them like long lost friends. "I just hope we can get this over with quickly so I can get back to that climate." He grinned as they all sat down at the board table.

Never one to sit around and chit chat, Tony changed the tone of the room to one of business. "What have you got for us?" he asked pointedly.

It was exactly what Nick had been waiting for. He knew that when Tony wanted to do business, his blinders went on and he zeroed in on his target. "I've got all the papers for this transaction. If you're happy with what you see, we can settle everything here and now." He stopped and looked directly at Tony, looking for any wavering or questions.

"No, I've seen all I need to and I think I can speak for Al in saying this is a sharp operation and one we'll be happy to be a part of. Vince here," he pointed to their plant guide and scotch dispenser, "is a gracious host and sure knows his stuff about steel pipe. I'm looking forward to being on the board of Frontier and Vince Armstrong has a big supporter in me." Tony turned and gave Vince a big thumbs-up.

"Well Mr. DiAngelo, and you Mr. Silvestro, have an awful lot of papers to sign, so I'll show you how I propose to go through this and if there are any questions, please just speak up. It's easier than going back and looking for something that bothers you. I don't care how small you may think it may be, please, speak up."

Nick then proceeded to lay out the papers in a row along his side of the table. Taking a notebook from his briefcase, he flicked through a couple of pages, settled on one and started to check each stack of papers on the table, speaking half to himself the names of each pile, to make sure he had the right ones in the right place. Once satisfied all was as it should be, he turned to Tony and Al.

"I've arranged these in order and turned them toward you. After explaining each bundle, I'll slide them across the table, one bundle at a time, and you'll see five copies in each pile. You'll have to sign them all." He then held up his index finger to make one more comment before starting.

"First, I want to know if either of you want independent legal advise. There are a lot of local lawyers, some very good corporate lawyers you can call on if you want. We can give you a list of four or five and we have the time to wait if you need someone in to go over everything with you. If not, we have these forms for you to sign waiving that right; either way, no problem."

Al spoke for the first time. "We were wondering if you

would ask that question. Tony and I discussed this on the drive in and we both feel if you're ready to wait while we get another lawyer to go over these papers, then you must have nothing in them that might hurt us. We'll sign your waivers."

Nick slid two papers across the table, pointed out pertinent details and handed Tony his Waterman's fountain pen. Tony slowly turned the long black beauty in his hand and admired the understated gold bands on its cap and body. He was smiling as he looked up at Nick from his chair at the table. "This is nice." he said.

"I like nice things," said Nick. "That was a gift from my wife so you can't have it, but when this is over, I'll get one exactly like it for you. Of course it'll cost you a drink or two."

"Done," Tony said as he slowly laid out his name on the waiver form in black ink. "I had forgotten how nice they move on paper." He again looked at Nick with a smile. "Thanks, I'm look forward to having one of these of my own."

The paper signing went on for an hour. Nick had waivers, statements of non residency, New York State papers by the handful, personal information packages and acceptance papers to be on the board of directors. During all this paper shuffling Nick had their secretary running in and out with things to copy. When it was all finished, Nick suggested there was one thing to do before they were done. He stood quietly and looked at Tony.

"I got you," Tony suddenly said with a smile and reached down beside him. He raised his very expensive leather briefcase and held it above the table. "I'm sure you're referring to this," and he laid it on the table, popped the clasps and opened it wide for everyone to see. "By the way, the briefcase is yours, that's for the pen." He smiled, knowing it was a fair trade.

There was a small gasp from some at the table because

two million dollars in cash, laid out in neat rows with stamped bank bands holding them together, is a sight few ever get to see. It was a hell of a lot of money.

"Do you want to count it?" Tony asked, with a grin.

"Don't worry. Frontier's bank will and we'll let you know if there's a problem." Nick grinned "although I'm really not too worried." And he reached over the table, took hold of the briefcase and spun it around as he pulled it toward him. "I've never seen so much cash so I want a look. I must say, it sure looks better than some little check. Here, Vince, take care of this, and remember to bring back the case for me." He said and shoved the money to the president.

"What time is your flight home?" Nick asked his two guests to break the spell of the cash.

"Not for about four and a half hours, eight-thirty, I think." Tony said.

Al chipped in "Yea, actually eight forty, so we have lots of time."

"Good, tell me, do you guys like chicken wings? This is the home of the world famous Buffalo wings and the original place where it all began, our Anchor Bar and Grill. It's just a few miles from here. You want to go and try the best wings you'll ever eat?" Nick had remembered Al commenting on one of the tapes his love for barbequed wings and how he was having trouble finding good ones in Phoenix.

Tony and Al thought it was a great idea and the meeting took the next fifteen minutes to wind down and move out into the hallways and foyer. There was a general jovial mood around the office and much handshaking and backslapping.

"You'll find this is somewhat of a family, here at Frontier." Vince said. "We take an interest in our staff and they sure take an interest in the company. We'll need photos of the two of you and we'll post a memo regarding you and Al joining the board. When you get home, call a good photographer and tell him to send us the bill. Our people like to know who's in control. You'll feel at home, the next time you come in. Now I think Nick wants to take you out for some wings. Enjoy, and I'll see in a few weeks. And by the way, welcome to Frontier Pipe." He gave them both a pat on the shoulder as they joined Nick and headed for the door.

Wanting to drive his guests himself and waste some time, Nick arranged for their car to be delivered to the Anchor by a couple of the film crew. He drove his guests along Hyde Park to Pine Avenue and took them through Niagara Falls 'Little Italy' district. They were surprised to see it, suggesting they would try out some of the good-looking restaurants when they came north for board meetings. From there he suggested a stop at the Falls but both had seen them before. Nick then drove past the Indian casino, pointing out theirs would be morc than three times as large, and then out onto the Robert Moses Parkway beside the Niagara River heading for the Grand Island Bridge. Within half an hour they were sitting in the Anchor on Main Street in downtown Buffalo, waiting for a pile of what were arguably the best chicken wings in the world. Their first round of drinks sat in front of them.

"It's not much of a place, for looks I mean" Nick said as they waited for their food. He had noticed them checking out the worn interior and the haphazard clutter on the walls and over the bar. "They've been here for ages and every time someone suggests a makeover, all the regulars go nuts. Actually, I like the place as it is. None of your cookie cutter glass and plastic eateries for me. This is where it's at." They were all laughing as the food arrived.

For the next fifteen minutes the three men stuffed chicken wings into their mouths with no more comment then a few moans of delight. Finally Al broke the silence with a moving testimonial to the fare of the Anchor Bar.

"Damn. These are the best wings I've ever had." And he went back to eating.

They had been drinking beer and the third round was half gone. Nick excused himself and headed for the rest rooms. It gave him a chance to call Alex for an update on their efforts at Frontier. They were doing just fine and expected to be done in about another hour before pulling out for north of the border. He also said their people in Phoenix were called the moment Nick was out the door. Asking his son to wait exactly five minutes and then to call him back, he headed for his guests. He needed an excuse to bail out and the phone call would do it.

Back at the table, the meal was done and the three sat groaning with pleasure. Two large bottles of Anchor Bar Wing Sauce sat in front of Tony and Al, brought by a willing waitress. "Nick, you were right. This place is the best. I've had wings all over the country but these win the grand prize. We're taking some sauce home with us." At that moment Nick's phone rang. He answered, listened to his son for several moments, said little, then "goodbye," and hung up.

"I'm sorry guys; I've got to be on my way. Something has come up and they need me. I'll get the check and if you like, directions to the airport." Nick started to get up.

"I already got the bill" Tony said. "I paid it when we got the sauce and happy to do so. This is a fun place and I appreciate you bringing us. Don't worry about us or directions. We should be able to find our way to the airport. Just get on your way. We'll talk in a couple days in Phoenix." He stood up and grabbed Nick's hand, shaking it firmly. "I want to thank you for your help in the casino project. I owe you, my friend, and someday I'll be there for you when you need me."

Nick lingered a few more minutes and then headed for the door. He wouldn't feel safe until he was across the border and fully updated on the Phoenix group.

Back in the restaurant, Tony was counting out a good tip for the waitress while Al was getting directions to the airport. He thought he'd call the airline to check the schedule but couldn't find his cell phone. Walking back to the table he asked Tony if he had seen his phone. He hadn't and it wasn't on the table either.

"Check the car. You might have left it there when we drove in." Tony said. It wasn't there either. Al figured he must have left it at the plant. "Call them." Tony instructed, "Ask them to find it and ship it to you. Their numbers on the map they sent us."

"I left the map on the table at the office. I'll get a phone book." He walked back to the front and asked for a phone book.

Al couldn't find Frontier Pipe anywhere in the phonebook so he asked for the restaurant's phone, with an offer to pay, and called directory assistance. They had no listing of anything even close to a Frontier Pipe within fifty miles of where he was standing.

Tony joined him at the front desk with a grin and put his arm around his shoulder. "Don't worry, I'll buy you a new phone, hell, I'll buy a whole phone company if you like." He was a little drunk and in a very good mood.

"I think we should drive up to the pipe factory. I mean, we should go right now." Al said it in a way that chilled Tony. He said "okay" and without another word, walked out to the car.

37

The Phoenix operation was prepared to fold up and disappear into the desert on a moments notice. Actually it started to do that within 30 seconds of the phone call from Niagara Falls. Three of the crew waited in the desert to remove the cloth banner from the sign and one call to them completed that job. Several more were at the office ready to complete the material removal they had quietly started several days before. Each had an assigned job and a set time to do it. LJ had outdone himself in planning this campaign maneuver. It was just after five in Phoenix and if all went well the plan called for everyone to be on the road heading home no later than six. LJ's major concern was leaving behind anything which could identify individual members of the group or where they may have stayed. He was adamant on this point and insisted every piece of paper must be collected, even to emptying waste baskets and taking the contents away with them in green garbage bags.

Part of LJ's "grand closing up shop plan" included the getaway, as he called it, and how it would be carried out. He didn't want a huge convoy moving down the highway much as they had arrived, so he designed different routes back to Florida and assigned some vehicles to each one.

One motor home and three cars took Interstate 10 back the same way they came in, heading east through El Paso, Texas. Another contingent drove straight up I-17, past the casino site with it's now blank signboard laying in the dust, on the way to Flagstaff. There they would turn east on I-40 for Oklahoma City and then south to Houston where they would pick up I-10 east into Florida. A variation of this had three cars taking State highway 60 east out of Phoenix all the way to Lubbock Texas and then down to Abilene and on east home. He even had several going up to Las Vegas in a one way rental car for a flight home and another couple going to Los Angeles to visit a sick brother. These arrangements, plus the half dozen who flew out of Phoenix on three different airlines, emptied the town of all except LJ and Harry, who had their own plans to get home. It was a well thought out program running like a Swiss watch. By the time the call came from Alex, half the group had left and were on the road.

The northern section went almost as well. During the shutdown Alex moved about his "movie set," lending a hand where necessary and congratulating his gang for a job well done. The group was in a good mood and jokes flew back and forth until someone found a cell phone lying with some papers on the boardroom table.

"Who left their cell phone in the boardroom?" Alex called several times as he walked amongst the boxes and furniture waiting to be loaded in their truck. Everyone checked and all phones were soon accounted for so Alex sat down, flipped open the found one and looked through the list of incoming and outgoing numbers listed in the menu. What he saw almost made him drop the damn thing. Not a single number had a Canadian area code. No 905's, no 416's, no 519's. This was the phone of an American and there had been only two in the boardroom that day. The owner was not one of the good guys from Canada. He was a crook from Phoenix and would be returning soon looking for it. It was time to get the hell out of there.

The crew of volunteers grasped the import of the find instantly and all joking stopped. Within minutes stuff was flying into the truck from all directions. Alex dispatched his spotter who had followed the villains from the airport out to the main entrance in his car with a two way radio. Her instructions were to park far enough away to be inconspicuous and holler if the pair from Phoenix arrived.

Alex and his crew raced through the dismantling process as their sense of panic grew. Everyone had their own mental picture of the two thugs storming in during the take-down of the set waving baseball bats or worse, pistols, demanding their two million bucks back. No one wanted to be there when that happened.

Somehow the loading was completed and all vehicles moved off the property before the dreaded call from the lookout came. Alex had just completed one last walk through, satisfying himself all was completed, and had stepped out the front door, turning to lock it. As the key slipped home his radio came to life. Alex's heart stopped.

"Targets just coming on the property," the young lady parked across the street from the onetime Frontier Pipe Company said calmly.

Nick hesitated for a second, then unlocked the door and slid back into the offices, throwing the lock back into place.

"Stay put until you hear from me. Just lay low and stay put, and keep quiet." he whispered into his radio as he saw the car swing wildly onto the parking area in front of the office. Alex made a dive for the boardroom and hoped the two wouldn't break in.

The car stopped violently and both front doors swung open in unison. One could almost see the steam puffing from their ears.

They had driven quickly, using directions from staff at the restaurant and giving no thought to the amount of alcohol in their bloodstream. As Al sped over the Grand Island Bridge he explained about the phone number, or lack of same. The rest of the trip was in silence, each man with their own thoughts and fears.

There was no relief from those fears. As they jolted to a halt, both jumped from the rental car and in an instant could see the only thing left were the white stripes on the tarmac. The parking signs were gone, as was the large overhead sign. Even the gold letters on the door were gone. The place was dark, cold looking, empty. Al swore and Tony kicked the brass plate on the bottom of the main door so violently Alex almost had a heart attack in his hiding place inside. Both men knew they were toast, as was their two million dollars. Heading back to the car, their anger grew with each step. Someone was going to pay for this great injustice. It never occurred to them that the sick feeling in the pit of their stomachs was exactly what all their victims felt.

Nick slipped back into Canada over the Peace Bridge after leaving the restaurant. Once through customs and driving toward Toronto on the Queen Elizabeth Way, he started calling LJ and Harry in Phoenix. He was still unaware Tony and Al knew they had been taken.

All reports indicated everything was going according to plan. Phoenix was empty and all participants on the road home. Niagara Falls was being cleaned out as well. Nick had asked his son to divide the money into two equal parts, pack it into two identical boxes, wrap them in brown paper and use some stout cord to tie them up. Alex then took both to the Pine Street Post Office in Niagara Falls and sent them off by ordinary parcel post. Everyone thought this was the best way to ship a couple million dollars. One box was mailed to Edward Fisher's restaurant in Bradenton, Florida. The other was shipped to Nick at the Hilton Garden Inn across the street from the restaurant. He would make a reservation for his next visit and ask them to hold his parcel if it arrived before he did.

Nick was elated by their success but his instincts told him hold off on any partying. It had gone smoothly but many things could still cause problems, so he just tried to keep calm. All the way home he drove with his cell phone in his hand, hoping it wouldn't ring.

It didn't for the moment, but as he was driving north, someone else was burning up the phone lines. He was of

Italian descent, Sicilian actually, without scruples, and mad as hell. In fact, he was more than mad as hell, he was seeking a vengeance of biblical proportions and he had already set the wheels in motion. He managed to finally get Frank DiPietro, his man from Miami, on the phone in Phoenix and gave him instructions to first check the casino office, and then to get the gang together for a meeting when he got in from Buffalo. Although Tony gave no details, Frank was astute enough to know there was a problem and he promised all would be at the office when they arrived. He also promised to check out the casino office as asked although he couldn't understand why. Tony simmered in the seat next to Al all the way to the airport where they barely managed to catch their flight.

38

Tony and Al marched out into the warm Arizona night to their waiting car at the arrivals curb of the airport where Harry Silver waited, as they did a few weeks before. Close examination would convince one these were not a pair of happy campers. Harry opened the back door and, still playing chauffer to big shot passengers, moved around to drive them into the city. As he pulled away Tony asked if the rest would be present and Harry said sure, don't worry, they knew better than to stay away, even at this hour of the evening. The rest of the drive to the office was in silence.

"Who checked their office?" Tony asked the seven men sitting in front of him. "Who checked the goddamned office?"

"I did boss," Stan from Cincinnati said. "As far as I could see, it's empty. There was a rental company here about four thirty and they took away all the desks and chairs. Things like that. I asked the movers what was going on, but hell, they didn't know."

"Okay, let's go over this," Tony said while walking back and forth in front of them. "A group of confidence men, and women, most of them old farts, move into our territory, set up shop, and target us for a big scam. We can talk to the office rental agent tomorrow, but we all know, these were professionals. They knew what they were doing and I'm sure they left few tracks. The big mystery is who the hell these guys are, where did they come from, and why us? Why the hell would they target us? " He stopped in front of his gang, hands on his hips and a look on his face that even scared some of the toughs facing him. "I want our money back and I want them to pay. Think, all of you. Think!"

"Well boss, we do take money from elderly people, maybe it was some of them." This came from Leo DiSousa, one of their enforcers who called Hartford home and wasn't known for his mental agility. His comments brought a few snickers from the others.

"Don't laugh," Al said. "Leo may have hit the nail on the head. It fits, Tony. Think of it. This gang was mostly old, except for Jennifer and that little weasel of a lawyer. They showed up on the scene after we arrived, they worked us just the way we do our marks, and then they disappeared with a pile of our money. Hell, if it was a group off old farts, you got to admire them. It was a pretty slick job."

"Slick or not, I want my money back and if you're right, I'm pretty sure I know where it is."

At least three of those present shouted 'where?'

"Florida." Tony said. "I think Leo's guessed it. Can you imagine the nerve? Some group of doddering old fossils with the nerve to out-scam us. Well they ain't as smart as they think 'cause I know where the hell they're from. They're from Florida. The damn money's in Florida. In fact, it's in the Bradenton, Sarasota, section of Florida. It has to be that group we worked last year." Striding back and forth before his men, hands waving and eyes gleaming, you could almost hear the wheels spinning in his head.

"The Palm Springs job was more than two years ago. If that bunch were going to do anything, they would have done it by now. The more I think about it, the more I'm sure. That money's in Florida and we're going to go and get it back."

"But Tony, it could have been the Palm Springs people." Al protested. "They were a lot younger than that gang of old fogies in Florida. Hell, most of them had trouble getting around, let alone mounting this type of operation. I don't know, I can't believe the bunch of dummies in Florida did this."

"You're wrong. They did it. They had some help, what with that damn bastard lawyer guy and the broad in the office. They did it, I know they did it and we're going to get our money back." Tony almost shouted. Al knew not to argue any more.

For the next hour Tony worked out the logistics of two operations running at the same time. He and Al would take Leo DiSousa and Frank DiPietro of Miami with them to Florida. Stan and Mario, along with Sal Papallia and Larry Silver, plus Alberto, Mario's brother, would stay in Phoenix and maintain the operation until they got back.

"Okay guys," Tony said as he closed his briefcase. "Now let's get some rest. Some of us have to get up early for our flights, the rest of you are going to have to double up here." Within minutes he and Al were in their car driving to their hotel. Neither had any doubt they would return from Florida with their money.

39

The phone must have rung six times before Nick's wife shoved him awake and told him to answer the damn thing. He groaned and rolled over, trying to focus on the clock beside the phone. It was 2:30 a.m. and he knew nothing good ever came from two-thirty in the morning phone calls.

"Hello," he muttered, hoping it was a wrong number by some drunk looking for a long lost girlfriend. It wasn't. It was Kitty.

"Nick, Nick, we need you. You have to come and help us. Nick, we need you." She went on and on, saying the same thing over and over, making it difficult to get a word in edgewise. He was instantly wide awake.

"Kitty, Kitty, calm down. What's wrong Kitty, shut up a minute will you," he shouted to his friend in Florida. "Just take a breath and talk slowly, calmly, and tell me why the hell you're calling me at this ungodly hour."

"Nick, they've got Harry and LJ too. They kidnapped them. Right off the street not far from our home and they're holding them for the money. Harry, it's those awful guys from Phoenix. They want all their money back. Our money. They say if they don't have every penny of it by six tonight, they'll kill one of them." She was an inch from total hysteria and it took Nick another minute or two get her back under control.

"Listen to me, Kitty, think carefully and go over the conversation you had with them. It's very important you do this. Try to remember every word, every instruction. Stay calm. Start at the beginning and don't leave anything out." He spoke calmly, trying to cool her down by being cool headed himself. It seemed to work.

Kitty took a deep breath and started her story from about 7 p.m., the night before. LJ had come around to pick up Harry. "They wanted to look at a used riding lawn mower up in Palmetto. They said they'd be back around ten." When Harry wasn't back home by eleven, Kitty began to worry and called LJ's wife. She had no idea what they were up to but she wasn't worried. By twelve Kitty was having a fit, pacing the floor, peering outside every two minutes to see if he was coming, generally doing all the things done by a worried wife.

She told Nick she was near frantic by 1 a.m. and decided to call the police. Just as she reached for the phone, it rang and she jumped two feet straight up. When she picked up and answered, a voice, male, quite rough, told her some business associates of her husband's had arrived from Phoenix Arizona that morning. He said they had come to retrieve something that had accidentally gone astray near Buffalo New York. He said Harry and LJ agreed it was all a big misunderstanding, he said they were right there, waiting for the items in question to be delivered. At this point Kitty started to cry.

"Take it easy Kitty. Calm down and stop crying. Tell me what else they said." Nick prodded.

He could hear her blow her nose, settling down enough to continue. She told Nick they put Harry on the phone for about fifteen seconds, long enough for him to say not to worry. The gruff voice came back on and said she was not to contact the police or FBI or anyone else and he would call her at noon to tell her how to deliver the package. Then he hung up. "Nick, please, you have to do something." She cried.

"Kitty, don't worry. We'll get this straightened out. Ann just checked the US Air site on the computer while you were talking. There's a flight out of Toronto at six-twenty through Pittsburg. I'll arrive in Sarasota at eleven fifteen. I'll be at your place before they call, and I'll have a solution. Now don't worry and try to get some sleep." He spent another couple minutes trying to calm her down, sounding much more confident than he was. Then he thought of another thing, "Kitty, do me a favor, please. After eight, call Ed, at the restaurant and ask him to come around to your place at about eleven thirty, get hold of Vince Strong and John Hardy to come over as well. We'll need their help. And don't worry, this will turn out okay. See you in a few hours."

Nick handed the phone to Ann and climbed out of bed. "See if you can calm her down, I have to start getting ready. It's almost three now and I should be at the airport by five and I have to shower and pack and think." He muttered this last piece as he pushed open the door to the bathroom and flicked on the light. He was worried.

His flights went according to schedule and Nick walked out of the airport into the bright Florida sun at exactly 11:30 a.m. He grabbed a taxi, figuring it would take too long to rent and if he needed a car he could borrow Harry's because he sure wouldn't be using his for the time being. On the way to Kitty's he went over his plan, hoping it would work. All the time he wondered how they caught on so quick to who was responsible.

Ed, Vince and John were sitting out back when Nick arrived and after a teary greeting from Kitty, he suggested they all come in to wait for the phone call while he explained his plan. It was now nearly noon and they didn't have much time.

"First," Nick said urgently, "we need some time. We have to stall them as long as we can so we can have a session on how to ultimately solve this problem. Kitty, when they call, I want you to tell them you don't know where the money is, which happens to be true, you don't. In fact, tell him no one knows because Nick the lawyer handled that himself while in Buffalo. Tell him you don't think Harry or LJ know either because Nick tended to keep these things close to his chest. Can you do that?"

"Of course I can." Her sniffles now stopped in the face of some decisive action being taken. "I have a minor in theatrics, you never forget how to use it, you know. What else should I tell them?" she asked.

"Tell them you've already tried to get a hold of Nick but he's on the road. If they ask what I do, tell them the truth, I'm not a lawyer, I'm a wholesale car exporter and I spend a lot of time on the road. Say it might take a few more hours to get me but for all you know the money may still be in Buffalo. Beg them for some time, you'll do what they say, you just need some time." Kitty was taking rough notes, nodding her head and looking nervous. At that moment the phone rang. Nick put his finger to his lips and directed Kitty to answer.

"Hello," she answered quietly, and listened. The expression on her face changed and she yelled "oh buzz off," and slammed the phone down.

"Aluminum siding salesman," she said as the phone rang again. "Hello" she repeated.

"Mrs. Stanton" asked the rough voice. "Do you have our property?"

"No, I'm so sorry but I don't," and she started to cry and wail like a banshee. Nick was very impressed at her act.

Calming down, she said 'okay' several times before she seemed under control. She told him exactly what Nick had suggested and he could see her smile and relax a bit. Nick thought they must be buying her story. The conversation went on.

"I promise I'll get hold of him and tell him what you said. Yes I'll be here if you call at nine. No, I haven't told anyone. No I won't. Please, tell Harry to take his heart pill. Yes, he should have them with him." This question and answer session went on for a few more seconds and then Kitty said 'yes sir" and "goodbye" and hung up the phone.

Her four male companions sat silently waiting for her to speak.

"He said we have another day. He wants the money by six tomorrow night but if I cry, we may get a little more time. He hates me crying. It really shakes him." She was much calmer now. "I feel better Nick. I don't think these guys are killers. I think they're just conmen who want their ill-gotten gains back. They can't go to the police but then, I don't think we can either. What do we do now?"

"We get to work finding our friends," said Nick, turning to the three other men in the room. "First off Kitty, give us all your cell number, we'll use that to leave the land line open. Next, Ed, I want you and John to go over to LJ's place. Ask if his wife has an address or a phone number for the riding lawn mower. If she hasn't, ask what paper they have delivered. Try and find the ad for a used riding lawn mower in Palmetto. Phone them. I'd like you to find the place, go there, check and see if they ever arrived. Get all the details, when they arrived, when they left, everything, and call me. We must know the general area these bastards grabbed them, and when. They called Kitty around two, so if we know when they were grabbed, we'll have some idea of how far they could travel. Now, get going." Nick waved them on their way and turned to Vince.

"Vince, I have a special job for you. It's going to take a great deal of finesse to get the information we need but I think you can do it. You're to go to the airport and visit the car rental agencies. These guys must have flown in yesterday. Not before that. They would have rented a car; probably a Cadillac, maybe a Buick, dark colored, remember, like the one they drove in Phoenix. It's likely there was at least two of them and possibly as many as four. You've seen them enough times so you can describe most of them. Find out who rents Caddies and try them first, if you have no luck try them all, find out what kind of car they rented, and the plate number if possible. It's important

Vince. It could be a big help in finding Harry and LJ. If you manage to find anything, call me right away. Now, you get on your way," he waved as Vince went out the door and turned to Kitty.

"You have to stay here, by the phone. You're to be our centre of communications and information. Get a pile of paper, or a notebook, several pens, pencils and set everything up near your phone. If you have to call out, to me or anyone else, use the phone on Harry's fax machine and we'll call in on your cell. If you want some help or support, call LJ's wife or one of the others." Nick was walking back and forth while he talked. "I think we can pull this off Kitty, so hang on tight, it's going to be a busy of couple days." With that he strode through the door and out to Harry's car. He had places to go and things to do. The only problem was he had to come back in and sheepishly ask for Harry's car keys. Then he was on his way. He wanted to call Miami for some help from a friend who had offered any help he might need, and he wanted to do it in private.

40

LJ looked with concern across the hotel room at his friend to see how he was faring. Harry hadn't brought his heart pills with him when they went to see the lawn mower and he was nearing his first twenty four hours without one. LJ was worried.

"How you doing over there, Harry?" he asked.

"Oh I'm fine, if I take it easy, relax, you know, I'll be alright. It's a shame I can't call the clinic for a read-out but we'll wait. I'll be fine, nothing to worry about." Harry smiled and waved as though all in the world was splendid. He was slouched in the armchair across from LJ and looked a little under the weather. Neither said anything for several minutes.

"What do you mean, call the clinic?" LJ asked.

"It's my pacemaker, the new one my doctors put in a year ago. If I have a problem or feel out of sorts, I call a special number; hold the phone to my chest and some machine at the other end reads my pacemaker. I guess someone looks at the information after I call in, because if there's a problem, they phone me back, tell me to come in for an oil change or new spark plugs, or go to my doctor, or stop bothering them. Well, not really the last bit." Harry smiled at his wit.

LJ looked at his friend and got up from the cot. "What the hell you mean, they call you back. How in hell do they do that?"

"With a telephone. It's a new thing that lets you talk to other people who are some distance from you; invented a few years after you were born. You should look into them, you never know, you might be able to use one." Harry now thought he was being very funny. LJ just gave him a dirty look.

"It's called 'Call display," Harry explained. "They have some kind of override software that lets them pick up any number coming in, no matter what or from where. It's quite a system."

"So if you called from here," LJ asked, "they would know exactly where you are calling from, right?"

"Sure, but why the hell would…" Harry stopped in mid sentence. "Wait a minute, what are you thinking?" He asked.

"Can you act sick?" LJ asked.

"Watch me." Harry suggested and mussed his hair a bit, wetting it with water from a glass on the side table and pulling it down onto his forehead. He then slid deeper into his chair and started to breathe with his mouth open. "How do I look?" he mumbled.

"Dreadful. Like death warmed over." LJ laughed quietly. "You look perfect, and dreadful. Now just follow my lead and play along with me."

LJ moved across the room and quietly explained what he was planning. Then he moved to the locked door to their keeper's area and started banging and hollering. It didn't take long before one of them yanked the door open and demanded to know what the hell all the noise was about.

LJ simply asked them to take a look at Harry, slouched in the chair on the other side of the room. He said he thought he may be having some trouble. The big one, Frank, the others called him, knelt beside Harry and asked what was wrong.

"Oh nothing," Harry mumbled. "It's just my hearts acting up a bit and if I rest I should be alright. I haven't any of my pills but I just need a little rest. I'll wait till they get the money here and then I'll get on the phone and have them reset me. Please don't worry, I'll be fine, lets just wait for the money," and he winced in pain and gasped a bit as he moved to a more comfortable position.

Frank got up and pulled LJ away from Harry, asking quietly, "How bad is he? I don't want the old coot dying on me. What the hell are these pills he's on about, does he need some medicine or something?" It was obvious Frank was worried.

"Not really, what he needs to do is set up a phone link so the heart center can modify his pacemaker. It doesn't take long, he tells me, and it may fix him up right away. He says sometimes he has to do it two or three times for the download to take effect, but when this is over, he'll need it right away, it's what he should have." LJ casually looked over at his friend and then back to Frank.

Frank was in way over his head now and didn't know quite what to do. "What do you mean? What the hell is a phone link?" he demanded.

"It's a new system." LJ explained. "See, Harry's an old fart with a bad ticker. About a year ago his doctors replaced his old pacemaker with a new computerized model. All he has to do is call from anywhere in the world, hold the phone to the pacemaker implanted in his chest, wait three minutes, then hang up. The machinery at the other end reads all the information about his heart through the phone lines and starts to analyze it. In five minutes Harry calls the same number back and the fancy heart clinic equipment sends corrections that the tiny computer in his pacemaker accepts, adjusting itself, and Harry starts to feel fine." He guided Frank over to the now-terrible-looking Harry and told the patient to undo his shirt. Sure enough, high on Harry's right breast was a small scar over a circular bump in the skin about three inches in diameter. Harry feebly pointed to it and Frank gingerly reach down and touched the bulge in the old chest.

"I'll be dammed" he said. "You mean that thing inside

him can really talk to some machine here in Florida? What the hell will they think of next?" He stood and shook his head in wonder, deciding how to handle this problem.

"Do you speak to anyone, when you make these phone calls?" Frank asked.

"Hell no, they don't want to talk to us plain ordinary humans," Harry said, "it's all just machines talking to machines and it all goes one way. Harry calls them but they can't call back."

"And you think it'll help him?" Frank asked.

"I've seen him do it once before and it sure worked that time. The upgrades they send back to him that download into his pacemaker changes the pulse rate and the force of the pulses. Almost instantly you can see the change. It may take a couple calls but it will work." LJ could almost hear the wheels turning inside Frank's head and he knew he just about had him.

"I'll get the phone but I'll be here every second watching you two to make sure there's no funny business. He just makes calls to his clinic and the phone goes nowhere near his mouth. Have you both got that?" Harry and LJ bobbed their heads in unison.

Frank stepped out and was back in seconds with the phone from his room, handed it to LJ and told him to plug it in to the empty jack by the nightstand.

Harry got out his wallet, extracted a laminated business card and passed it to Frank for examination. It was the card of a Sarasota Heart Clinic and on the back was a number under the heading 'Pacemaker Hotline'. The tension and suspicion slipped from Frank. The card was all he needed to know he made the right decision in letting Harry call for some help.

Over the next thirty minutes Harry made four calls to the Hotline number, holding the phone to his chest each time with his left hand, while he studied LJ's large wristwatch in his right, checking the second hand for accurate timing.

Within minutes of the last call he was as bright as a new penny, standing and chatting to LJ and Frank, asking for a cold drink. Frank and the other thug guarding the two were dumbfounded at the change.

"I'll be damned" said Frank. "I just wouldn't have believed any of this if I didn't see it with my own eyes. That has to be the most incredible, most fantastic new medical thing since the heart transplant. Man, it's like watching a Star Trek show. What the hell is next? Maybe they're going to beam you to the hospital or something." He unplugged the phone and left the room shaking his head in disbelief. It wasn't until the door had fully closed before Harry turned to LJ and gave him two thumbs up.

41

The technician responsible for the pacemaker monitoring unit at the Sarasota Heart Clinic stood quietly reading the print-outs from her hot line printer and couldn't understand what the hell was going on. After some indecision, she figured this problem called for higher-priced brains so she phoned her superior for guidance. She had worked in the PMU for three years and this was the first time she had ever seen someone call in three times in a row. While she was waiting for Dr. Hunt to arrive the unit rang again like a fax machine and started to spit out another stream of data. She walked to the catch tray and couldn't believe her eyes. It was another print-out from the same patient, he had called again. As she checked the number to be sure, Dr. Hunt entered the unit.

"What's up, Rebecca?" he asked with a smile. "I don't hear from you very often. What happened, get lonely down here and feel the need for some bright handsome male company?"

"Hell, if I wanted male company down here in the bowels of this building I'd call that cute new young intern you just hired. I sure wouldn't call an over-the-hill heart surgeon, even if he does own the joint and has more money than God." They both laughed at this. Rebecca was one of those brassy girls you either liked or hated. Brian Hunt liked her style and got a lot of good laughs out of her comments and good natured barbs.

"Well you better have a good excuse for calling me down here, wasting my time and making my coffee go cold. Otherwise, it's the pink slip for you, me lass," he fired back.

"I should be so lucky. Here, look at this." And she handed him three print outs only minutes apart and almost identical. As he checked them out she retrieved the forth one from the machine. "I've never seen anything like it."

"Did you call the number?" he asked.

"Sure, right after the second one came in. It's the Holiday Inn on Riverfront Drive. I talked to the desk clerk and he's positive there's no Harry Stanton, or any other Stanton in the place. Actually, the guy was quite helpful. He rechecked his list of guests for me but nothing came up. By then the third one was coming through so I called you. Weird, isn't it?" She was serious now.

"He's one of our regulars, isn't he? You have this guy's phone number on file, haven't you? Let's get it and call to see if anyone's home," Dr. Hunt suggested as he looked over the print-outs. "Odd, he seems to be okay," he muttered as went to the phone.

Rebecca found the number, dialed it and handed the receiver to her boss. As she did, Kitty answered.

"Mrs. Stanton, its Dr. Hunt from the heart clinic, is Harry there?"

"Not right now, he's out on business. Is there a problem?" she asked, concerned.

"I don't think so. We're trying to contact him and we thought he might be home or you might know where he is. We'd just like to chat with him for a minute or two about how he checks in with his pacemaker. It's nothing to worry about," the doctor soothed.

"Doc, don't con me. What's going on? Has there been a recall? I'm his wife. I have a legal right to know why the top surgeon at Harry's heart clinic is looking for him and I don't want any cock-and-bull story. Now tell me, what's going on?"

Dr. Hunt only hesitated a second before deciding to give her all he had. He knew she was aware of everything in the pacemaker program; all wives were. Kitty had a card with the clinic's number, just like Harry, so she could call and hold the phone to her husband's chest in case he couldn't. It was best he just tell her what happened over the last hour. He wasn't ready for her response. She didn't want to know how his heart was; she wanted to know *where he was*!

"Where did the calls come from?" she demanded. "I know you can track them and your printouts always have the numbers at the top. Please, where did the numbers come from? Please, I have to know. Now. Doc, believe me, it could be a matter of life and death." She was breathless and excited and almost shouting.

"Sure, sure, Mrs. Stanton; I'll tell you anything you want if you can stop him calling the damn hotline every five minutes. The calls came from a Holiday Inn on Riverside Drive. We phoned them but your husband isn't there and that's why we called you. He could be somewhere else and there's some kind of phone glitch but as far as we know, the number listed on our printout is the number of the hotel. Listen, Mrs. Stanton, get hold of him and tell him to knock it off, will you? There's nothing wrong with his ticker and he's just using up valuable machine time." She said she would and hung up, leaving the good doctor holding a dead receiver.

It took Kitty about ten seconds to find Nick's phone number and start dialing. When he answered she almost shouted the news. All Nick said was 'that's great' and 'thanks, I'm on another call and I'll get back to you' and hung up. Her trust in him was so great she smiled as she hung up the receiver. She wasn't as worried about Harry as she was a few minutes ago. She knew exactly what the old devil had done and why. With a big grin and a much lighter step she went into the kitchen to put on the tea kettle.

Nick returned to his original call and relayed the news of Harry's whereabouts to Orlando Chevas, his client, friend and sometimes Spanish teacher in Miami.

"Sorry Orlando. That was Kitty in Bradenton. She found

out where Harry is. I don't know how but we have an address. When do you think your friends will be here?"

He had called Orlando, told him of the group's activities over the last several weeks and how they thought they had pulled off the perfect job until today. Orlando laughed heartily and congratulated Nick and his friends on such a brazen caper. He said it didn't seem like too big a problem and he knew a couple nice young Cuban boys who could be of some assistance. He assured Nick they would be in Bradenton within five hours, ready to follow Nick's instructions. He also said he should explain the situation clearly to these fellows and then step back, not question their methods, and let them do their job. They were experts in the field of convincing people to do things their way.

Nick thanked him several times, in English as well as Spanish. He promised Orlando his next ambulances would be very cheap, and hung up smiling at his Cuban friend's last words. Just before hanging up in Miami, Orlando said thanks but it didn't change the fact that Nick's gringo Spanish was still pretty stinky.

42

Nick sat, beer in hand, with John and Vince, at a table in the back room of Ed's restaurant, going over how they would handle the coming rescue of their friends. He had called them all back in as soon as he got off the phone with Orlando in Miami. Vince was ready because his job was done. He had found the rental company Al Silvestre used and because the local manager was a fellow Rotarian, Nick sat with a slip of paper in hand with the make, model, color, and plate number of their rental car. The note also included Al's home address, phone number, local address, credit card number and driver's license number. Vince felt he hit the jackpot but Ed drew laughs when he noted Vince didn't have Al's shoe size or whether he preferred boxers or briefs.

John and Ed were well on their way to matching Vince's success when they found the lawn mower seller and discovered the two kidnapees had been there. LJ tried out the lawnmower, liked it, bought it, and left the owner a hundred dollar deposit to clinch the deal. Harry and LJ left the mower vender's home around 9:45 p.m., and LJ had asked for the nearest gas station. Ed and John had been checking these when Nick called and asked them to hurry back to the restaurant. Within forty five minutes they pulled onto the parking lot.

"I called a friend in Miami and asked if he could give us a hand. He's sending a couple of his business associates to help us. They'll be here anytime now," Nick said.

"Who's your friend, who's he sending and what kind of help do we need?" Ed asked as he walked into the room with fresh beer.

"My friend's a reputable car dealer in Miami and I have no idea who he's sending. Orlando said they were nice young Cubans who would be a big help. He said they would know what to do and we should let them do it. I thought we needed some help because this thing may be a little out of our league." At this, a waitress with a curious look entered and whispered something to Ed. He turned to Nick.

"You said you had friends in low places and I think some are here now. My girl says four well dressed guys are asking for you and they seem a little out of place. She also said they don't look like nice people. I'm not sure what you got us into but you've done well this far so I guess we'll go along the rest of the way." He waved to his girl to bring the gentlemen in. All rose to greet them.

Their guests were different than expected. All obviously had a Latin heritage, all in their late twenties or early thirties and all were very polite. Any similarities ended there. The point man, an incredibly good looking Cuban, was wearing a suit worth almost as much as Nick's car. Everything else about him was expensive, smooth, and indicated very good taste. This was a man with exceptional knowledge of the latest fads in expensive menswear and the ability and style to wear them well. The picture was perfect except for his eyes, which were like black ice.

His friends were somewhat different. Standing behind this movie star was a short slender fellow in a blue blazer over a black turtleneck. About five foot five with dark glasses over a pencil thin moustache and rat-tail on his collar, he calmly checked out the room and everyone in it with an bemused look on his face. Next to him was a nondescript man in jeans and windbreaker who needed a haircut and had eyes that never stopped moving. Although young, his face looked like three miles of bad road. He was not pretty.

The fourth member of the quartet looked like a Mexican

Sumo wrestler. He almost had to turn sideways in the doorway to enter the room. At close to seven feet tall with shoulders three feet across, he was the biggest man Nick had ever seen. He wondered which tentmaker made his clothes but thought better of asking. Their leader stuck out his hand. "Hi, you must be Nick. Orlando described you quite well." He spoke quietly with the diction of a person educated up north, Boston or New Haven possibly. "He also told me if I wanted a laugh, just get you to speak some Spanish." This was said with a smile and a chuckle from his compatriots.

"Wait till I see him," Nick laughed. "I suppose he told you the story about me paying for lunch?"

"Don't feel bad. He's done that to every gringo he's met. Same story; you have to learn some Spanish. He says he will help you, teaches you to ask for the bill, and then takes you to his favorite restaurant to score a free lunch from you. The restaurant staff have seen it a dozen times and when Orlando walks in with a non-Latin, they know what's up. Oh, by the way, my name is Miguel and I've done some work for Orlando from time to time." He was pleasant, charming and very self assured; certainly not what any of them would consider a tough guy.

Nick introduced his small group as did Miguel and everyone sat down to await the beers Ed had ordered in. They sat in silence until the waitress closed the door behind her.

Miguel started: "Orlando said you found the guys who grabbed your friends. Where are they?"

"They're in a Holiday Inn on Riverside Drive, not far from here. We haven't gone near the place. We're pretty sure there are four of them, that's what the car rental agent at the airport figured. We have no idea if they are armed."

"Doesn't matter" Miguel said. "Orlando told me most of the details but nothing about the bad guys, can you give me a run down on them?"

Nick gave a pencil sketch of Tony and Al, the leaders, but had no idea who was with them until he got a look at the hotel. They spent half an hour discussing their problem before Miguel decided it was enough talk and time for action.

"Here's what I think we should do," he said. "It's getting near supper time and they'll probably split up to eat. You guys should come with us, point out who we have to chat to, and then get out of the way and let us do the chatting. If we can separate them and take one or two out first, the rest of the job will be easy. We'll simply explain the error of their ways, get them to see things our way, and end this nonsense. Just stay a little behind us and let us do the job we're here for. Any questions?" He looked at Nick, saw agreement and turned to his co workers. "You guys ready?"

All three just smiled. Julio, the slender one with dark glasses, and George, the non- descript one in jeans, reached into their jackets and pulled out the largest handguns Nick had ever seen. Both checked them for ammunition and action. Their weapons looked like the 44-Magnum used by Clint Eastwood in the 'Dirty Harry' movies.

While Miguel slipped a clip into a small automatic hidden in an armpit holster Nick asked the two with the cannons what it was they were holding. The giant sitting quietly in the rear didn't move.

Julio, with a grin reversed the gun and passed it handle first to him. "It's a Smith and Wesson model 500 X frame. It's fifty calibre and considered the biggest handgun in the world. Just the sight of it is usually enough to make people listen to reason." he said with a chuckle.

Nick understood why. As a Canadian he had little exposure to guns, particularly pistols or revolvers and he had never seen one this big. Hefting it he commented on the size and weight.

Julio took it back and slipped it into his shoulder holster. "It's fifteen inches long, weighs four and a half pounds and makes as much noise as a stick of dynamite. I had to have a custom holster made by a guy in Miami and I had a hell of a time finding a tailor who could make a blazer to accommodate the size. It's a bit of a nuisance but I find I seldom have to use it and when I do, I just fire into the ground. The noise scares the hell out of anyone in front of me and usually brings them to a dead stop. No pun intended."

Julio stood and buttoned his jacket but the bulge could still be seen. He pointed to George, saying "Now his is just a little Colt Anaconda. He's not big enough for a real gun like mine." Noticing the monster George was sliding into his holster as he laughed, Nick was glad these guys were on his side.

Juan, the giant, stood and Ed asked if he carried a bazooka. Miguel burst out laughing and Juan grinned. "Juan doesn't like guns; he uses AGA to get people to see things his way."

"What the hell is AGA?" Ed asked.

"It stands for acute gravitational attack. He just reaches out and makes people fall down," and the four Cubans all laughed. Ed looked at the huge hands and understood.

"Let' go then." Miguel said, getting up. "You guys go in your car, we'll follow, and if you see their car in the parking lot, get as close as possible. Nick, from what Orlando told me, they might recognize you so find a ball cap and dark glasses. When we get there, rather than eight of us marching in, you go in first with him," he said, pointing at Ed, "to the front desk and ask about rooms and rates. You other two, drift into the lobby store. We'll follow you in and if you see any of your friends, point them out; we'll take it from there." With that they left for the hotel.

Nick parked three spots away from Al's blue Buick and Miguel pulled up opposite. As instructed, newly disguised Nick and his group wandered into the hotel and started to check it out. He had been at the front desk for several minutes when the elevator doors opened and Al Silvestre stepped out into the lobby. Nick signaled to Miguel as Vince did the same with Julio. Both casually turned to follow Al as he walked through the lobby. By the time he reached the front doors, Julio was on Al's right and George had been signaled by Miguel to slip in on his left side. He was boxed in between the two sets of doors into the hotel.

"Excuse me sir," Julio said quietly, causing Al to stop to see who was talking to him.

"If you look down at my right hand you'll notice a very big gun. If you don't want to see how it operates, just do as I say." Al looked at the talking man and then down at the gun. He went very pale and looked like he might collapse in a dead faint. Turning to the man on his left, he saw him holding open his jacket. His huge gun still hung in its holster but looked just as menacing.

"What do you want?"

"Just be quiet, act natural and come with us and you won't get hurt." Julio said as he guided him through the hotel door and out onto the parking lot. At Miguel's car they pulled a roll of duct tape from the back seat, made Al sit down and proceeded to wrap his feet and hands together and tape his mouth shut. Without ceremony they shoved him over onto the back seat, threw a blanket over him and locked the doors. Both men returned to the lobby with nary a glance back at their handy work.

Passing through the entrance doors they saw Juan step up to another man as Miguel moved toward him with his hand inside his expensive silk suit jacket. The expression on the face of the man looking up at Juan was much the same as the look on Al's face a few minutes before. Miguel didn't even bother to take out his pistol.

Nick stepped forward just as Julio and George joined the group and removed his sun glasses. "Hello Mr. DiAngelo, we meet again." he said. The fear vanished from Tony's face, replaced by rage and some understanding.

"What the hell's going on? What have you done with Al?" he fumed, looking like he may make a fuss right there in front of the elevators. Miguel touched Tony's arm and pointed at Julio and George, standing with their jackets open, revealing their guns and instantly cooling Tony down.

"We are going to get back in the elevator and go up to you room, Mr. DiAngelo," Miguel politely informed him, reaching over to press the button. "You're going to help us get into your room without any problems, that way Julio and George won't have to waste any of their expensive bullets. Then we're going to discuss this kidnapping thing you and your group are involved in." The elevator door opened, they politely stood aside, waiting for it to empty, and then all nine men got in. Miguel politely waved a couple hotel guests to the next elevator, saying they were full as the doors slid closed. As it rose through the floors, Julio and George, standing with backs to the doors, silently got out their guns, checked them and took off the safeties. Miguel did the same, all in plain sight of Tony. There was no question these men were pro's who knew the psychological value of a large weapon, a calm exterior, and an air of professionalism.

At the room Tony knocked, identified himself and said he had forgotten his car keys. He was then pushed aside to the care of Miguel. Mario opened the door and found himself staring into the barrels of two huge handguns. Those holding the guns held their fingers to their lips and pulled Mario out into the hall where he was encircled by a giant with hands like hams. He saw a sullen looking Tony being held at gunpoint by a good looking young man with his finger to his lips as well. Mario didn't make a sound.

The two gunmen, one crouching low and the other standing, aiming their constantly moving gun with both hands, moved into the suite, looking for the fourth kidnapper. Julio silently signaled George and pointed to the washroom door as the toilet flushed. Taking position they waited for the occupant, who stepped out still doing up his zipper. Seeing Julio near the floor and then spotting George standing five feet away, he casually shrugged, finished zipping his pants and asked: "What's up?"

"Our boss wants to talk to you and your friends. Move slowly over to the sofa and sit down. By the way, we were told you own a gun, where is it?"

Frank pointed to the chest of drawers and Julio retrieved an automatic and slipped it into his belt. "Any more?" he asked and when Frank shook his head no, he called: 'all clear' and the rest of the group came through the door to fill the room.

"Please sit there with your friend," Miguel said to Tony and Mario, pointing to the sofa. "George, take Juan and get the other one from the car. Take his tape off. They should all be here for this conversation. Now gentlemen, where are the captives?" All three pointed to a door to the adjoining room. Nick walked over, turned the handle and pulled it open.

"Would anyone here like pizza and beers for supper?" he called into the room. It only took a second for the reply.

"The hell with you," Harry called back. "We phoned this morning and we're still waiting. Your delivery service is too damn slow. Get lost." This last came as a grinning Harry and LJ strode into the now full room.

"Hell Harry, a welcoming committee. You guys didn't have to go to all this trouble you know." LJ laughed as he shook hands with his friends.

George and Juan finally arrived with Al, pushing him through the door into the suite and directing him to the sofa. The room quieted down as Miguel stepped forward to stand in front of the four men squeezed onto the one hotel sized chesterfield. It was time for the conversation to begin.

"Gentlemen," Miguel politely started, "a friend of mine in Miami asked me to come up here and give these people a hand. We have done that and our job is almost over. I'm aware of what has gone on, both here last year in Florida and over the past month in Phoenix. You have to admit this is a pretty feisty group of seniors you've run up against and I think they got the best of you. Now, you've taken your best shot and these people have done you in at every turn. I would suggest you accept the fact that you've lost, give up this quest to retrieve your ill gotten gains and get on with your lives." Miguel was the epitome of sense and sound reasoning.

He continued in the same tone, "Now, what you are going to do, is go away. You're going to pack your bags, now, while we wait. You will give me your rental car contract and I will call the Bradenton Airport location and change the return location to Tampa Airport. When you finish packing, we will escort you downstairs to the lobby, you will check out, leave, and two of you will get in your car along with Juan and George. The other two will ride with me and Julio. We will drive to Tampa Airport together, with us driving directly behind you. At the airport you will buy tickets to Phoenix and fly out tonight." He paused to let his words sink in.

"Now, do you all understand these arrangements?" All four heads bobbed up and down. "Good, because if any of you vary even the slightest bit from these instructions, we will hurt you. In fact we will take you someplace private and we will hurt you more than you could possible imagine. That is not a threat, it's a prophecy." No one in the room, including Nick and his friends doubted Miguel's words for one second.

"Now, one at a time, start packing." Like obedient children, the four men looked at Miguel, then Juan and the other two with belief and understanding on their faces. Frank stood first to get his bags.

While the packing got started, Nick introduced Harry and LJ to Miguel and his merry band of do-gooders. He still didn't know their last names, nor did they offer. He did offer that Orlando and Miguel's father had escaped from Cuba when Castro took over and their families had been tight all these years. Miguel was involved in some form of export and import business, and seemed to be doing very well.

When the packing was complete with the bags sitting at the door, Miguel took Juan and George aside, giving them instructions about taking the luggage down to Tony's car and putting them in the trunk. He then turned back to Tony and his small group of totally subjugated villains.

"You're all very lucky to get out of this with all your bones intact. I would suggest you leave Florida and make no plans to come back. I understand you're from Miami." Miguel spoke directly to Frank. "Good. I would think you may have heard of Ernesto Dominguez?" Franks eyes grew wide and he seemed a shade paler than a moment before. "We sir, are business associates of Senor Dominguez and tomorrow night, at dinner, I will let him know how much you have cooperated. I might suggest while on the plane to Phoenix, you explain to your friends how lucky they are to be leaving Florida sitting upright. Also, you should consider resettling out west. You stole two million dollars and those you stole it from came and got it back. You are even. Now go away and save yourself much trouble." Turning to Julio, he said "You take Mr. DiPietro to the front desk so he can check out, we'll take the others to the cars. Is everybody ready? Good, let's be on our way." Miguel nodded to Juan to open the door and the exodus started. Nick couldn't believe it was over.

The movement from the room to the cars went without a hitch and no one at the hotel knew of the drama unfolding. Before he left for Tampa, Miguel took Nick aside and asked what they were going to do. When told nothing more than have a few drinks and get a room at the Hilton in Bradenton, he handed Nick a business card. "Call me in the morning and I'll fill you in on the rest of this evening." He said. "You and your friends are fine now; these dummies will never bother you again. They're confidence men, just a notch above purse snatchers. They know if they ever bother your friends, you call Orlando, he will call me and Senor Dominguez will okay our quartet having a more vigorous discussion with this scum. Believe me, it will cost them far more than a couple million of their ill gotten-gains." Nick believed him. He shook hands all around as did his partners, hopped into his car and with a cheery wave, followed Tony's car onto the street.

Nick and his five friends stood watching the two cars disappear toward I-75. They hoped it would be the last they saw of the hoods and all six of them felt it would be so. Miguel was much like a Panther and none of them disbelieved a single word he said.

Turning to his friends, Nick, with a big grin said: "Come on you two kidnappees, I know of a couple wives who would like to see your ugly old faces. Let's not keep those poor misguided souls waiting."

Epilogue

Seven days after the rescue of Harry and LJ, a final meeting of all victims was convened in the back room of Ed Fisher's restaurant. It was one happy group as this was when they got their money back. This was 'We Did It Day'.

Harry and LJ sat at the head table with Nick on their right. Piled in front of them were a couple stacks of large brown manila envelopes. Each envelope had a name printed in black felt marker across the front. Inside each were several tightly bound, neat little bundles of crisp green and white paper. Every piece of paper had a picture of Ben Franklin on it and many were still held together by their original brown paper bands, complete with the stamp of various issuing banks, some in the United States but most in the Caribbean. Few had been touched since Tony and Al delivered them in Buffalo. Harry raised his hand to speak and silence swept across the room.

"Back in the beginning, while we were wondering what we were going to do, each of you gave me the amount taken from you by those crooks. It's been a long time coming but I'm happy to say, each of these envelopes contains the exact amount you told me you lost." Harry was drowned out by applause and cheering at this point.

After several minutes he was able to continue. "As I call out each name, please come up for your money, and remember, dancing, skipping, and shouting loud hoorays *will* be tolerated." With a big grin, he began calling names. Members of the group, no matter how old, sat happily watching each couple moved to the table at the front to accept their envelope. Good natured calls were tossed about as the grinning recipients turned to face their friends, tightly gripping their envelope, most waving it overhead. One joker got a big laugh when he yelled that Tony

Axeworthy would have to remove his shoes and socks to count his money. Tony just stuck out his tongue and happily escorted his wife back to their seats. Only once was the levity set aside. It occurred when Harry called the name of Bella Brown. The applause was thunderous and no one bothered to hide the tears as she came forward.

Within a few minutes Harry and LJ had handed out all but one of the envelopes. None bothered to open their envelopes or count their money, they simply held it close, a symbol of what they had accomplished. When everyone was quiet again, Harry patted the remaining envelope.

"This last one is what was left over. You see, when we added up all that was stolen, it came to a little under one poit eight million. Our generous friends from Phoenix were good enough to give us an even two million for their share of the casino. LJ and I discussed with several of you what to do with the remaining two hundred and fourteen thousand. We've decided, after covering all expenses, and with the approval of all of you, exactly where it should go." He paused for a moment for dramatic effect and to hear if there were any objections. He knew there would be none.

"We covered the expenses and party for Nick's son and our friends in Canada. Their efforts on our behalf at the pipe factory were outstanding and I won't tell how much their party cost but believe me, any rumors you've ever heard about Canadians' ability to drink are true. It must have been one hell of a bash. Nick, you're going to have to tell me where you guys learned to party."

"We've arranged a week at Disneyworld for Bob and his family because they would accept no money for the rooms at the motel or all their help." This drew much applause. "I know they're closer to Disneyland in California but bringing them here gives them a chance to see their parents because the package includes tickets for them. Besides, it will give Amanda a chance to see the guy she has a crush on." And he turned to LJ amid much laughter.

"There are two other helpers you haven't met, from Paterson, New Jersey. They are the sons of LJ Livingston, the guys who so brilliantly took care of all our printing and signage needs. They too wouldn't accept anything so when LJ told me one liked single malt Scotch and the other fancied fine Cognac, I sent them both a case from all of us.

"Many of you suggested something charitable and we finally settled on the idea of an educational scholarship for the Bradenton-Sarasota school system. We're setting aside twenty-five thousand dollars to provide an annual scholarship of fifteen hundred dollars for excellence in writing and literature. We want to name it the Richard T. Brown Scholarship because Richard did such a good job on writing his own eulogy and everyone here enjoyed it so much. So Bella, that's for 'he who can't be here tonight'." The applause after this announcement was thunderous, and Bella, tears in her eyes, stood to thank everyone.

When the tumult died down and everyone was ready for more, Harry continued. "We also figured everyone gets an extra twenty five hundred to cover expenses in Phoenix." More cheers and applause followed this news. "That extra, by the way, is already in your envelopes. The total for all these items is slightly over one hundred thousand dollars." Harry paused here, taking time to rearrange papers in front of him, getting ready, so it seemed, for his final comment.

"I'm glad you're all happy with these arrangements. The only problem is, what the hell do we do with the one hundred thousand dollars that's left over?" Harry looked around the room, knowing he was on pretty solid ground.

"We think, LJ, Ed Fisher, Bella Brown and a whole lot others, that the rest of the money; one hundred thousand dollars, should go to the man who made all this possible: The man who convinced us we should try to get our money back; who made us believe we could, and who dreamt up a wild idiotic plan to do just that." Harry picked up the last envelope and turned, still speaking, to Nick.

"And when we ran into trouble, he called his family and friends to come and help us out. Nick, everyone here wants you to take this envelope, enjoy the contents in good health and God Bless you and yours for what you have done." The room burst into loud applause and cheering.

Nick couldn't believe his ears. Looking around him, he saw a group of proud old people, happily forcing one hundred thousand dollars on him. Some of them were shouting 'yes, yes;' others simply beaming with tears in their eyes. He was overwhelmed.

Standing at the end of the table, tightly holding in his right hand the envelope with his name blazoned across the front, Nick looked out over the room. Not many men ever got this kind of ovation.

When the applause and cheering finally ended he found his voice. "I can see there is no sense in arguing with the lot of you. You're all too stubborn and set in your ways and I know it's useless to try to change a mob like you." This prompted laughter and a few comments that only added to the jovial atmosphere in the room.

"I'm surprised at this" he held the envelope high above his head "I can't say much more than thank you and perhaps finish this little gathering with some news from the recent past and an announcement of something coming up.

"I heard from some sources of mine that the four desperadoes sent packing from the Holiday Inn last week were arrested at Phoenix Sky Harbor Airport when they got off their plane. It would seem those guys were truly a worse bunch than we imagined. Each had in their luggage a large quantity of heroin plus a few other nasty drugs. How the authorities found out is beyond me, but I have a feeling they will be a lot older than any of us when they finally get out of prison. So be happy, we will never be bothered by them again, nor will others like you." This brought the longest applause of the night. Wives kissed husbands, friends slapped backs and fists were thrust in the air. Nick couldn't believe the genuine happiness and enthusiasm.

When they had finally settled down he continued. "That was the news of the past. The news of the future is this: Exactly one year from tonight, this room is booked for the first annual 'Geezers Bash'." This brought a huge cheer. "I expect you all to be here because I'm inviting our well armed Miami connection, the fantastic film fabricators from Toronto, and the fearless Phoenix four-some of Bob and his wife and Amanda, and Jennifer, the world's greatest receptionist. I know you guys will love that." This last brought cheers from the men and wifely comments from the women. "And this will make it the best party ever," he shouted, holding his envelope high overhead.

"If any of you ever have a problem, something you may need help to solve, just pick up the phone. Look around you tonight and *believe*. Everyone here will jump to your side. Few in this world have what you have."

"Last," said Nick "I want you to know what a privilege it's been to work with all of you. You have accomplished much over the last many weeks and I have learned a lot. It's amazing what a group of unconnected people with various talents can do if they set their mind to it. Thanks for listening to me in the beginning. Thanks for keeping me in the picture during the implementation," he added, waving his envelope to the cheering throng. A roar of laughter greeted his closing quip: "And most of all, thanks for the cash… my wife is going to have a ball with it." Some jokes, like some people, never really seem to get old.

Manor House Publishing Inc.
www.manor-house.biz 905-648-2193